Praise for *Among the Ten Thousand Things*

'Explosive...what makes Pierpont stand out is her writing: understated yet intense, it captures each family member's emotional vicissitudes with an acuity that is devastating and funny; confirms Pierpont as a bold, self-assured new voice.'
—*Sunday Times*

'A whip-smart dissection of a crumbling marriage...astonishing...Pierpont excels in sharp dialogue and deft pen-portraits.'
—*Financial Times*

'Bold.'
—*Daily Mail*

'A novel you can dive into on the plane and lose yourself in until you come up for air a few days later, looking at all your holiday books suspiciously because can they ever truly compete with this one?'
—*Stylist*

'[An] assured debut...Pierpont avoids the obvious...sifting through the strains on loyalty that betrayal imposes on children.'
—*Mail on Sunday*

'Ten out of ten.'
—*Spectator*

'Fast-paced...poignant and convincing...[an] accomplished and clever debut novel.'
—*Irish Times*

'This book is one of the funniest and most emotionally honest I've read in a long time.'
—Jonathan Safran Foer

'Remarkable...Julia Pierpont displays not only wisdom, but real tact as a writer, knowing how much to say, how much to leave out, how much to imply.'
—Colm Tóibín

'A luscious, smart summer novel...written by a blazingly talented young author whose prose is so assured and whose observations are so precise and deeply felt that it's almost an insult to bring up her age.'
Review

'An emotionally sophisticated, nuanced examination of a splintering Upper West Side New York City family...*Among the Ten Thousand Things* rises above for its imagined structure, sentence-by-sentence punch, and pure humanity... Pierpont has written a debut so honest and mature that it will resonate with even the most action-hungry readers—perhaps against reason. Her story is the one we'll be talking about this summer, and well beyond.' —*Vanity Fair*

'[A] sharp, knowing dissection of an unraveling marriage... Like the best fictional alienated-children-of-New York—Holden Caulfield; the Brooklyn kids in Noah Baumbach's film 'The Squid and the Whale'; more recently, the teenager at the heart of Peter Cameron's novel *Someday This Pain Will Be Useful to You*—Kay and Simon exude an irresistible blend of worldliness and vulnerability, knowingness and cluelessness.' —*New York Times*

'Poignant, surprising, and fiercely intelligent, *Among the Ten Thousand Things* is about the sturdiness and tremendous delicacy of the bonds between parents and children. Don't miss this powerful debut.' —Megan Abbott

'A vicious and enchanting portrait of a fragmenting family that will leave you hungry for whatever Julia Pierpont does next.' —Courtney Maum

'Sharply observed and deeply illuminating, *Among the Ten Thousand Things* marks the beginning of what is sure to be a brilliant career.' —Elliott Holt

'Why aren't there more first or second or seventh novels like *Among the Ten Thousand Things*? That's what I asked myself as I read—actually, devoured—Julia Pierpont's debut. My conclusion: Very few writers, at any point in their lives, can produce prose of the sort you'll find here.' —Sean Wilsey

'*Among the Ten Thousand Things* succeeds in being both heartbreaking and funny: It's a wry, sly look at a privileged New York upbringing and the ultimate loneliness at the heart of it.' —Mary Gordon

Among the Ten Thousand Things

JULIA PIERPONT

ONEWORLD

A Oneworld Book

First published in the United Kingdom and the Commonwealth by
Oneworld Publications, 2015

This paperback edition first published by Oneworld Publications, 2016

Copyright © Julia Pierpont 2015

The moral right of Julia Pierpont to be identified as the Author of
this work has been asserted by her in accordance with the Copyright,
Designs, and Patents Act 1988

ISBN 978-1-78074-830-6
ISBN 978-1-78074-764-4 (eBook)

Printed and bound in Great Britain by Clays Ltd, St Ives plc
Book design by Liz Cosgrove

Excerpt from "Little Sleep's-Head Sprouting in the Moonlight" from
The Book of Nightmares by Galway Kinnell, copyright © 1971, and
copyright renewed 1999 by Galway Kinnell. Reprinted by permission of
Houghton Mifflin Harcourt Publishing Company. All rights reserved.

This is a work of fiction. While, as in all fiction, the literary
perceptions and insights are based on experience, all names,
characters, places, and incidents either are products of the author's
imagination or are used fictitiously.

Oneworld Publications
10 Bloomsbury Street
London WC1B 3SR
England

For my parents,
as a matter of course

Little sleep's-head sprouting hair in the moonlight,
when I come back
we will go out together,
we will walk out together among
the ten thousand things,
each scratched too late with such knowledge, *the wages
of dying is love.*

—Galway Kinnell

PART ONE

New York,
the End of May

Dear Deborah,

Do you go by Deborah? It sounds so uptight. I bet you hate Debbie. I hate Debbie, too.

Jack calls you Deb.

This is a letter about Jack.

I began sleeping with your husband last June. We were together for seven months, almost as long as I've known him.

We did it in my apartment. Or I went to his studio, a lot. One time at the Comfort Inn in midtown, last August. He used his Visa. Look it up. I know about Kay, her getting bullied at school, and I know about when Simon got caught shoplifting at the Best Buy. I never asked to know about your family. It's just that sometimes, he needed me.

In movies, when the woman is dumped, one thing to do is to take all the love letters and pictures from photo booths and old T-shirts, and to set them on fire. This is to help the woman move on.

I don't have any pictures from photo booths. What I have is email, and a little blue folder on my hard drive called "Chats." So, look what I did. I printed them, at a FedEx on Houston Street. $87.62. I haven't had my own printer since college. The hours and hours made pages and pages, none of it so romantic, a lot dirtier than I remembered. I bought a handle of Georgi at the liquor store so it would really burn—the Jamaican behind the register gave me extra bags because it was hard to keep the pages together—and I carried everything back, the sum of my love rolled in black-and-gold plastic, and dumped it all out into the bathtub.

But it didn't seem fair, that I should be left with the mess, when I use this tub, when I stand in it almost every day. So I got this box together, to give to him.

And then just now I was looking at it, and I realized whom I should be giving it to. You.

Falling in love is just an excuse for bad behavior. If you're fucking someone in a way that you mean it, the rest of you is fucked also. Did I care about you, your children? Did I care about my work? Ask me if I cared. If I care, even.

The thing that kills me, that I can't get over, is I didn't do anything to make him stop wanting me. I didn't change. I held very still on purpose. I weighed myself the other day for the first time in a long time. I thought for sure I'd gained weight, like twenty pounds. Twenty pounds is maybe enough to change the way someone feels about you. But no.

You get migraines, right? He told me you do. I get them too, Deb. Do you think maybe it's him? That the migraines are coming from him? Like if we drank the same dirty

4

water and got cancer, or if we both lived a block from 9/11 and got cancer, or if we did anything the same and got cancer, then we'd trace it to the source, right, and expect a settlement, wouldn't we. What are you settling for, Deb? How much did you get?

There were things you learned early, growing up in the city, and there were things you learned late, or not at all. Bicycles were one of the things Kay had missed, along with tree swings and car pools, dishwashers and game rooms in the basement. The only style of swimming Kay knew was the style of not drowning, any direction but down. Instead of a dog, they had a cat, and before that a cockatiel and a cockatoo, sea monkeys, lizards, gerbils that made more gerbils, one regrettable guinea pig.

She made up for what she'd missed with things New York had taught her. Like how long you had to walk after the DON'T WALK started to blink. The way to hail a cab (hand out but still, fingers together). She knew where to stand in an elevator depending on how many people were on it already, when to hold the poles on the subway and when it was okay just to let go and glide. She knew how to be surrounded by people and not meet anybody's eye.

"If you push harder, you won't shake so much." That was what the other girls all said. They kept a few yards away, pigeon-toed, with hands on their hips or as visors over their foreheads. It was the Sunday morning after a sleepover. Their eyes worked at pinching out the sun.

"Just bike to here, Kay." Racky, on the only other bike, made figure eights around the rest of them, Chelsea and the Haber twins with their twin braids. It had become a group project at these New Rochelle playdates, teaching Kay to ride. She could never get past the wobbly, the fear of falling. That jelly feeling would hit after the first pump, and her foot would come down like a gag reflex, like the time she smacked the wooden stick out of Dr. Frankel's hand when he tried to depress her tongue with it, her foot would hit the pavement and drag her to a stop. Cycle, stop. Cycle, stop. Twenty minutes of this, most weekends, and finally the others would get bored, would propose trips to the multiplex, to TCBY, to the kitchen for facials with an issue of *Allure* and someone's mother's old avocado.

"I can't." It was a hot day and probably there was something good on TV, in the air-conditioning. Central air seemed the greatest of suburban luxuries. It was like living inside a Duane Reade. They had AC units at home, wheezy ones that dripped puddles under the windowsills.

"If Kay bikes to here," Racky said, "she can choose what movie we watch."

"I don't want to choose what movie."

The girls whispered, negotiating behind long strings of

blonde that they tucked behind their ears as they came up with new terms.

"If Kay bikes to here," said one of the twins, "she can choose the movie *and* if we get pizza or Chinese."

"I don't care what we eat."

"Lo mein, Kay."

"I can't."

Racky rang the bell on her handlebar. "If she bikes to here," she said, counting off on her fingers, "she gets the movie, Chinese, *and* twenty bucks."

The Haber twins laughed. Kay understood that no one expected her to make it, that they were already telling the story on Monday in the cafeteria, the great lengths they had gone to teach Kay, how hopeless she was.

She pushed off the pavement with the girls still laughing and forced herself to pedal a second time, through the uneasiness. For once, she wasn't afraid to fall. If she fell, then at least this all would be over; they'd stop laughing, maybe even feel bad.

She rode right past them—past them!—went another eight or nine yards before sailing into a curb. But still, she had done it. Been bullied into it, but still.

She chose *Harry Potter* and beef lo mein. She never did get the twenty dollars from Racky, but then she never asked.

It was half past nine by the time Racky's mom's minivan pulled up in front of Kay's apartment building. "Your mother's going to have me arrested for kidnapping."

8

"She won't care." Sometimes Kay caught herself making her mother sound neglectful for no reason. She said thanks, for the ride or the weekend generally, to the whole of the car and worked the handle to slide herself out. She could feel the minivan waiting for her to reach the lobby before it lurched away.

Kay's favorite doorman was on. She never called him by his name, although she knew it, had heard other people address him this way. She was afraid that in her mouth it would come out wrong, that she'd been mishearing it all this time—what everyone else was saying *sounded* like Angel, but no one was named Angel.

"Okay, Kay," he said when she came shuffling through the lobby, backpack heavy with weekend things. She got to the elevator door just as it opened, and inside her button was pushed already. A magic trick Angel liked to perform. Kay stuck her head out to gape at him, as always, the suggestion of applause, and Angel laughed high and long, different from his laugh with the adults.

The door was sliding shut when Angel held up a finger—wait—and ran around to the service elevator where they kept the packages. He came back with a box.

"For Mommy," Angel said.

Riding up in the elevator, she turned the box around in her arms. Its flaps were tucked instead of taped together, and there wasn't any postage or even a street address. And another thing: It was addressed, in black Sharpie, to Mrs. Jack Shanley. No one called her mother that except for Kay's grandparents, her father's mother.

9

In the light of the hall, she noticed something pink where the flaps left an opening. The one thing she would not confess to after that night, for which she would always feel a flush of shame, was the thought that inside the box was a present for her.

Her birthday was not until September, and they observed Easter only in candy aisles the day after. However. If it was a gift for her, she didn't want to wait until the fall to get it, and if it was for her mother, or her father, or for Simon, then there wasn't any harm checking.

Inside, it was just paper. So many pieces of paper, thrown together like tickets in a raffle.

i went to that dinner party in red hook tonight. all the talk was about what's happening in syria, what's happening in egypt, and i can only think about what's happening with you.

The feeling that her domino eyes were running over something she wasn't supposed to see. She tried to make them stop, or to see without reading, but they could not, would not stop.

i can't explain why i get so sad when you make me so happy

i've been thinking of how you pressed my hand against your neck

show me your cunt

And right there, slid off the top, the winning ticket, the pink that had drawn her in: an envelope. This, too, was addressed to her mother, but it wasn't sealed, and so she opened it. The letter was the only thing in the box that had been written by hand.

10

Dear Deborah,

And:

I began sleeping with your husband last June.

And:

I know about Kay.

She redid the flaps, held the box under her arm, and let herself into the apartment. Clenching all her parts as she passed her mother and brother in front of the television.

"Kay?" her mother called. "Why so late?"

Quickly to her room, head down to hide her face. There was that little guy in her throat, the one that hurt when she wanted to cry.

Her mother's shoes clicking nearer, she buried the box under a tangle of shirtsleeves on the floor of her closet just as the door swung open. "Babe? What happened to you? I tried Arlene." Kay pretended to look for something in her bottom dresser drawer. "She never picks up. I don't like that woman." Kay was moving handfuls of clothes from one end of the drawer to the other. "Did you hear me?"

"She's a good mom." She hadn't meant to defend Racky's mother. Feeling herself start to cry, she dug deeper into the drawer. Nightgown. Where was her yellow night-gown?

"Baby, did something happen?" Deb's hand touched her shoulder and Kay twisted away. Her mother was quiet and so pretty, with her shiny hair and tiny waist, the evenness and natural tan of skin that Kay had not gotten from her. "Did you have a hard time with the girls, with learning the bike?"

The bike, the sleepover, those things seemed small and

11

far away now, but remembering made everything worse: yet another place where her life was not as she wanted it to be: She had unkind friends. But in a way it was good to remember, it allowed for her tears. Her mother held her, and she let herself be held, in the orb of Deb's Deb-scented perfume.

"Did you fall?"

Kay nodded. The wet skin under her eye stuck to her mother's arm.

"Where does it hurt?"

She could follow instructions and give the box to her mother. She could throw it away. She could give it back to Angel, have *him* throw it away. What she couldn't do, she knew in that moment, was go to her father, who might never tell her mother, if he had the box, because how could she live with him then.

For now the safest thing to do was nothing. The box was a secret she kept, the whole next day at school. She found herself in history, in math, in science, not knowing how she got there, not remembering the halls. Lockers slammed too loud, and Racky, the twins, everyone was always laughing about something, and what was so fucking funny all the time? She felt faraway and alien, her teachers going on about fractions and photosynthesis and the Underground Railroad. What did these things have to do with her life, where did they touch her?

It wasn't Sunday but Monday that everything happened, and Simon might have been slightly, vaguely, barely, just approximately high. A little tiny bit.

He'd skipped the bus home and gone to the Short Stop diner down the hill from school, where the kids sat drinking bottomless cups of coffee with their omelets and buttered toast, tired-eyed teenagers who hibernated through breakfast every morning and so made up for it in the afternoons, ruining the dinners their mothers or housekeepers were making for them at home. Seniors held court over the seven booths, leaving the underclassmen to share barstools, cheek to cheek. Simon was fifteen but arrived with a senior from his religion class, Jared Berkoff, with whom he'd been partnered to present on Confucianism, a topic they'd drawn at random from Mr. Dionisio's just-rinsed, still-damp coffee tumbler. Jared was a stoner, always high except on the social ladder, though the JAPs still invited him to their parties, and when one of the more inspired jocks discovered

13

the effect of switching out a letter in Berkoff, a mascot was born. There were worse people for Simon to show up with. The diner was where deals were struck, where everyone went looking for drugs or for play. Jared was looking to score both.

Both arrived in the shape of Elena Gorbunova, a junior with a broad forehead and pretty, space-alien eyes. Simon had seen her before in the cafeteria, knew the tight turtlenecks that hugged her so that waist-up she might have been a figure skater.

"Gorbunova," Jared said, flipping shut his phone. Clearly she was the one he'd been texting since they sat down in the back booth, next to a quiet senior who did studio art and whose cuffs and cuticles were always edged with paint. "Gorbunova's going to smoke us out."

Elena, with the slightest bend of her knee, managed to curtsy. Probably she and Jared had something—or used to have something or were about to have something—going on. She led them out the door, all hip bone, tonguing a sugar packet.

Elena got a steady supply of weed from her brother, Gorb, now a student at Manhattan College, which was in the Bronx, near their school. Gorb had been expelled from high school his sophomore year, but before that he'd been a star of the varsity fencing team, which practiced in the middle school gym. Simon remembered him, padded white and huge, like a walking sofa bed, with a wispy mustache and a silver mask under his arm, whipping a foil around the breezeway.

In the parking lot beside a shuttered tanning salon, the

three of them squatted behind a car, and Elena set a yellow glass bowl on the ground. She pulled the weed apart, packed it herself. Sticky on her fingers, but she worked fast. She might have been failing out of PE, but clearly there were things she knew.

She took the first hit, quickly, as though she was just getting it started for them, and passed it to Jared. Simon noticed a mark on the back of her hand, an almost-star, all but the last two lines drawn. Thin, white lines. A knife, or a razor blade. He watched the star twinkle at him as she fingered another sugar packet. When it was his turn to take a hit, he realized he'd forgotten to watch how it was done, and he'd never smoked anything before. Why couldn't it at least have been a joint and not this bulbous, lemony thing?

His fingers felt clumsy around it. He saw in flashes how it might fall to the ground and ruin everything, the privilege of being there so new. On the inhale the air came too easy and felt like nothing.

"Here," Elena said, moving his finger over the hole on the bowl's side. Like a music teacher, she was patient. "Tap."

He looked at Jared, mercifully unaware, picking something off his tongue.

When Simon pulled it into his lungs, the weed turned to orange embers, darkening again on the release.

"Hold it in," Elena said, and put two painted fingernails, pink and green, to his lips. It burned him up bad on the inside, but he would never cough onto her rough little fingers, her star scar.

The smoke had to come out somewhere, though, and it

came out in his eyes. His vision blurred and tears trembled in the corners, waiting to fall the moment his head tipped a centimeter this way or that. Elena, with no expression he could read, kept her fingers to his lips, almost cruel—was she trying to kill him?

When she finally did take her hand away, Simon tried to keep his choking on the inside. Was he high? Was this high? He was happy and afraid, but this had more to do with Elena's knee brushing his where they sat Indian style on the poured concrete and sharp bits of pebble and glass.

Now Elena took a long, slow hit and let the smoke out smoothly, as if it were only hot breath on a cold night.

How he knew he was stoned had to do less with a feeling and more with the fact that when he smiled he went blind, eyes so small. Jared's eyes, at least, were red, but Elena's were round as ever, calm, curved pools, surface life on the plane of her face. Maybe she'd built up a tolerance for weed, or a total immunity. That would be sad. Or maybe she was high all the time and had one of those miracle faces that never showed it.

"Look at fucking Simon," Jared said. "He's turning Japanese-a."

They both started to laugh. You're blowing it you're blowing it you're blowing it. Stop smiling, you idiot. You have nothing to smile about. The sound of Elena laughing made the cotton in his mouth sink down into his stomach and grow. This helped some, brought his cheeks back to normal, though his eyes still felt small, like pink and green fingers pressed to his lids.

Jared clapped his hands together. "Your face is amazing, man."

"He's cute," Elena said, but like she felt sorry for him.

Simon's mouth was dry and probably he had to throw up. He felt like a science experiment gone wrong, and what if he just cried in front of them.

Elena leaned closer. "You are cute to smile," she said, her English worse than it should have been. Had he ever even heard her speak before? Was this the first time he was hearing her voice?

Before he realized it, she was kissing him, once, not long but sweetly and sweet, sugar granules pressing off her lips, that thick, musty smell on both their mouths stronger when multiplied, and Simon did the worst thing he could have done. He smiled, so that she kissed his teeth.

She straightened up, wiping her mouth, the star a comet across her face. She leaned her head back against the car door and closed her eyes. Jared had done the same. Simon sat and waited for someone to do anything, but they seemed to have gone to sleep. He cleared his throat. Jared scratched his nose.

Simon saw himself out.

On the subway home, he cursed himself for the smiling and the dryness of mouth. Also, for not buying a soda at the bodega on the corner, that was a mistake.

It was half past six when he got off at the Eighty-sixth Street station and started for home. Coming up on the corner of Broadway was the supermarket where a hundred times on the train he'd imagined himself buying a can of Sprite, but before he reached it, he saw his sister, sitting on the wooden bench put out by the ice cream shop. She was looking down, apparently into her belly button, and her short, feathery hair fell forward, hiding her face. She hadn't seen him, and the Sprite was so close.

But she looked very small, his sister, and very sad, and he wondered for a second if she knew something, if someone at the school had seen him. If Jared and Elena had been arrested, his name would have come up. The school or some precinct might have called the house, and his mother might have sent Kay out so she and Simon could talk alone. That was how Simon buried himself, in the middle of Broadway, because of something he saw in the curve of his sister's back, what had made her so heavy.

"What are you doing here?"

"Buying ice cream."

She didn't see him look pointedly from her place on the bench to the ice cream shop and back. "You know, you have to go inside for that."

"In a minute." She strangled a shirt button by its thread. The shirt was a leftover from elementary school dress code, white but graying, and she hadn't matched the holes up right. Simon remembered the early mornings when she'd fought against these shirts, before the big middle school privilege of getting to wear what you wanted. The novelty had worn off, though—freedom of expression was another kind of nuisance—and she'd gone to wearing bits and pieces of uniform again.

18

Simon had meant to avoid Kay's looking at him closely, in case his eyes were strange, they still felt strange, but she was almost crying now, and he sat on the bench beside her. "How much did Mom give you?"

"I had money from lunch."

"You didn't eat lunch?" So it was something that happened at school. Simon remembered that high people got paranoid. This wasn't about him at all. Still, what it was about, she wouldn't say, so he touched her shoulder like someone she didn't know was there and said *hey* and nodded toward the white light inside the ice cream shop, where the menu hung glowing from the ceiling.

Ice cream helped, a little, even though Kay let most of her grasshopper pie run down her fingers and gather in the cave her palm made. Simon got butter pecan, his favorite, which their father called the geriatric flavor, but he felt wrong to enjoy it with his sister so upset. Plus, he knew, marijuana made pigs out of people.

It was a great test of his burgeoning manhood, but his affection for his sister, or maybe just curiosity, kept Simon from stopping for the soda he wanted. Kay was moving now, dropping bits of cone into the corner trash can, almost home, and he followed her.

The doorguy was helping some building people load luggage into a taxi, a relief to Simon, who liked the doorguy but not always the banter that came with him, how much he joked with Kay. In the gold-green light of the elevator, he stared into the brass plate that framed the buttons, where he and his sister reflected back at him, warped around the engraved numbers, their bodies strange of size.

Their eyes were the same in this light, over-small and under-bright. Simon forgot to press the button. But Kay remembered.

Their mother was in the kitchen with a pot of spaghetti and a head of broccoli. Sometime that year she'd started making dinner every night, which meant less meat. She didn't like to handle it. Their dad was still at work. He was never home this early.

It was the smallest decision Kay could think to make, smaller even than doing nothing, which felt like deceit. Showing Simon would be like showing herself, because he was theirs too.

He sat on her bed with the box in his lap. Kay knelt behind him so she couldn't see the changes in his face but could see what he was reading, how slowly he pored over the letter to their mother, he must have read it three or four times, and the sudden speed with which he read the rest, *thank you for yesterday,* until he was crinkling pages, probably getting only the gist of things, *i can't explain why i get so sad when you make me so happy,* pushing through the sea of it, careless, so that some spilled over the cardboard sides. He was angrier than she thought he'd be, and when he'd read enough, without saying anything to Kay, who was about to ask what did he think, without even a word to her, he pushed down on the pages and lifted his chin and shouted: *"Mom!"*

She didn't even look at most of it. That was something Simon couldn't believe, how his mother didn't pore over every page. As furious as he was with his father, he was furious with her too, for reasons he couldn't explain yet but that had something to do with how her reaction was not enough, not nearly enough. Though he didn't know what would be.

This is a letter about Jack. This is a letter Deb held against her lap, in case her hands wavered. *I began sleeping with your husband last June,* and Deb began feeling grateful her children could not see through to her stupid heart, how it lurched there. *It's just that sometimes, he needed me.*

You get migraines, right? He told me you do.

From Kay's bed, she lifted her face to where her son was standing, defiant with his arms crossed, defiantly *not* crying, and where her daughter was shrinking into the wall, trying to press through plaster.

"Okay, just." She stood. "Guys, I need. Just give me a minute." She picked up the box like it was furniture and considered it there, as if deciding where it should go, as if the whole idea wasn't to be with it somewhere her children weren't. "I'll be right back in a minute."

Simon and Kay watched her go, listened to her footsteps travel the hall, heard the bedroom door creak a little open, then closed. They waited like it was all Kay's room was for, waiting, like they should have had magazines. Each minute took all its time.

Above the bed, Deb weighed the box in her arms and tried to decide if the pages were a lot or a little, for all those months.

"Where'd she *go*," Kay moaned at the floor.

"She didn't go anywhere."

"But what's happening?"

"She's upset, dork. Be quiet."

Kay was and still Simon said, "Quiet."

Subject: about yesterday

somebody braver would do this on the phone, or in person.

Deb wanted to protect her children. She wanted to put shoes on their feet and coats over their shoulders, coats though the weather had warmed already.

22

yesterday might be something you do all the time. i've never been married—i don't know what that's like.

She wanted to carry her children someplace safe, her mother's or the movies, carry them though they were fifteen and eleven and too big for her to carry.

i've been thinking of how you pressed my hand against your neck. it seemed like such a kind thing to do, like you wanted to make yourself vulnerable to me too.

But her first impulse about the box had been to hide it. She was the victim, yes, but in front of her children, she understood at once what else she would become, which was a guilty party, and she began to notice her breathing.

Their mother's private sounds grew more and more frightening, the longer it seemed they'd never stop. Sometimes just a page turning, and they wondered which page. Or when something slammed—a lighter object colliding against a heavier one, a cascade—what was that? A hand, a fist, a stack of books.

The wound which Deb had tried to tourniquet had reopened, and she'd been so stupid for thinking she could tie it off there, and what were these words her kids had read, these awful words they'd seen? *show me your cunt.*

show me your cunt.
hi! i'm working
i can see your bald cunt.
haha no you can't

23

i close my eyes and i see it. you're wearing the white skirt and no underwear.

She imagined Simon reading it, and she could scream. Kay reading it, and she could hammer Jack's head into the ground. She pictured them together in some small, dark space, reading, and they were younger in her mind, both somehow three or four, before they even could read. The ages they'd been when she sat with them on the ugly old sofa they used to have to watch PBS and eat. When Jack came home, he'd ask what had happened to the buttons on the remote, the surface of everything shining from grilled-cheesy fingers. They were taller and tougher now, her children, more angled—Simon especially—but it was those kids she imagined the words hurting, growing them up in the worst way.

And she hadn't done anything, but that was the problem. Stupid, idiot woman.

A shrill sound pierced the air, making them jump, what both hoped, horribly, wasn't their mother's voice, what turned out to be the smoke detector singing.

Deb came running out to the kitchen, and Simon and Kay found her at the stove saying, "Shit shit stop it stop," bullying the pot of pasta that gurgled hot foam onto the range. She flapped a dish towel at the little white disk mounted near the ceiling. "Could someone please open a window please!"

Simon leaned over the sink to push out the pane of glass, which got the air to where it was almost circulating. Deb

24

went on flapping. Within their panic it was a relief to have a small, solvable problem, something actionable. When the alarm stopped, the other problems were still there.

She got them both to the table. Simon sucked down glass after glass of soda, so that Deb eventually brought the two-liter bottle out from the fridge and left it to sweat on the wood. Kay wound pasta into a mass on her fork, her face intermittently crumpling into the mask of tragedy. Deb wished she could hear what words rang in her daughter's ears, what thoughts kept breaking through, breaking her pink, round moon face. She began to doubt even this decision, dinner, a sad stab at order where it did not exist, and got out of her chair to crouch between them. She touched the backs of their necks, which felt hot, or maybe she was cold.

Simon was watching the bubbles cling and lose their grip inside his glass. "You're going to get a divorce."

Deb could feel all the insides of her throat, saying, "When Dad gets home—"

"I don't want to talk to him. I hate him." So Simon wouldn't talk and Kay couldn't, could make only a wet whistling sound with her breathing.

"Don't cry. We—" And here Deb looked at Simon too, stressing the word. "*We* didn't do anything wrong." The sharp eyes her son made back at her made her wonder if he disagreed, if maybe he thought she had done a few things wrong.

They gave up on dinner. Kay cried in the mirror, watching herself brush her teeth. Deb gave her two Tylenol PMs and sat with her as she fell asleep. She touched her daughter's face with a bent finger. The girl's skin felt like a wettish peach.

In the living room, Simon splayed out on the floor with his videogames, the buzz of his hair silhouetted against the light of the screen. Deb stood over him. The time glared on the cable box: 9:28. Jack, so near an opening, would not be home for another several hours. "Which game is this?"

"*Battlefield.*"

"How does it work?" On-screen it was a gray day, and the camera bobbed through torched forests, past patches of fire and ember. There was the sound of footsteps and a helicopter overhead. Deb flinched at gunfire.

"You kill people." He pressed so many buttons. "It's the Vietnam War." There was shouting in a hard, alien language (real Vietnamese?) and more shooting. A hand that was Simon's reloaded his gun. An American shouted *Grenade, get down!* The color washed out, and the point of view fell to the ground, on its side. "Fuck."

Deb looked at her son in a way he could feel.

"What? I died." Already he was alive again. KILL ASSIST +10 flashed on the screen.

"Who are you playing against?"

"Uh." His words came from far away. "It's live, so. Just anybody."

"Strangers?"

"Uh. Yeah. I mean, I don't know them."

. . .

26

Later he went to bed, or at least to his room, where, from the hall, Deb could see the strip of white light underscoring his door. Probably he was online again. Probably had never been off.

The box she'd left in their bedroom, under a blanket on the rocking chair by Jack's closet. That was where it greeted her now, tipping a little forward in the current the window conspired with the open door to make.

you are tracing it with your two fingers, up and down, slowly. are you doing it?

my roommate is in the kitchen

you're doing it

This Jack she knew. He'd said things to her, maybe not quite so dirty. People were less dirty in the nineties, or it felt that way. They weren't typing it yet. But Deb remembered talking on the phone. She'd had a roommate then, Izzy, another dancer in the corps, who was always around, walking through her room to the kitchen, peeing with the bathroom door open to still see the television in their dark one-bedroom converted to two.

now put your fingers inside. get them wet. are you wet?

Deb wondered if he bit her too. This faceless girl, touching herself, who was she?

i'm so hard for you. i've got it in my hand so you can see.

And where was he, writing these words? Here, while she was in class and the kids were at school? *i'm sliding in you. i slide right in you because you are so wet.* He wanted to know about other men, how the girl touched them, let them touch her. *did you like his cock in your mouth? did you*

27

suck his balls? These were the kind of questions he'd asked Deb when they were new to each other, when the memories of other men were still fresh in her mind. She'd tell him about a boyfriend who liked her to drag her teeth up his shaft or dance a finger around his asshole, and the next time they were together, he'd ask for teeth, for assholes. She thought it was cute, that he got jealous, and curious, that jealousy made him want it. "Don't you want to hear my stories?" he'd ask. "Don't you like hearing about things I've done?" No.

I'll be a little late tomorrow, picking up Kay's cake. Let yourself in, take off all your clothes, get down on the floor, and wait for me to make you cum. Deb saw smooth legs opening somewhere in Jack's studio, on the drafting table maybe, and she saw the white skirt.

To call her mother, she went out through the yellow lobby, past Angel, who hopped off his stool, and into the early-summer air that cradled her.

"Hello?" Ruth always picked up. "Hold on a minute; let me turn off the set."

Deb held, wandered the block. Dark around the First Baptist Church, where a woman she worked with at the college had gotten married. The outside was beautiful with its rose windows, stained glass rainbowed like oil in a puddle, but the little room where they'd had the ceremony had plaster walls and low ceilings. For two twenties Simon had helped videotape the wedding.

"Okay, hi, dear." To Deb's quiet she said, "What is it," her voice weighted with every possible wrong.

"They know. The kids. About Jack."

"You told?"

"What? No, of course not."

"Then what, Deborah? Slow."

Deb told her, slow, passing under the warm neon of the twenty-four-hour burger place where they used to give the kids balloons. Deliverymen sat waiting at the green tables and chairs on the sidewalk.

"And you called David?"

Deb walked faster down Broadway, with a snap that suggested purpose. She crossed against the light. David Currie was the divorce lawyer she'd gone to in January, really a friend from high school who had grown up into a lawyer. "I just wanted so goddamn much to be done with it." Her throat had closed up. Past the Korean grocery, where the grapefruits and green peppers outside seemed to glow. The streetlights were orange and red and swam in her eyes.

"I know." Ruth sighed into the phone. "Oh, don't I know," as if she was thinking of her own past.

"I just can't believe it. I just can't fucking believe he did this." That wasn't true, so why did she keep saying it?

"He's a son of a bitch, Debby. We knew this."

"I don't even want to fucking talk to him."

"So call David."

Back in January, what David Currie had told her was to wait. He had been through a divorce himself; they were

29

long and sometimes people changed their minds. "You'd not believe," he'd said, "what people get over." He told her about a woman who'd stayed with her husband after his sex-change operation.

"I keep thinking about how someone might say it's my fault. For not doing anything." And because she did know what it was like to lose sight, behave badly, and she was afraid of bringing in the mud, the ugly, afraid of what might be used against her if she pressed Jack, and if he tried really to defend himself. "I should have, I shouldn't have been—"

"But you *did*. You *were*. Honey, no good comes this way. Listen. Look. Lie down. Take a rest. He isn't home yet?"

"I'm out."

"Where are you?"

"Can't you hear I'm outside?"

"What does it matter? No, I couldn't hear."

"I'm not coming over. Relax."

"You could come."

"I know, you'd love that. Look, I'm sorry I woke you."

"I was eating."

"Well, you shouldn't eat so late," Deb said stupidly. "I'll call you tomorrow."

Outside the Seventy-second Street subway station, sprinkles of people were gathered in pairs or posed alone against columns, waiting for other people. A red stroller rolled across the square, a woman with short hair leaned on its handlebars. A comfort to find life in other places, people who didn't know him, who'd read his write-ups maybe, in *New York* or the *Times,* but who didn't give a fuck about Jack.

30

That time the girl let herself into the studio, took off all her clothes, and got down on the floor, Jack was two hours late getting there. And when he did arrive, he couldn't get in because the girl, in one of her moods, had fastened the last remaining lock, a chain he busted his shoulder getting through, charging the door like a ram. He found her at the sink, washing her hair. Bare from the waist up, that was why she'd used the lock, *for peace of mind*, and the running water was why she couldn't hear him shouting.

So instead of fucking on the floor, he was on the couch, on his stomach, enduring the girl's crude massage. *You couldn't relocate a shoulder if it hit you over the head. What are you trying to do, kill me?* He left her there, in almost tears, to go home to his wife, with her years of physical therapy, who knew how to touch what felt broken.

But all that was, what, last fall? The pain in his shoulder had gone mostly away, though there were still no locks on his studio door. Especially risky because he'd found already, the time he forgot his building key, that by squatting he could unlock the downstairs without it, hooking his arm up and through the poorly engineered wrought iron.

He didn't replace the locks. It amused him, to know how easily a stranger could come in off the street. It made him think of baby elephants, how they are tethered to stakes when they are young and weak so that years later, when they are big and strong and could pull the stakes out no problem, they don't. At some point people in first-world countries had come to accept the idea that all doors to private properties require keys. And Jack's work was valuable now, more or less. It was of some value. A person could clean up with what was in his studio. It tickled him to walk out onto the street and look at the people passing by and think, if you only knew, you dumb elephant.

The neighborhood, anyway, was changing, back to some earlier version of itself. The methadone clinic across the street had reopened. Maybe he *would* get a lock. There was that woman again, hanging around outside, chain-smoking in a flowered housedress with snaps. The dress reminded him of his mother-in-law.

On the train ride home he thought of his work the next few days. This was his favorite time, the week leading up to an opening. But the first night at the gallery was also his favorite. Then the interviews, reading the listings, sometimes articles—that would be his favorite, the buzz in his ears for weeks after, until the magazines and newspapers quieted down and the show closed. His least favorite time. Then he began again.

Jack liked to hammer a lot of thoughts out on the train.

The hardest part of a marriage—of living with anyone—was those first ten minutes after walking through the door. Questions about his work, his lunch, his trip home, which in his mind had barely ended, and answers to questions he'd not asked, so many words flooding him, and there was the news to discuss, not just U.S. but world news, and then not just that but local news, gossip, about professors Deb knew at school, and not even professors but administrators, sometimes. Administrators, quite frequently.

The impending barrage was on his mind as he flipped through his keys under the building's hunter-green canopy. Past midnight, Angel had gone home, leaving the lobby locked up behind him. Late nights like these Jack wasted a lot of time under the light of the awning, looking for the right key. He had about a dozen, and they all looked the same. He had the lobby key, the mail key (easy because it was small), the two for upstairs, the building key to the studio, the studio mailbox key (again, small), the ones to the studio's broken locks, and another series for the old house in Rhode Island where they hadn't been in years. Every night he thought to take them off the ring, and upstairs every night he forgot.

In the elevator he checked his BlackBerry and lost service, per usual, somewhere between the fourth and seventh floors. Deb would want to know why he hadn't answered the phone earlier. She'd been slow to believe him about things since Christmas, even though, since Christmas, he'd really done nothing wrong.

The living room lights were on when he let himself in, but she wasn't on the sofa watching cable news or in the grandma chair, reading and waiting up for him. He listened for her in the kitchen: not there either.

Plates of pasta were still out on the table. Sometimes Deb made noodles too *al dente*. Jack recognized his daughter's handiwork, the spaghetti a ball of yarn on the end of her fork. Like a Rosenquist close up. There was something a bit eerie about everything left uneaten, as though they'd had to go somewhere in a hurry. Eerie and irritating, because of the condensation from the soda bottle that was leaving spots on the Biedermeier. Jack licked his thumb and rubbed at them.

Out the window, the Empire State Building was blue-blue-blue. The three tiers of light, in ascending order, had been green-green-green for Saint Patrick's Day, and red-pink-white for Valentine's before that. He didn't know what blue-blue-blue was supposed to mean. When was Rosh Hashanah?

He toed off his shoes and pincered a few strands of pasta, dangled them into his mouth. Cold, but not so hard.

The hinges groaned when he put his palm to the bedroom door. The light was on here too, the little Tiffany lamp with amber fireflies that splashed the books half in yellow glow. Deb was on the bed, not in it, on top of the bedspread, head bent to just miss the pillow and wearing all her clothes.

A box sat gaping at him from the edge of the bed. Not much could be read off the flap, the writing sideways and half in shadow, but Jack recognized the hand from the notes she used to take, pages left to collect footprints all

34

around the studio. He knew that annoyingly small print, child's print, more labored than Kay's or even Simon's, whose penmanship, as a boy's, had been naturally impeded.

Deb was sitting up now. Her dark hair hung thick over either shoulder, like doll's hair, all of a piece and with that familiar crease in it, testimony to the one bun she'd fastened since childhood. Halolike, especially with the firefly eyes reflected, lighting a crown around her head.

"What's going on?" He willed himself to ignore the box, as if somehow to keep her from noticing it.

Deb rubbed small circles into her temples and tried looking at him. Jack was halfway between the door and the bed, standing with both arms at his sides and open to her. She was thinking that he'd put on a couple of pounds, and that he'd never been traditionally handsome and still wasn't but that he was, on the strength of his voice and stature, the declarative bridge of his nose and thick curls, graying now, becoming salt and sand—she was thinking that he was, to women, very much attractive. More now.

Jack noticed not for the first time the dimples around her mouth that deepened whenever she made her worried face. The dimples were girlish, but she'd always have them. And he thought her eyes were on him in that critical way he'd seen more of these last few months. "Tell me what happened," he said, "so I can—"

"Tell you? I should tell you? No, you tell me. No, I don't need you to—"

"Have you been drinking?"

"You were so sexy at the gallery this morning," she read, *"teasing me in those boots."* The page she'd whipped out

35

from nowhere, something she'd been sitting on, armed with. *"Tomorrow I'm going to bend you over—"*

"Deb."

"—I'm going to bend you over and show you how dirty you really are."

"Please."

"I couldn't sleep last night, getting hard thinking about what I had for lunch, which was you. I haven't been drinking, you shit."

"Now come on now, all that's over. I ended it."

"Bravo," she said as he came closer. "Really, well done!"

"Let me see," holding out his hand.

"What for? So you should know how much to admit to?" She lunged forward on the bed and swung the box up and to one side, though kneeling as she was he had only to reach farther forward. "Think she left something out? I don't think so, she's very— *Hey!"*

Hey! because he had the box, and right away she was on her feet and after him. Jack rounded his back at her, her arms flying at him, and he didn't know what to do. What he needed was to think, and so he spun around into the nearest place, their bathroom, and turned the lock behind him.

"What the *hell*." Deb smacked the door from the other side.

He put the box on the counter and pulled the pages out in heaps, dumping them into the sink.

"Jack!"

It was the dirtiest stuff that worried him. Things he'd forgotten writing that made him feel foreign to himself. *i*

36

want to cum between your tits next time. Not that they didn't sound like him.

"Open the goddamn door."

He wanted more than anything to make them go away. The girl was crazier than he'd thought, and it was impossible to talk to Deb with this between them, this prop. But there was only the wastebasket, which was small and from which they'd be retrievable, and the toilet, which would clog the pipes. They should have kept matches. Instead he pulled open the small window that looked out over the gravel courtyard, the building's glorified air shaft. An illogical thing to do, holding handfuls of paper out the window and letting go. He watched the pages fall and catch the air, wafting white into the dark blue, flitting and flipping acrobatically, one or two sailing into open windows.

In the current, the sheets turned as though someone were reading them. That he could hear them turning, flapping against the updraft, made him realize that Deb, in the bedroom, had gone quiet.

When he opened the door again, there was only Travolta, the cat, just wandered in, touching her nose lightly to the corner of bedsheet that had wilted toward the floor.

Jack carried the empty box out to the living room, where the dishes had been stacked and the spaghetti scraped onto a single hulking plate. Deb was standing in the middle of the room, running the charm at her neck taut along its silver chain and watching the time under the television. 12:44. 12:44. 12:44. 12:45.

"Hey," he said. There was a streak of pasta sauce bloodying her neck. He tried to pull her into a hug, to

37

squeeze her arms that way he did when a fight was over, that way that said, It's me, remember? Never forget it's me. I want to hold you, and you want me to. He squeezed her arms, reminding her that she had arms, and a body, and what had happened to her body?

"Don't." She pushed him off. It was exactly the only way she hadn't wanted to let him touch her. She felt her arms shaking and thought, Good, let him see me shake. She wanted the whole room to shake and for him to know it was from something he had done. He saw her see into the box, with only a page stuck at the bottom. "Find the prize inside?"

"It's history, Debby. Ancient." He waved the box as he spoke, and the last sheet fluttered out like a final gesture. "Over."

"You have no clue."

"It's *been* over."

"You sad shit." She spoke softly, but her teeth were sharp at him. "You know who gave it to me? *They* did."

Jack bent over to collect the escaped page. "Who's they?"

"'Who's they?' People you barely know. Your children."

He stayed stooping, face to floor, the paper in his hand. When he stood, things would be different. Or, things were different already, but this was pause, this space of floor, this page. *Maybe bring some food on your way so we won't have to go out*. The girl had shown up with a can of Pringles and a watermelon, like she'd never bought lunch before, never heard of sandwiches. He'd laughed about it at the time, though he'd been annoyed, and she had laughed too, though he could tell she'd been embarrassed and might have cried if he hadn't then taken two of the chips and stuck them half into his mouth so they made a duck's beak. That was a long time ago, when watermelon was in season. It was about to be in season again. Year-old melon and a thing of chips: how he would pay for them now, the moment that he stood.

"Don't act like you don't hear."

"I'm not." He stood. He hadn't made the decision to, only it was a reflex, to answer her, and now here he was. "Who told them to open it? Was it addressed to them?"

"How does that matter?" She pushed past him and carried the stack of plates to the kitchen. Dark in there, but she knew her way around. At the sink she ran the water. On low the faucet made a shrill sound like a whistle or a soft scream.

Jack switched on the light over the counter where they let mail pile up. "What'd they say?" She squeezed green soap wheezy out of the plastic bottle. Her answer was too quiet for him to hear. "What?"

"They don't want to talk to you."

"I can't hear you," though that time he could.

"I said they don't want to talk to you." She was scrubbing a pot.

"Christ—could you not do that now? I mean are you kidding, doing that now?"

She stopped the water and retreated to the bedroom, flicking drops from her fingers as she went. He thought she might have been about to cry, from how she'd kept him from seeing her face.

Travolta trotted out as they came in, the loose of her belly swinging side to side. Deb looked all around the room. "What did you do with it?" She looked into the bathroom and saw the window open. "You did *not*."

"I didn't know what else to do. I don't know what to do."

"Go clean it up. Someone will find them."

He told her he didn't care who found them, the idiots in this building.

"*I* care. I see these people every day. I ride elevators with these people, I see them at the goddamn supermarket."

"Okay, all right. I'll get the pages, and I'll—I'll throw them away."

"It doesn't matter what you do with them. They won't ever go away."

I hope that's not true, he wanted to answer, but it seemed better not to say anything. "I'll be back. Deb? I'll be right back."

She sat on the bed with her head bent and would not show that she'd heard.

The door to the courtyard was through a long hall in the basement, past the boiler room that hummed, the fluorescents bright over the white washing machines, the playroom with its plastic castle and alphabet foam floor. In the basement, as in the elevator, Jack lost reception, but got it back in the open air of the shaft, where he crunched across the gravel and stood amid the litter that was his words and dialed the girl.

The phone rang awhile. It was late, but she stayed up.

He'd never been afraid of her, but he was a little now, waiting for her to answer, afraid of his own anger, of what letting himself be angry would do.

He never found out, because she didn't answer. And so he went around picking up her pages, which were cool on the ground and made him realize for the first time that the night had grown a bit chilly.

i want to cum all around your mouth like lipstick and i want you to lick it up.

In some other context, he could have gotten hard, reading it all over. He thought if she had only sent the letters straight to him, he might even have fucked her again. But that wasn't what the girl wanted, sex. Probably it wasn't ever what she wanted. Women were always deceiving him about that. He was always lowballing their demands.

He got the stack of papers pretty near assembled, if worse for wear. Certainly there were a few pages missing, coasted onto ledges or into the bathrooms and back bedrooms of their neighbors. A nice surprise those would be for someone come morning.

Jack tipped back his head and looked at the square of sky the building made. Starless city sky, just barely distinguishable from the building, silhouetted black and dotted, as his eyes ran down the brick, with squares of yellow, cheerful warm.

He hummed to himself, to the night. Things would turn out okay. For him, somehow, they always had, and so they always would.

. . .

Upstairs again, Jack cradling the pages, there was a moment, pre-words, where they only looked at each other, and he wondered if maybe they were post-words, post all the things that words could do.

"You fuck." Wrong. Deb had words. "I could leave you for this. For less than this."

She was still perched on the bed, and he didn't yet dare sit next to her. "I know you can," he said, easing gently into the rocking chair, trying to keep from swaying.

"Or I can stay, because, I don't know, you want me to."

"Of course I do."

"No, you shut up. I'm not asking what you want. The point is I could, I could do the easy thing, or I could do the hard thing. I don't even know which would be harder. Divorce? Do you know what a nightmare? And I *want* to be married. I got married because I want to be married, Jack. Why did you?"

"Because I love you."

"You don't get to love me right now. That you could sit there and tell me you hope I forgive you, that that—"

"I *do* hope."

"God and I hate that you make me say this, these cliché things. People actually talk this way?"

There was a lot of talk after that, talk that led to nowhere, because it was not one of those problems that talking could fix, and so none of it came in any order they could remember, and all of it went on forever. At one point Deb definitely said, "Do you even know, how much I gave up for—this?" "This" meant "you," and no, for worse or for better, no one could ever know that. And later, when

42

she'd made herself sad: "I have a hard time believing it matters to you." This was in response to the question: What did she want?

He said he would sleep at the studio, and she told him no. She didn't want him in bed with her, but she didn't want him out of the apartment either, leaving her to wonder where he'd gone.

"I'll be in the living room then."

This they hadn't done before, slept in separate rooms, not even last winter, when she first found out. Jack took the saddest of the pillows—he would have dragged it behind him if it were long enough—and went out to the sofa to lie down.

It felt warmer than it had in the courtyard, warm enough to sleep with the windows open. Outside he could hear echoes of happy birthday to you from some rooftop garden or fire escape. Voices from faraway parties, somehow always female—because men were raised not to sing in public, not to really sing—reaching their apartment on the eleventh floor from however many buildings away.

How they met. At a party. "I almost left early," she used to say. "And you almost stayed home." Would it have made a difference? Would they have met some other way? He knew she'd liked thinking about it. The way we met, the way we were. He told her he was married. His wife? No, his wife wasn't there. Didn't like parties. She arched her back at him and asked about his work. Strappy black dress and dusky skin, sharp shoulder blades. They shared a cab home, nothing more. She stood under a canopy until the car pulled away and took the train to where she really lived. She had so wanted to be on his way.

He heard from her a week later. She wanted to meet somewhere and talk. Just talk. His marriage was not exactly well. He let her press her knees against him under the table.

She began visiting the studio downtown. To see how it was done. She took off her underwear and sat for him. "I am married," he told her. She said to sculpt her with his hands.

They spent afternoons in her apartment. He could feel the power in her young legs when they were wrapped around him, reminding him that, if she wanted, she might never let him go. Like a horse but in a good way, good teeth and hair and strong seeming. Her breasts could barely fill a martini glass, but in his hands or in his mouth they felt like enough. He made her sit across the room from him and touch herself. It never affected his work. Impressive even to himself that he could keep them separate. The work existed on some higher plane. With his head between her legs, he thought about form, the shapes of things.

That one day he walked in and found her crying, he didn't have cause to think it was any different from the other times she'd cried. And when she told him why, he thought, isn't this what you wanted? Or maybe he didn't think it; maybe he said it out loud, from the way she started shouting and the way he heard himself apologize and the way he held her after.

Seven months later Simon was born.

And now Simon, this person they'd made, this Simon wouldn't talk to him. Deb had been right about that. The next morning Jack, in his T-shirt and underwear, sat up in the living room, pillow cool across his thighs, waiting, and when Simon finally did come, it was not to his father but to the door, to leave. He was dressed already, backpack on both shoulders, like an armadillo.

Deb followed behind him. "Are you sure you don't want me to zap them?"

"I like them like this." Simon smacked a foil packet against his palm.

"It's so early," she said.

"I told you, I'm meeting somebody. We've got a presentation thing first period."

From the couch Jack offered something short of a wave, almost a salute, and his son's eyes flew to him but then away; he wouldn't look.

Deb followed the boy out, saying tiny things Jack couldn't hear. She stood in the hall while Simon waited for the elevator. From his spot on the couch, Jack could see her arms rise over her head and tense in stretch. She clasped her hands behind her head, elbows forward, and maybe she was whispering something. With everything lifted like that, her long sleep shirt became almost inappropriate for the hall. As a dancer she'd never been shy about her body, which was narrow and less tall than it seemed. Sometimes Jack thought it would do to be a little shy about it with the kids. His children would never see him walking around like that. But it was different, too, with men.

There was the chime and warble of the elevator, then the clack and near echo of both locks snapping shut. Jack watched Deb walk back toward the kitchen and did not expect her to stop, which she did.

"I have nothing to say to you," she told him. In a way, good news. Like saying, *No, I can't hear you,* or, *Yes, I'm sleeping.* Jack even smiled a little.

Deb bent forward, resting her hands on her kneecaps. "Are you crying?"

Was he? Well, he was smiling a little and crying a little,

too. Surprising, to find his eyes wet. He blinked hard and squeezed out a tear. It wasn't a bad thing, to cry. If there was ever a time besides funerals, it was now, here. She looked into his face, and he held it out to her, open as he could make it, hoping to be solved by her. Whatever fix she found, it was important she think it her own.

He began to imagine that she was waiting for him to blink, so he tried not to, and his eyes watered more. She released the sight of him and walked to the kitchen. Jack pulled on his pants and went after her.

Kay was at the sink, her penguin pajamas rolled to the knees, using a spoon to strain extra water from a bowl of instant oatmeal. There were eggs on the counter in pink Styrofoam, and Deb began cracking them into a mug. Use a glass, Jack wanted to tell her. Easier to check for shells.

What he saw of the future, the next few weeks at least: His wife would fight with him, really just yell, because who can fight with a spineless thing? A misshapen, regretful thing that curls up and sleeps with white flags waving like windshield wipers. She'd get sick of yelling, of crying. When she cried, Kay cried, Simon cried. They'd speak to him only when his physical presence was an impediment, when he was blocking the refrigerator and they needed him to move. And then they'd be overpolite.

"Excuse me, please," said Kay, and he let her by for the milk.

For a time, they'd live this way.

Back in the living room, he thumped his bare feet into shoes, pushed his head and arms through the same neck- and armholes as yesterday. When he closed the door, he did

47

it quietly. He pushed for the elevator and watched his face in the hall mirror. He rubbed his cheeks, which felt porous and muggy. He rubbed enough that some oily bits of skin rolled up under his fingers. The elevator came, and Jack felt the bulk of his wallet in his back pocket. He would keep out of the house during the day. Officially, because Deb would want Simon and Kay to wake up and come home to what she called *a neutral space*. But he would have gone anyway. He didn't know how to face them, his kids.

Ballet III began at 1:10 in the Barnard Hall Dance Annex two days a week. Deb watched in the mirror as the girls trickled in, clinging to each other and giggling. These past few weeks their arrival could be timed by the sun, the hour it chose to angle itself through the high windows, warming the dark floor and bouncing off the corner mirrors. College girls, some carried their leftover lunches with them, salads in plastic bowls.

Deb set Delibes spinning on the stereo. "Legs turned out. Keep them out," she called, walking down the aisles of them. She saw her presence recorded in ripples where she passed, backs straightening, chins lifted a little higher. "Nice. That's good."

A joke to try and do both, college and ballet. With modern dance you could, maybe. Five years of teaching, and not one of her graduates was still dancing. Not that they kept in touch. She liked the girls, they seemed like such good girls, but she never let them get close. She had the best résumé on faculty—City Ballet spelled success—and so her classes were always full. But she knew her reputation: accomplished, chilly.

"Okay, now remember your legs. Turn. No twisting."

Sometimes they asked about Isabel Davey. Did she know her? A little.

Deb and Izzy were at SAB together. They entered the corps the same season, danced the same shows. They shared an apartment in Chelsea before it became expensive and climbed the ranks together, though Izzy climbed higher and faster and, unlike Deb, never broke. When Deb quit, she was about to turn twenty-seven, and *we all have to quit sooner or later*. But Izzy was still dancing. She'd grown a career as old as Simon, and she was a star now—her name appeared in bold type now.

"That's good, Hannah. And, arms arabesque." The girls lacked form, discipline. Even the few who'd shown promise as first years, the serious and naturally turned out, were worsening. That was why Deb kept her distance. She corrected their arms, tapped together their heels, but rarely did she learn where they were from, what dorm or what state, and when they asked her advice, she had a hard time meeting their gazes. To encourage them would feel like a lie, because really, she didn't approve, wanted to whisper in their ears: *Quit now*. Better off spending their time in economics or history, pre-med, pre-law, pre-anything. To watch them try depressed her. They'd compromised, with their families, with themselves, their ambition. They had lives outside these rooms. Whereas when Deb met Jack, she was virgin enough to still be proud she wasn't one.

She'd known since Christmas, when they'd gone to see Jack's mother and stepdad in Houston. Their last day, while Charles was showing model trains to his not-quite grandchildren in the attic and Phyllis was popping tubes of crescent rolls in the kitchen, Deb listened to Jack hold half a conversation on the other side of the bathroom door. Half had been enough. She raised her arm and hit the door three times, hard, not with her fist but the flat of her hand, like a POW tapping out code, blows that echoed in the quiet wood after. There was a pause, and when Jack opened the door her eyes were hot but there wasn't time to scream or say anything, because there was Phyllis, her hands in a dish towel, asking if something had dropped.

In Houston, then, Deb hadn't been able talk to him. Her anger became unspeakable in that house where Jack was everywhere, in picture frames, in mirrors. She'd excused herself from dinner, citing a headache, and in so doing found it was true: Her head did hurt. Then on the plane home, they sat apart, their seats two and two. Only when they were home could she tell him, with perfect calm, to get the hell out.

But by then Jack too had had time to prepare, and his counter was a triumph, deft in just the way she should have known it would be. He had been immediately grateful. Thank God she'd found him out, to shepherd him from all he had already come to regret. He'd been on a wild horse, and she'd lassoed him in. Thank you, Deb, for saving us.

That night, he answered the questions she wished she didn't have. Questions made it seem like the answers could matter, if they were the right ones. Still, there were things she couldn't help wanting to know. Do you love her? (No.) How long has it been? (Less time than you think, but too long.) And you'll give it up? (Yes, I will, yes.) How'd it start? (She's a kid. She just wanted to talk to me.) When did you know you would? (I didn't, honestly. I never meant to.)

She tongued the corner of her mouth where she could feel a cold sore coming. "Arabesque now. Reach."

Deb envied everyone. She envied Izzy and she envied these girls, looking to her now out of the corners of their eyes, gripping the barre, their arms bent in fourth position. They had no idea yet how old they were in the dance world, just as Deb, at their age, had had no idea how young she was in the real one. At twenty-two and twenty-three, at parties with regular people, nondancers—they'll coo over you like a rare bird. Which you are, to them. You are sinewy grace and bone, everywhere tight, from your tied hair to your pointed toes. And you'll feel yourself a liar there too, because in the corps you are one of so many. Your own mother needing binoculars to pick you out. The only time Deb didn't feel like a ballerina was at the theater. That's the rude surprise. Like your father used to say, a pinhead in the crowd.

"Good, ladies. Again." She thought they had so little in common, yet here she was, in the room with them.

Was it after a fight, or some night I said I was too tired? (No, Deb, no, don't do that to yourself. Who knows anymore?) Were there others? (Nothing, nothing that mattered.) How many? (It doesn't matter.) How many, a

52

number. (I don't know.) What is it you do with them that you can't do with me? (It's nothing like that, Deb. There's no comparison. I don't compare them—Hey, don't—what, Deb, Debby, shh.)

The period did somehow pass, and as class was ending, Deb's cellphone rang. It was an unknown number, and she didn't want to answer it, but that was the thing about having kids.

"I don't get it—you never call, never write. You get my email?"

"How are you, Gary." Gary was Jack's old roommate from the Rhode Island School of Design. There was the long-told story of how they met their first year in an experimental film class. Gary had nudged Jack awake during a screening of Brakhage's *Mothlight,* which was actually a mass of insect wings taped together and run through as a filmstrip. *Now I know what life is like for a bug zapper,* Jack had said.

"I'm good." Gary was always good. "I'm just looking at my calendar, thinking of making it down to the house." The two men had bought a ramshackle house together while they were still in school, a fixer-upper where they both could paint and Gary could go fishing. Gary had since married and divorced a wealthy woman, and then another wealthy woman, and lived mostly alone now, mostly in Boston, halfheartedly selling real estate. In the summers he was always trying to get them out to Jamestown, to the vacation he was always on.

"It's just been a little crazy these days."

"I know, Jack's opening coming up!" Gary had left the art world, or it had not come to him, but still he liked to keep track. "He nervous?"

"Listen, can I call you back?" Behind her the girls were filing out, texting, eating their salads. They shoveled leaves into their wide-open mouths like brontosauruses, or was it brachiosauruses.

"Real quick—I tried your husband."

"Oh?" Though it wasn't unusual these days for Jack to ignore Gary's calls. At some point the history between the two men had hardened.

"Left a voice mail, I know he hates those. Anyway, would you tell him I said good luck? Good luck with the show."

"Why don't you try him again? He should be at the studio."

At the studio, Jack had a long leather couch. No shower but a basin he could lean into and wash as far as his armpits. When a piece was going well, he was there all hours, through the night. He'd fall asleep on the swivel stool, hunched over the drafting table sometime near morning. When his head and his hands were running on all cylinders, it became impossible to scrape him out.

That had happened more often in the early years, when he was hungry and everything was on the rise. For a while he lived and worked the way he'd imagined doing while at RISD, five or ten pieces always going at once. So many ideas, he'd only had to go out into the world, among the ten thousand things, and there they would be. He saw strange symmetry in everything. It felt like stealing.

More recently he had begun to ask why, and, what for. At least to wonder. He sometimes caught himself standing idle and oafish among the fuel tanks and torches, unformed sheet metal, sharp dust crowding everything.

He was standing like that now.

He walked to the big window and tipped it open as far as it would go, breathing in the mild midday air. No. He would not not work.

It would go against the grounds on which he'd married. Family was meant to make things easier. He'd seen other artists, rivals and friends, how they struggled when they were alone. Forgot to eat. Lived in their studios, gave up their homes. Or the homes became the studios. They got too thin or too fat, too everything. They drank and didn't exercise, except with girls they brought home from other people's shows, and even then it was only an hour, two tops, before the girls pushed out from under their heavy arms and wriggled away. Drugs and they never knew what day it was. His painter friend Richard stopped taking the medication that kept his hair in his head, either couldn't remember to, or it conflicted with the drugs he was on already, Xanax and Percocet, Valium, special K. Those he never forgot. Richard had been taking SSRIs for twenty years without a prescription. What he paid for in place of health insurance.

Jack had had it with the benders, had his fill of them by age forty. The sad and unglamorous truth that he knew and people like Richard didn't was that it's no good living like the art you're trying to make. Art is work. It is getting up early and working until you are tired and after, and it is surrounding yourself with things that keep you in a healthy state. People. Life on a schedule. This was why Richard the painter was bald and Jack still had a thick head of hair.

So: He would not not work. Only he couldn't start any

real project until he knew the consensus on his last. That was another thing he'd developed these last few years, a reputation. His reviews were read now, and it made him careful.

There was one job he could do, a commission from a university out west. The director of facilities at the art school there, a woman, had given him almost totally free rein. The director's name was Jolene, but call her Jolie, and she laughed at simple questions like they were good jokes. That and the syrupy twang of her disembodied voice had him thinking she was fat and flushed easily. He'd told her the name of the piece he was chewing over: *Sculptural Improvisation*. Jolie had laughed. It would be in braised bronze. "That sounds just right," she'd said. "Just right for the space."

He'd been getting more commissions, more attention from better galleries, steadily over the last nine or ten years, ever since the controversy, the September series he'd made, also bronze, in 2002. You'd know it. Even outside the art world you'd have seen it. Three pieces. There was the man sitting, bent over and hugging his knees. There was the woman crouched, eyes closed and arms out, hugging an empty space. And there was the other man falling, presumed falling. He was upside down, his head twisted as though just pressed against something. His bronze suit was rippled and rushing, filled with metallic air. They were put out in Bryant Park. By the fourth day, two of the three had been vandalized and had to be cleaned. By the sixth day, they were covered in tarp. Then they were carted away.

Jolie would use terms like *site specific* about *Sculptural*

Improvisation's size and position in the surrounding quad. Jack foresaw university tour guides noting how Shanley's piece forced the visitor to "*acknowledge the space.*" They would talk about the movement of the thing, even though there wasn't any. Sometimes with these big pieces he felt he was pissing all over everything, marking territory. Very few people know anything, and the ones who do don't know much. Students would meet by it, sit on its low bend in springtime and wrap its ends with scarves in winter. Maybe screw on it the night before graduation.

He started the circ saw but kept stopping, thinking he heard his phone. It was impossible to hear, with the machine going and his earplugs in besides. But he swore he heard it, worming its way into his ear, that phantom tone.

The September series turned out, years later, to be how he met the girl, a graduate student at NYU who wanted to interview him. For her thesis, she said. Censorship in art. Probably won't even be published, she told him. "I can come to you." She didn't have a Dictaphone or anything like that, so they recorded the interviews on his computer for him to email to her later. She kept coming, and eventually he stopped sending them. She was the kind that goes around all day with buttons undone and doesn't know it. She kept coming.

In the studio now, he tried not to think of her, but it was hard, the number of times he'd had her there. He tried at least not to think of her by name.

His first marriage had been fucked from the start, but this time, with Deb, he'd married the right woman. He had.

Marrying Deb, having the kids, all that was right. It was

he who'd gone wrong, or the world. He'd felt it these last few years. Something to do with the Internet and jihad and all the natural disasters they'd been having: There was a buzz in the air that made it harder to move forward, a feeling that they were living in a time with no future. And then there had been that girl, in her see-through blouses with the breasts under them, soft and pointed up like curious things. With her full lips and full ass, and how did she stay so full when everything else every day was being depleted, when—

Listen, look:

It's not like I killed anybody.

That was it. Jack did not really, in the end, believe he'd done anything so wrong. With the girl he'd been careful to make no promises. He'd encouraged her to date. Deb would need time and patience to forgive him, but here, alone with his tools, he could feel he was forgiving himself already.

True, it was hard on the kids, but that was why he wanted to explain to them, explain how much it was not about them. Maybe that was the painful part, that not everything in their parents' lives could be.

The girl was a channel that let him be a better man at home. Like a soldier, I do on the outside what I need to keep the inside safe. That was the truth of how he felt, something to be kept down and buried deep.

(But what stays buried? Even heavy things have that way about them, of always coming to the surface—*especially* heavy things do—and when it did happen, when it did all come out, that Jack had been sleeping with a woman who was not his wife, not once but many times, a woman who loved him or thought she loved him, everyone knew. Deb, the kids, their grandmother. Even the building knew, because of something Simon said in the elevator, when a neighbor woman from the top floor had asked how is everything, and Simon, who was meant to make his answer about school, Model UN or SAT prep work, had said that his parents were getting divorced and that probably they would be moving.

Actually it was not so bad as that. Worse too, but also not so bad, in that it hadn't been totally Simon's fault. Because there, on the elevator bulletin board, where the co-op posted its newsletters and petitions against nearby construction sites, where tenants pinned lost socks from the laundry room, tacked *there,* for all to see, was a piece of paper, slightly creased.

Across the top, in red pen, like a bad mark from a teacher, the words: *PLEASE do NOT drop TRASH into the SHAFT.*

Simon didn't know how the page got wherever it had been, or who had found it, but he knew what it said, approximately. Approximately, he knew the words.

So he hadn't had to look at it very carefully, not like the mom from 16B, who'd smiled at him before leaning close to the board and squinting to read. She bent further forward in the stretchy pants she always wore, purple and made of something like crushed velvet, gloving her body in a way that embarrassed him.

Simon hung back against the wall, squeezing the elevator rail behind him, and watched as her features crowded together in the middle of her face. Her size and her boy's haircut made her elfish. He thought of a *Peter Pan* they'd seen one summer on a family trip to the Berkshires.

"God," she said. "Gosh, that's horrible. They shouldn't have that up in here." She sucked the air between her teeth and tried to share a cringe with him.

Simon stared blankly back and watched her become awkward about the words they'd been confined with, she and this person who was still more boy than man. Her eyes clocked the door, though it was closed, had been closed, the floor already lurching up beneath their feet. "So, you must be all done with classes."

"Almost."

"Bet you're pretty excited."

"Uh-huh." Simon paused. "Actually I haven't thought about it too much, since my parents have been splitting up? I don't know if you—? No no, it's totally fine. I mean things got pretty rough but, it is what it is. Better this way."

As he spoke the neighbor woman did too. "Oh," she said, "No, I," "Gosh, I had no," and "Well." She spoke to bridge the gaps, to keep him going. She could not have stopped him anyway; Simon could build his own bridges. Or could sink his own ship. Whatever the expression.

"Happens, right? We'll probably be packing and moving all summer, so but that's fun. I wasn't going to go to camp anyway, this year."

"I'm sorry." New light fell on her face, light from the hall. The elevator had stopped. They'd reached his floor. "I'm going to write to your mother," she was saying, the moment that Simon, one leg out the door, lunged at the board, tearing down the page and sending the tack flying.

He watched 16B's face, all surprise, as the elevator closed. His mother could probably not expect any note.

In the hall he reread the message along the top of the page. The *S* in "SHAFT" was the fancy, curling kind. And "TRASH" was clever, how it could mean two things. Someone had taken the time.

He took the page to his room and closed the door, though it was not yet three—he'd skipped his last two periods—and no one else was home. These were the words that he guessed had embarrassed 16B: *Spread. Tits. Cum.* Also, maybe: *Open. Fingers.*

He folded it five times, bent it a sixth, and buried it in his underwear drawer. Hard to say why he'd taken it at all.

Not to protect his parents, their privacy. And Simon's words to 16B shouldn't have meant much, shouldn't have reverberated very far. Shouldn't have but would; he knew they would, enough for their next-door neighbors to hold vigil for signs of cardboard boxes in the stairwell, to wonder where the support beams were, to calculate the dimensions of new living rooms when their two apartments became one.)

In most of them, Jerry and Elaine fell in love. More recently, Elaine and George had been falling in love, and that had been more interesting. Elaine and Kramer would never fall in love. Kramer was not a very well-rounded character. He was not very *dimensional,* as her father would sometimes say about art. Kay's middle name, Ellen, was very like Elaine's name, Elaine, a fact that Kay liked about herself.

She didn't know how it started, only she was sure she didn't know it was a thing until later, when she found the forums. By then she'd seen all the episodes, which were on every day after school, sometimes two at the same time on different stations, and she'd already written a few herself, though she had recently learned that her formatting was not yet in the standard way. But in the beginning she thought she'd invented it. And in a way, hadn't she? Invented it to herself. The best was that she could write them anywhere, whenever she was bored, and become not bored.

She wrote them in the back row of math, or she wrote them in the back row of history, or she thought up new stories on the bus ride home with her head bouncing off the window that rattled and her knees pressed against the fake leather seat in front of her, torn in places and patched with tape.

Now in her room after dinner, while her brother played Xbox in the living room and her mother did dishes, Kay wrote ideas in the notebook where homework was supposed to go.

- Kramer goes to a foreign country (Turkey?) and Jerry promises his apartment to Elaine and to George. Fight. Or: they move in together? Love?
- Elaine buys a vintage dress that is white and she doesn't realize that it is a wedding dress until she goes outside and everyone on the street makes jokes like: Where's the groom? She likes the attention and she thinks it makes boys imagine marrying her. This backfires somehow.
- Kramer dies?

There was a crashing sound in the kitchen, a plate breaking. "Shoot," Kay heard her mother say.

- Elaine has an unbreakable dinner plate that breaks and that she has been trying to return to Bed Bath & Beyond. But the guy behind the counter looks at the bag with the pieces of plate in it and says they can't take it back because she dropped it on too hard a floor. The guy says: "Sorry, your floor's too hard." Elaine makes a face at him like, what?

Kay went to bed without finishing her homework. Deb came, as she had been doing these last few nights, to sit with her daughter in case she cried, which mostly Kay didn't. She'd been going to bed earlier each night because it was taking her longer to fall asleep.

For her mother Kay had always been the more difficult, difficult because she would not make herself so. She would not speak up as Simon did, and so it was impossible to know what she thought and felt, how much she understood. Deb knew that adults were always underestimating what an eleven-year-old understands, but she was too far from that age to remember how much.

She had tried. "It's okay," she'd said that first night after Simon had gone to his room (part of his *prerogative*, those days, to be always the first to leave). Sometimes a married person meets someone new, someone they think is nice, or exciting, and sometimes they'll make a mistake. Lots of married people, women too, but mostly men, lots of them do this. "But it doesn't mean anything. And it isn't about you."

And Deb left her daughter to sleep, not knowing that she'd said the wrong thing—so easy to do when you are a parent. Where she'd gone wrong, it was just a word, how could she have known. What she should have said: It doesn't mean *everything*.

Instead she'd said that it didn't mean anything, and Kay

had lain awake picking paint blisters off the wall, trying hard to believe that the things her father had done were okay. If this was the world that was waiting for her, it would be a good idea to stick a toe into it now, let her body adapt to such a future, which was cold, not at all a place she wanted to be.

Everyone does these things.

You know what was a lie, then? Television was a lie. *Friends* and *Everybody Loves Raymond,* where married dads didn't have sex with other women. Maybe they did and just never talked about it. Too obvious to get its own episode.

When she was little—Kay's stories often began this way, with the old people in the room always shouting, "You're *still* little"—but when she was little, maybe four years earlier, Deb brought home a DVD of *The Little Mermaid* from a peddler down by Battery Park. Only it wasn't the version she'd seen before: Here the Ariel was blond, and her name wasn't Ariel but Marina, and instead of Sebastian the crab there was a dolphin named Fritz. It was the original fairy tale, not Disney but Hans Christian Andersen, and in the end Marina turned to foam, was happy to turn to a clear, fine sea-foam so that she could float or buoy or do whatever sea-foam does near her prince. Kay had cried at the television, "Don't they know kids are supposed to watch this?" (Adults loved that part of the story, that she'd said that.)

If that was a fairy tale, what was *Seinfeld*? She knew she'd been watching something, not the truth, but not something entirely foreign. Life wasn't like television, but did it have to be so different?

Stranger things happen. Stranger things happen than this.

So the girl was not answering. So what? That was like her, to blow a storm in from nowhere and then just disappear. How many calls back in winter had he let go off in his pocket? How many messages had he let sit weeks, unplayed, until one came in for work, something he needed? Only then had he cycled through the others—*thirteen* of them— the beginnings only. "Hi, I—" "I don't—" "You never—" "What—" "People d—" "*You sh*—" How she changed! And came entirely around again, so that the second-to-last one was back to "Hi," and the very last was nothing, was "............................" Jack had listened to them, had not listened, on the streets, so that it felt like nothing he was doing, so that it was like—what?—just walking, just going place to place.

And now—trying to lure him to her, that was what she was doing. So fine, if it was what she wanted. Confrontation. Maybe it was what he wanted. Look at what you've done—to *children*. She'd think she was getting her way, at first. She'd see him there, through the peephole, and think she won. That Deb had left him and that he'd come back to her, maybe that he needed her.

He took the train down to Astor Place and cut across on St. Mark's, where neon from the shops and bars made brighter the night sky, would have made it almost day if not for the packs of people, nighttime energy the light could not break through. A little after midnight but still warm, the tourists out with their tiny backpacks, the freshmen from NYU just starting to make themselves sick drinking, many sets of legs that began at the hip, ended in towering heels.

He passed the hot dog place with the phony speakeasy inside. Fifteen-dollar cocktails, and who for? What Lou Reed wrote about wasn't around anymore. Sally can't dance. The whole strip was like one of those living history exhibits, commemorating an old war that was lost and over now, only nobody wanted to know it was over. Because it had been a sexy war and it was hard to let go.

Avenue C was quieter. The girl lived on the top floor of a six-story walk-up. She used to get scared and call him on her way home. Someone's following me. Stay on until he goes away. Then: Stay on until I'm inside, until I feel better, it's scary here, alone, I'm making tea, stay on. Stay on until.

He buzzed 6B, Garcia. Still the old tenant's name on the number.

After a minute he buzzed again, but he didn't have to wait. Another tenant, a small, deeply tanned woman, came out through the lobby, trailed by a leash and then an old husky. She held the door, and Jack took it, remembered having patted the dog once or twice. "Late night for a walk," he said, looking down.

She smiled. "I spoil him."

"Lucky dog."

She walked away still smiling. Around forty. Tight jeans, tight ass. Probably never married.

The stairs he climbed a few at a time. He used to be better at them, was now winded by the fourth landing. Two more to go. He stood a minute to breathe outside her door.

Knocking.

She was out, or was asleep, or? The lights were on under the door.

He turned and looked up and down the hall, trying to remember where she kept the secret key—under one of the other apartment's mats (less obvious, she said)—when he heard the chain slide open behind him.

There was the roommate, a short, stomping thing always in yoga pants. "Oh," she said. "It's you."

"Arabella." Her name was easy to remember because it was so at odds with the rest of her. "I hope I didn't wake you." The thing about those pants: he could never tell if they were pajamas.

She stepped back, crossing her arms, the upper parts rashy with chicken skin. "You know your way around."

All the lights in the living room were on, and somehow it seemed they'd been on a long time. The TV, too, at commercial.

The girl's room was dark except for the table lamp from IKEA he'd put together for her, shining into a mug of coffee that was cloudy at the surface, like a blind eye. Her makeup bag was turned over, glitter dusting the desk and colored pencils rolled halfway over the edge. She'd started wearing more makeup, toward the end. He remembered the last time, when he knew and she didn't that it would be the last, that she hadn't washed; he could tell by her hair, where it was matted and stringy.

The bed was the same, same sheets, unmade as ever, the comforter in a heap on the floor. And over the bed, that painting, one of those Chinese ones they peddle all over Times Square, her name in watercolors, letters shaped from flowers and birds: J*O*R*D*A*N. A gift from her parents the time they came to see the New York life she'd made for herself. He hated how it brought out what was tacky and juvenile about her. "But it's pretty," she'd said. She liked looking at it.

The overhead came on. "You can tell her I want this month and next," Arabella said behind him.

He looked at her like who was the crazy one. "She isn't here."

"No shit, Sherlock."

"Do you know when she's back?"

"She's with you." Arabella shifted her feet. "You aren't here for her stuff?"

He said, "No," and clearly that was the wrong answer.

"That fucking—cunt." She began unfolding and refolding the waist of her pants. "I don't even. Monday she said she was going to the *vet*."

The guinea pig, Jack realized, was gone. The albino puff with red eyes that he'd tried to keep away from but that still got its little hairs on everything, had made Travolta distrust him before anyone else did.

"Look," he said. "This has been a mistake." Arabella was starting to sweat in front of him.

"But you have to know where she is."

"No." He moved in reverse and she forwarded. "I'm the last—believe me, she wants to talk to me even less than—least of all people. I mean, you don't think she'd do anything, to hurt herself, do you?"

New rashes began to blossom on her chest and the rounds of her cheeks. "I could call the police."

"You should." Backtracking along the hall, arms out behind him. "I think you *ought* to call the police."

"Yeah and I'm sure they won't want to question *you*. The married boyfriend."

"Hang on, okay? Hang on." He saw the backs of his hands and realized he'd put them up. "Let's see if I can make this easier. What's rent for her room, like six hundred? Six fifty?" He began to feel into his pockets.

"Nine."

"Christ, *nine*? Okay, okay, wait." He pulled a billfold of twenties from his back pocket, then smaller denominations from the front of his jeans, balled up and crunchy. "I've got . . . one—one twenty . . . one thirty . . . seven. A hundred and thirty-seven. Dollars. For you, from me. A gift."

She did him the favor of taking it.

The next morning, Jack's studio looked like the set for a movie or TV show, the pieces of house laid out the way he'd have them in the gallery. The movers were coming that day for the walls. Really they were blocks, but Jack thought of them as walls, and lining the space of the gallery, they'd look like walls. He was still packing them in felt and tarp when the buzzer rang. Four guys and a couple of mattress carts.

When everything was loaded, he took a cab to the gallery and met them there. He'd wanted to ride in the back of the truck, but the muscle men told him no, there wasn't room, what if one of the blocks fell over. "I'll fall *you* over," Jack muttered, but hailed a taxi anyway.

At the gallery the staff left him alone to set everything up. Even the little receptionist out front he made leave. He listened to her heels clack across the hardwood of the lobby and out.

Then he mixed the plaster, rigged the explosives. Peering at angles through the walls' windows, he adjusted the furniture inside. He turned over a chair he'd welded himself, broke a ceramic dish into the ground. He brought out a stuffed animal, a tiger he'd found in their building's playroom. The one found object in the space. With a good pull he tore a leg off and let the stuffing cloud out of the stump.

Around lunch he got a falafel and carried it to the park, tahini sauce dribbling out the foil. He sat on a bench near the playground, a school group shrieking. It was a cool day for playground weather but their little bodies kept hot, running and jumping and swinging. Jack watched them and wondered how anyone could doubt that human beings came from monkeys. At the slide, kids at the bottom end scooted up the wrong way to go again.

He'd been up front about not wanting children, and Deb had been afraid to tell him in the beginning. But then, life, and she was having one, they were, and it surprised them both how it changed him. Most infidelities happen during pregnancy, when the woman is a whale and cries all the time. Maybe that isn't true but you did hear stories, eight months along and the husband out the door. With Jack it was never that way. When Deb was sore and bloated and soft in places she hated being soft, when her whole body felt like meat and when she was most afraid, that was when he had loved her best.

There was a small, pretty Mexican woman watching him from the bench nearest his. She had a fat blond cherub bouncing in her lap. The women at playgrounds were all sitters. A few reminded Jack of the Latvian woman who'd been their nanny after Deb's maternity leave with Kay and

74

before Simon was big enough to be in charge after school. Jack was proud they'd gone so long without succumbing to a caretaker.

The pretty Mexican had begun to glare at him. Jack balled up his foil and headed back to the gallery, remembering that there were rules about grown-ups in playgrounds, how long men without children were permitted to sit.

At six o'clock Nicky came. "'Sup, boss?" Lanky Nicky in his hoodies and caps, his videographer, twenty-four and twice arrested for vandalism, both times with Jack to bail him out. Today he wore a shirt that boasted TEIAM PLAYER, which Jack wouldn't get until later. He had his equipment bag heavy on one shoulder, a skateboard and a tripod in his arms.

Nicky was a shy kid and quiet most of the time, qualities Jack found common in street artists, which would have surprised people but shouldn't have; the art required them to disappear. And Nicky disappeared well behind a camera. That was what Jack liked about him.

Nicky set the tripod where Jack told him. He gave a thumbs-up when they were rolling and Jack fingered the detonator in his hands. "All right, steady." He'd done a number of practice runs at the studio, but still there was no guarantee that the walls would break along the right lines, that the impact wouldn't subtract too much or too little.

He'd wanted to save the explosions for opening night, for an audience, but the safety people wouldn't let him unless they were behind glass, which showed how little they understood.

There was a slight lag when he pressed the button before

plaster shot off in all directions. Clouds of it got into his clothes, into his lungs, would have gotten into his eyes but for the goggles. Good he'd had the extra pair for Nicky.

They went section by section, stopping to set up the next shot, a new angle.

They waited for the dust to settle.

The air puffed and swirled milky around them. Particles sank into small heaps on the floor. The rubble was good. He'd keep that. Jack thought the walls had all gone off without much problem. A piece by the window on block #3 had not blasted all away, but it looked okay that way, maybe better. That was one thing he liked about the blasts, how they allowed for happy accidents.

Even with the goggles, Jack's eyes had watered. He went out to the lobby to breathe.

There he took a sheet of letterhead from the receptionist's desk and wrote a note. *NO ONE MUST TOUCH THE DEBRIS.* He tucked the page into her keyboard, between the keys.

Nicky was at the window, reviewing footage by the blue light of the dying day.

Jack came up behind and looked over his shoulder. "What do you think?"

Nicky frowned. "How do you want to project these?"

"A few screens in back. Have it on a loop. I don't want anyone to see it until after they've been to the house." Yes, from blocks to walls, Jack had built a house that day.

Deb's cold sore bloomed, and the rest of her lip chapped. Not a natural chap but the kind she did to herself, biting and bothering, an adolescent habit that had made it past adolescence, past gnawing her toenails and cracking her back. The lip hurt, but not in a way she minded. Anyone who'd danced had an unusual patience for pain.

"They're just impenetrable to me. I don't know when that happened," she called from the slipcovered couch. "It's like, if I say jump, they say, you know, *no*. They lie down."

At Ruth's, she had no choice but to face her mother's kid, herself. Ruth lived in a junior one bedroom downtown, in an apartment complex that made it seem hard to get to, and with each visit Deb startled at the number of photographs laid out, how the place seemed always to become more a shrine. There, on the bookcase nearest the door, was Deb, age five, performing a handstand stoically against a wall at home in Tenafly, and at nine, eating frozen custard on the boardwalk at Point Pleasant when her father was still alive.

A pink-tulled sweet sixteen was under way on the mantle over the television, all her ballet friends posing beside pizza and sparkling cider in Dixie cups, Deb with horrible aqua eyeliner and a mouth full of braces. Her career at City Ballet was born atop the CD changer, where she was beaming backstage in red and blue for *Stars and Stripes,* and died with *The Nutcracker* in the carousel frame between two wicker chairs, the season she'd danced Marzipan. Beside that a rickety wood-veneer liquor cart collected not bottles but Simons and Kays at all heights and ages, enough for a flip-book.

"Maybe you could try sending them to somebody," Ruth said in the kitchen.

"I think that ship sort of sailed." Simon had gone to a psychiatrist the year before, after what happened at the Best Buy. He'd come home complaining that the lady was half-deaf and smelled of vitamins. She'd told him he could talk about whatever he wanted, so Simon had talked about videogames.

"So they don't like to talk." Ruth came out carrying a mug with a thumb rest and a handful of her pills. "Well, they're definitely yours."

"What's that supposed to mean?" Deb asked as Ruth delivered the pills, then the mug, to her mouth, swallowing with a sharp backward kick of her head. "Really, Mom, do you have to take them like that?"

"How am I supposed to take them?"

"Nothing, just it's dramatic."

"Deborah." Ruth put a hand in the air, palm out, where it tremored and failed to make her point. "What is your problem? Say."

"I don't know. It seems ridiculous all of a sudden. That I *wanted* to work it out."

Ruth sat and leaned her hand with the mug on her daughter's knee. "What changed?"

"Reading it? I don't know, believing? And I *want* Kay to be able to tell me what she's feeling. I don't *want* Simon to think of me as a person who lets these things happen."

"You want to set an example. But everything's black and white at their age. Give yourself a break. You'll make yourself crazy. Not everything is so cut and dry."

Deb was thinking, why does everybody cry. Stupid to cry; what does it do? What does it get out? "Do you know, I keep thinking of what you told me, when you knew I was pregnant." She meant the first time, when her mother had tried to talk her out of it. You're twenty-six, Deborah. I'm old enough. He's a married man. I don't care. What about dancing? Dancing is who cares. Dancing over.

"What did I say?"

"You said, 'What do you want a child for? You will never again know when it is safe to feel happy.'"

"Sure," Ruth nodded her small blond head. "Like having your heart walk around outside your body the rest of your life." She stood and walked back to the kitchen. "Am I wrong?"

"No."

"I can't hear."

"No, you're right," Deb said louder.

The refrigerator opened, tinkling bottles and jars inside. "So what about tonight? Are you going or what?"

The kids would not come. They'd missed Jack's shows before, been kept away from them because of content, things she didn't want their young eyes seeing—nakedness, the suggestion of blood. So there had been a precedent for that. Ruth would call them around six to check in, see if they needed anything. And Deb would be home by eight.

Of course, she had thought about not going herself. But she wasn't going for him. She was going because she thought the girl might.

In the lobby of the gallery, people were starting to gather, bodies in black or white. Plastic cups of wine hovered, deep cherry and blond, catching the light. The warmer days were taking everyone by surprise, and the AC was not quite strong enough, so that the show cards were fanned and fluttered, made to produce small currents. The receptionist girl was there by the door, her hair slicked back with dark grooves, bite marks from a comb's teeth, the furrows deep and clean and even. Here, too, was art.

Jack mingled.

"I thought the show was called *Bait*," said the woman from *KIOSK*, "like with an *i*." They all said the same things. Jack laughed and touched their elbows, if they were women, refreshed their drinks if they were men. He laughed and looked to the door and continued to not see her.

Deb pulled out her phone, checked the time. Walking was taking longer than she thought it would, but she was in no hurry. Let him wonder. She knew how he got, wired, before an opening. So in a small way she was surprised, how this time he had gone through it alone, that he had not even tried to enlist her. Though if he *had*—she imagined the things she would have said to him, if he'd come to her now with that worry. Sorry, buddy. Not my problemo. You should have thought about that before. She would have especially liked that part, saying that.

"Hate to tell you this," Stanley said. "I know Deb's running late, but we gotta open up." Stanley had been director at the gallery for more years than Jack had known him, and Jack had known him a long time. They stood shoulder to shoulder, facing out, Stanley's eyes running inventory of who had come, how long the most important people had been waiting.

"Oh, yeah," Jack answered. "Sure, that's fine," and turned toward the room.

For the first eight or nine minutes, only Jack would remember, the show was well received. *Bayt* was a home in no specified country. It could have been an Israeli home or a Palestinian home. It could have been in Iraq. It took people longer to realize that it could have been in America, too. The books flung from the upended bookcase were blank, and the art knocked from the walls, photographs of fields that Jack had taken years ago in Houston, were of no discernible nationality. The house was filled with things that could have come from anywhere. The target was from no place and every place, and so the enemy too.

When people saw the house they became reverential, as though something really had happened there. Heads poked through the broken windows and holes in the walls. The bolder ones began to climb through the larger opening, exploring. Let them. Others followed. They looked for clues in the way the teacups were painted. Let them.

Jack was by the door when the last explosive went off toward the back of the room, a large bang. A woman screamed. He thought at first that something had been knocked over. Then he saw the smoke and heard another scream, and people were leaving the house, trying not to run, or else they were gathering around one woman, who held her arm strangely. Stanley motioned to security. People were ushered out. An ambulance was called and the woman, five or eight years older than Jack with hair she'd let mostly gray, sat on the ground, clutching her arm and crying.

Jack went over to her, asking, "What was it?" The receptionist teetered in with a box of first aid. "What did you *do*?"

The woman just cried. "It doesn't matter, Jack," Stanley said. He had one arm around the woman's shoulders.

It didn't matter either when Jack said that he'd realized the problem, that it was with block #3, the bit that had not blown all away. It didn't matter when he said he was sure that explosion was the last one, that all the others had gone off and that it was safe now for everyone to come back. None of that mattered, except to him.

The gallery was far west, near the river, but Deb was a whole avenue away when the first show cards began dotting the street like bread crumbs. She took one, catching the corner with her nail, and walked with it, big block letters, *BAYT*, bobbing in view. In smaller print, the Hebrew and the Arabic, and below those the English: *House*.

A police car pulled past her, no siren but lights revolving red and blue, which looked less threatening, candy colored, in the still-daylight.

The police stopped just before a small crowd. There was an ambulance too, its rear doors swung open and an old woman sitting in back.

Stanley was near the entrance, talking to an officer. He gesticulated, his hands cupping a small, round space and springing outward, fingers wide.

Through the lobby and its people, some she knew who called to her. The doors were propped open, and she smelled smoke faintly, the beginning or tail end of it. One of Stanley's assistants put a hand out to stop her. "I'm married to the artist," she said, and the girl let her pass, but Deb had heard herself too, the strange claim she had on this other person that let her go places, that demanded she did. It had brought her into a room marked off with caution tape, and there was Jack, his arms wrapped around himself like a boy in a fit, the position so at odds with the size of him, the large man he was. "Larger than life," he used to say, collapsing on top of her, pinning her to the bed.

"They won't listen." He rubbed his face.

She thought she would reach out, touch his shoulder, but didn't. And then he moved, out of reach, to the caution tape, which he took a tall step over. "Jack."

He touched the wall with just his fingers, then with the whole of his hand. Deb watched him walk up and down, crouching, reaching, now running his palm along the surface, as though looking for a wire to trip. Then inside the house, and he was only feeling things, and she imagined ducking under the tape and stepping through the large hole on the side to follow him.

Thinking it, she found she had. In the room now, she bent down and picked up one of the books he'd made, leather bound, the pages creamy and blank. She thought it would make a good journal for Kay, cleaned up.

Jack was sitting in a chair he'd built on a carpet he'd hired someone to weave. There was a second chair, on its side, and Deb thought she should turn it right and sit with him, take his hand. But on the floor, too, was a toy, the Tigger with the missing eye that she recognized as Simon's, something she thought they'd lost or thrown away. The leg was torn off and she didn't know where he'd found it.

She stood and turned slowly toward the door.

"Deb?"

She didn't like the bits of glass under her shoes or the air she was breathing. She could not fix the Tigger any more than she could fix anything else, and wasn't sure anymore that she wanted to.

What Deb wanted was to go home to her kids, but the apartment was dark when she got there, except for a green light, minute and glowing on the living room floor, the Xbox Simon always left on. She dialed his cell.

"Hello" was how Simon always answered her, soberly, never betraying that he knew who was calling. It was something she'd always meant to ask him about, why never "Hi, Mom," why not even "Hey," like she heard him answer his friends.

"Where are you guys?" She tried to sound sunny. There was a lot of ambient noise wherever they were.

"Everything's fine."

"That's good. Where's that?" She carried her bag to the counter in the kitchen and switched the light on.

"Just a diner." Plates clattered around him. "With Grandma." Ruth used to be Ommy, a name Simon had shied from over the years, saying it less often and more quietly before stopping altogether. Kay took the cue from her brother not long after, and thus was Ommy replaced with the generic.

"That's good," Deb said again, pulling open the refrigerator. "About how long do you think you'll be?"

"Well, we just sat down."

"Which diner?"

"We ordered already." The soft magnetic strip suctioned the refrigerator shut the rest of the way. "I mean, come if you want to."

"Nah, I'll just be here when you get back."

"Or we could bring you something—"

"No, please, there's plenty of food in the house." Simon was speaking to someone. She thought she heard her mother's voice. "I've got all that fresh broccoli and avocados from yesterday."

"Hang on. Grandma wants to talk to you."

"Tell—say I'll call her in the morning. And say I might go to bed early so not to come up."

"Okay."

"I love you. Tell Kay I love her."

"Hey, Mom loves you," Simon said unceremoniously. Then, "Yeah, she loves you too."

"Okay, I love all three of you."

Simon hung up, and Deb, as though he could see her, went about enacting the things she'd contended she'd do on the phone, setting a pot of water to boil on the range. She fished an avocado out from its crinkly produce bag and cut it open lengthwise, turning it in the palm of her hand. She hit the pit with the blade of her knife and pulled it out this way, a trick Jack had taught her.

She wouldn't go to bed early. She'd call Stanley in an hour, ask what had happened to that poor woman. Could Jack be charged for a thing like that? Assault?

She wished the kids were there with her. They would have been nice to come home to, just to feed and to sit with while they read or played or groaned over their homework. It would have been so obviously the better decision, Simon and Kay and the living room, instead of Jack and the gallery and his rubble. Her mother was always going a step too far. Deb had asked her to check in with the kids, not to take them somewhere away. Now she was alone in the house, alone with the box, sentient on the rocking chair in the back bedroom.

She was picturing it, slicing avocado in parallel lines, when she heard a key in the door.

At the diner they ordered like it was the last supper, but no one could eat. Simon got waffle fries, and Kay got waffles, and they both got milk shakes even though one would have been enough, they were so big and came with extra in frosty metal cups. Their grandmother ordered a bowl of matzah ball soup, cutting the ball in two and spooning the bigger half onto Simon's plate. Ruth was five foot nothing, bird boned, and it was sometimes strange to think of her as their protector now that even Kay stood taller.

When she first turned up, around five-thirty, Ruth said she'd been shopping in the neighborhood and needed to use the bathroom. She stood at the living room mirror and ran a comb through her dyed blond bob in little pulls. Simon and Kay sat on the couch and listened to the soft rasping sound as the teeth of the comb brushed through hairspray. She didn't know anything, they didn't think, and for a horrible moment, each thought the other would break and tell her, but neither did, and by the time they'd climbed into the mauve vinyl booth, they felt secure that neither would. And their grandmother, they were quite sure now, knew nothing at all. Her indulgences with them required no special purpose. She loved to be Ommy, to bring parties wherever she went, mainly in the form of chocolate and cake.

They used to sleep at her house every New Year's Eve while their parents went to this and that social function. Ommy would buy poppers of confetti and plastic hats and those cookies with the rainbow pieces, and they all three would watch the ball drop together. The first year that Simon defected, to go to a party of his own, Kay promised her grandmother they'd always spend New Year's together. "No," Ommy had said, "you'll go too, to your friends'," and when Kay protested, Ommy had added, "It's natural you should go with your friends," and still Kay had sworn inwardly that she never would. But this past year she had, to a sleepover at Racky's where the girls drank sparkling cider in plastic champagne glasses, played Cranium, and gossiped in corners about each other.

"Terrific," their grandmother muttered. A small child at another table had started to wail. Ruth brought her hands up around her ears. She loved children but only her own, her own's own. Babies crying, big crowds, people walking on the wrong side of the street—*tumult*. "Oh no. Not good. Why do they bring them into restaurants?"

"*Rest*aurant," Simon repeated, mocking, his point being that this wasn't one. He thought he'd meant it to be funny (had he?), but it came out rude and cruel.

No one said anything. Kay's fingers webbed with maple syrup and her thighs stuck to the plasticky booth. Across the room the child howled.

Jack was kneeling on the bathroom tile where Deb had gone to get away from him. He was six one and solid and slow moving; the floor did not come naturally. He covered his face. She hated to see him cry and hoped she wouldn't, that he'd keep his hands where they were until she'd slipped away again. A bad place to have a scene, the bathroom. Too bright. The bathroom was where they'd first kept Travolta when she was still kitten enough to get lost or trapped under things. They set out food and water, a blanket and a litter box, made sure the toilet seat was always down. They took turns sitting with her, letting her learn the feel of their hands, the smell of their skin and cuffs of their jeans.

"Deb. Deb Deb Deb Deb Deb."

Some new creature filled the space now. Deb looked away, looked back at him, closed her eyes, stared at the bare bulb over the sink and followed the afterimage as it drifted. She was holding this new thing up against the rest of their life, certain memories. She had to decide what she could live with, what could fit, be made to fit.

"How's the woman? They take her to the hospital?"

"She's fine." Jack breathed into his hands, the sound of

snot and expelled air against and between his fingers. "Her arm—it doesn't matter. I don't care."

"Don't be stupid. You better care."

"Deb."

"What."

"I went to the park."

"Just now?"

"Yesterday I went. I watched the kids climbing. It made me think of us when we used to take them. They were so little."

"Kids are little."

Again they fought and again it went the same place as before. How many times can I say it? Everything I do is wrong and I don't know how. It's just so much more than I thought it was going to be. I'm sorry. More and also worse. I feel like I've been sleepwalking, like I was two people and one died and forgot the other. The kids were so little and you were so old and you *what*, Jack, you felt jealous of them? What time is it? I'm sorry. I love you, do you believe me that I love you? God it's almost ten. I'm sorry. I'm sorry. I'm sorry. The word had lost meaning to Deb somewhere in the air, she suspected to both of them. Sorry, sorry, sorry. Like a wrap—what are those, a sari? Like a wrap for everything.

"Get off your knees," she said, louder than she'd meant to.

She didn't want all this sorry in her life, in her bathroom, her bedroom, the kids' rooms. She climbed into the bathtub and leaned her head against the wall. There were long hairs, her own, stuck dead to the sides of the ceramic.

She didn't clean the drain out, and Jack never said anything. So, see. She wasn't so easy to live with either.

When she was pregnant, in this tub, Jack had washed her hair. He changed a million ways but that was what she remembered most, that at some point both times he'd started climbing into the tub and washing her hair, one hand cupped over her forehead to keep the soap from running into her eyes. When she remembered it now she couldn't even picture him, behind her, just the faucet skimming the waterline—two bodies upped the level—and the water falling in little splashes behind her and his hands learning the shape of her skull.

"The kids, they treat me like I'm a stranger." He was still on the floor.

"Well, you've made it very hard for them to feel like they know you."

"I've ruined everything." His voice was flat.

He had made so many mistakes. Maybe her own was to think of the past, or maybe the past was not to be discounted. But she could feel it softening her. She used to do okay on her own. More than that. Only after she'd met Jack had she ever felt really lonely. Lying awake on that awful twin bed in her first apartment and him asleep for barely an hour beside her, she thought she'd made a terrible mistake, loving. She'd wanted to go brush her teeth, but that would have meant getting out of bed with his warm body, and she hadn't gone.

She thought about what she would say next. It was a bit of a gift. "But hopefully, they could get over it."

Jack nodded as if to say yes, he'd thought of this, they

were kids, their hearts were open still, there was time to make it up. "And you?"

Deb was in the tub, which was a boat, and Jack was on the floor, which was an ocean, and she had to decide if she would let him drown or bring him aboard. Maybe. She had to be practical. If he swabbed the deck, she thought. There was so much hair in the drain.

Ruth took them the eight blocks home in a taxi. While the cab idled outside their building, a roll of tissue materialized from inside her blouse and opened up to reveal a smaller roll of bills. She gave them each two tens, which they stuffed into their pants pockets, and put the tissue in the zippered front compartment of her purse.

Simon wanted to kiss his grandmother and whisper to her, Sorry, sorry for how he'd behaved at the diner, poorly, but Kay was between them, so he couldn't kiss her, and if he'd whispered she wouldn't have heard. It wasn't just that she was generous—Simon knew, though wasn't supposed to, that his parents gave her money—but that she'd put the roll of tens there, wrapped in Kleenex, when she was getting dressed that afternoon before coming to meet them, and that it had been there all the time, even when he'd been mean, and for what? So she could give it to them like this, not from anyplace so vulgar as a wallet but from actually almost her heart.

"Call me when you get upstairs so I know she's home," Ruth said.

"She's home."

"You two didn't eat." She was the smallest person in the world and also probably the very best, the most concentrated good in one package. She just loved him. His mother loved him too, in that open oozing way that she must have learned from Ruth, but his mother's love embarrassed him, made him feel somehow pathetic.

"I keep—it's crazy, but I keep thinking about what it would be like, to have another baby with you."

"Don't."

"Yeah, I know, I'm just. I miss it, is all I'm saying."

She was almost disappointed to hear him back away from the idea so quickly, because she understood what he meant when he said he missed it. She missed it too. Not that it was a thing she'd consider—it would be too obvious a distraction from what was wrong, like making a window out of the mirror they were standing in, just so they wouldn't have to look at their own reflections.

It had been a little that way the first time she was pregnant. The timing was terrible—she said it, everyone said it—but inwardly she knew the timing was also so good. It was the summer after Izzy made soloist, and everyone was moving up the ranks or moving on, south or west, to start families or join smaller companies. Deb had been in the corps seven seasons without any sign of rising up out of it, and it thrilled her to think of never going back, that her ticket out was growing inside her.

Children brought new problems, a respite from the old ones, and made them tender toward each other. It had been true with Simon and again with Kay, though not as much maybe, the second time. It was possible that with a third there would be less still, and there was the fear of diminishing returns. Because if that didn't fix everything then nothing would, ever.

"Maybe," she said, "you should be more concerned with the kids you have now. You don't just screw up a pair and have another."

"Don't say that, Deb. Don't tell me I've done that."

The avocado had browned and would have to be thrown away. Simon and Kay were surprised to find their father in the back bedroom, sitting up on his side of the bed, head lowered even when they stood in the hall and he knew they were there. Deb came out from the bathroom, her face and her hands a little wet from washing, and shepherded them to the kitchen.

"Hey," she whispered, "your dad wants to stay here tonight, but I want to know what *you* guys want." It was true. She could not bear the burden of a wrong decision, and whatever her children wanted was inherently right, for all of them. "Hm?" She bent down between their two heights. "Whatever, seriously. He has the studio, he's more than fine. I have no problem sending him." She snapped her fingers, *like that,* but they didn't make any sound.

"If he goes he'll just do it again."

"Sy."

"What, won't he? You don't think he will?"

Deb looked at him. "No, I really don't."

"Yeah, and you didn't think he would at all, so that's how much you know."

Deb wavered a little in the air. Here was their son and they'd made him so angry. Jack, maybe mostly, but she had too. What would Simon say if she told him how she'd known already, known for months, and had done nothing. That she'd tried just to make it go away. Probably he'd say she was weak, and dumb. And what if Simon knew the facts about how his own parents' marriage had started? Probably he'd say she was dirty. And deserving, now.

"If that's how you feel," she said. "He can stay out here, on the couch. Okay?"

Simon nodded. His mother's face was damp from the water she'd splashed on it and he could see the pores on her cheeks in the light from the window. Again he'd been cruel.

The talk was over without Kay saying anything. If it had been left to her, she would have had her father stay at the studio. She was afraid of running into him in the kitchen or coming out from the bathroom. She was afraid of what he might try to say. The house seemed a so much safer place when it was just the three of them. But she never would have thought of what her brother said, about her father doing it again, she didn't have a mind like his, and she guessed it was better that he had been the one to answer.

It was late, but still no one had really eaten, and so they ordered Chinese food, too much, enough for six or seven but more important, enough for four. Simon, then Kay, then Deb, marched a plate out to the living room to sit in front of the TV. Deb left the food containers and an empty plate on the counter like a live mouse trap, and before long Jack came creeping out from the back of the apartment where he'd spent the last half hour in a state of self-imposed but well-received quarantine. He took an empty space on the couch just behind Simon, who was stretched out on the floor, and neither child elected to break the tunnel vision that ran invisible between *The Daily Show* and their General Tso's chicken.

Jack ate hunched over with great, heaping mouthfuls, like an animal afraid his food might be taken from him. The size of his portions offended Deb in some way she could hardly explain, and she caught herself scowling. She grew angrier watching him watch the television, his attention also nearly ravenous, invasive somehow. She was too angry for this, and regretted the peace offering, regretted it until Simon, at the first commercial, picked up his dinner, which he'd hardly touched, and left the room, stopping for no one, even when she called his name. Her son's anger deflated her own, as though serving as her proxy, and Deb again felt sorry for Jack.

That night the kids kept clear of the hall for their father's lonely procession, living room to bedroom to living room again, and Deb got into bed with the mangled pages, her husband's words.

The dirty stuff didn't bother her so much as when he was sweet, though she supposed that was a predictable thing to feel. Before a weekend trip to D.C., the girl had

97

written to him that she didn't like Washington, that everything about it had a hum. Jack wrote back, *Hummmmmmmmmmmm. Thought of you the whole day.*

Deb's heart also quickened anytime she saw mention of herself on the page, and she always went back and read that section slowly, coming to her name in natural order. *Deb's asleep early. Just me in the living room, lonely for this afternoon.* She wasn't sure if it was out of superstition or if she got some sort of perverse pleasure in the delay, in making herself wait, but she did the same thing when she saw the names of her children. *Promised to go to Kay's play Friday.* That was in November, and it hadn't been a play but a dance concert.

There was a knock at the door, and Jack shuffled in to the closet where they kept extra bedding.

"I wish you wouldn't keep looking at that." He pulled down a gray blanket, one of those fleecy ones nobody liked the feel of, and was leaning forward on his toes, reaching further back. She watched him tug the corner of one toward the bottom and send the whole pile onto the floor. "Sorry," he said, bending down and popping up again with a thin, yellowy quilt that might have been white when they bought it. "I saw on the calendar, Kay's got a field trip?"

"So?"

"Mind if I pick her up?" The quilt had been Simon's when they first moved him crib to bed, and she wondered if Jack realized, if that was why he chose it. Probably not, no.

"You do what you want."

He nodded, quilt aloft, and went back out to the living room to sleep.

I want you to sit for me tomorrow around noon. Bring that belt from before. I'll only have a couple hours but I think we can get to everything by then.

Ninety-two percent of Americans disapprove of extramarital affairs. Deb had done some research, online. Sixty-four percent would not forgive an unfaithful spouse, and sixty-two percent would divorce one. The site did not explain the other two percent, who neither forgave nor divorced. Catholics. Catholics or possibly black widows.

She'd taken her lawyer friend's advice. She'd waited. Time was the trick everyone else knew already. Hold on long enough, let the heaviness dry in the air, and it does not seem necessary to do anything at all. Jack was fifty-five to her forty-one and had seen firsthand what time could do. "Do me a favor," Ruth had whispered as the kids turned the bulbs on grandma's menorah. "Don't talk to him unless you're sure."

And in the interim, what had happened? The sex had gotten better. Or at least, they'd started having it again, rougher and for longer, even if sometimes she wanted to slap him across the face when he pinched. Deb made changes, but they were with herself, part of a decision to work at being happy.

Jack used to make her happy. She was twenty-six when they met, a young twenty-six. You had to choose between dancing and living, and up until that point she hadn't lived. Her only boyfriends had worked in offices, done things with money she didn't understand. They'd liked to show her off, hadn't liked that she always went home early. They hadn't known how to touch her, afraid of breaking her or, worse, wanting to. Jack had never been that way; he hadn't had to be, and for that she gave herself willingly to him, throwing dance away just as it had begun to fail her, and it was a lot to ask of a person, maybe, to let you make them your whole world. His work she felt she understood, art that was like hers except it lasted, didn't disappear behind a curtain. The best a dancer can do is bring life to another person's steps. Jack didn't have steps to follow. He made his own. An artist seemed the greatest thing one could be, also the purest, and her whole life shrunk next to that, her father the salesman, her mother the secretary. She hadn't learned to look for the difference yet between what one did and who one was. Hadn't even known there was a difference.

Things are usually described as better in the morning, and maybe they are, for some people. Jack preferred the night, when everything seemed at last to be at a close. He was out in the living room, yes, but he was home, and the day was over—the nightmare, he thought, over. There goes everything, the show, the career. There, my life. I'll never speak to anyone again, not to the guy from the *Voice* or the woman from *KIOSK*, not to Stanley, not even to Nicky. But at least, sleep.

But then, morning, and instead of speaking to Stanley never again, here he was speaking to him now. Jack had wanted only to stop the incessant buzzing by his head, to shut off his phone's alarm, but the alarm had started talking, and in a voice very much like Stanley's.

Like Stanley's, but harder. Colder. All-business Stanley. "The woman seems all right, but she'll press charges."

"She said that?" Jack rolled onto his side, propping his

head up on his hand and squinting in the morning light. Blinds would have ruined the picture windows.

"Right now she says she won't—*most likely,* she says—but she called a lawyer in to the hospital."

"She's still at the hospital?"

"I think she needed a scan—"

"What they should do is check her into the psych ward."

"I think it would help if you released some sort of statement. We could do it on your behalf, but—"

"If I make a statement, do we reopen?"

There was a pause, and Stanley sighed. "What you aren't getting, Jack, is that everyone who was in that gallery last night could sue for something. And they wouldn't be going after you."

"Then why don't you sue me, Stanley?"

"Be serious."

"Look, say what you want to say. Write up any little release you want, and I'll sign it, all right?"

"We don't need you to sign—"

"You know what? I don't have time for bullshit; do what you want. Just make it go away."

Stanley hung up, but Jack stayed with the phone to his ear. He checked the time under the TV. Not yet seven. Stanley was one of his oldest friends, but what kind? He'd gotten rid of Stanley, but he wasn't really done talking, so he called Nicky.

"Nicolo! You're awake," Jack boomed, detecting a whiff of subdued life on the other end of the line. "I'm glad I caught you. Meet at the studio? I can be there in an hour."

"I have work."

"Right, right. Shit. Where're you at again?"

"Man, please, do not come to my work."

"What? Maybe I want a Frappucino."

At half past nine, Jack was at the coffee shop at Astor Place. He ordered an americano.

"What size?"

"Whatever, large."

"Come on, boss, you know the sizes."

"Venti. Nicky, look, it's clear you've been hibernating the last fifteen hours, but at some point while you're up for air, you're going to hear some things about last night." A line was forming behind him. "Ring me up for one of these biscotti things too."

"Was the video not okay?"

"We didn't get that far." He fished a credit card out from his back pocket. "Listen, you remember that girl, Jordan Esberg?" Last October, when Jack was starting to worry things were getting too serious, he'd wondered out loud why the girl had never shown an interest in Nicky. Maybe they should give it a shot. They were about the same age. The girl had stared at him; Jack had smiled. What? He really did just want everyone to be happy. "Do you think you could reach her for me?"

"I don't even think I have her number still." That Halloween, while Jack and Deb stayed home distributing fun-size candy bars to ghosties and junior pirates, Nicky and the girl had gone to a costume party. "Can't you reach her?"

"She's been ignoring my calls."

"If she doesn't want to talk to you, I definitely don't think she'd talk to me. I don't get it. Why would she be ignoring *your* calls?"

Another employee appeared behind the register, the manager in a green corporate visor. "Friend of yours, Nick?"

"I'm a customer." Jack wielded his biscotti.

Nicky handed him back his card and receipt. "Your drink'll be at the bar, sir."

At the bar Jack ate his stick of cookie, which was stale and crumbed on the keyboard of his phone. The day after Nicky and the girl's date, All Saints' Day, Nicky had turned up at the studio with a pair of sparkling black wings that she had left at his apartment that morning, tiptoeing out while he was still asleep. A few hours later the girl had come to Jack and when she did he teased her about it, her obvious intentions, to make him jealous. He made her angry, then made nice with her, pushing up her short sleeves and kissing her round shoulders, the knobby back of her neck, until she began to smile and tell him about her night, sliding out of her clothes and into her wings before leading him to the sofa, floating glitter and doom all behind her.

The trial by dinner had not been a total catastrophe, but it had helped Deb to make her decision, and the next morning, on the walk to Simon's subway station and Kay's school bus, she wedged herself between them to talk about What Next. Again she found herself using old standards, the clichés, like, *people make mistakes,* and wondered if the kids recognized them as such, or if she could get away with it because of their ages. Were they too young to know the words were rewarmed?

"What your dad did has nothing to do with the two of you," she said at the corner, barricading them back as she looked both ways. "It isn't about you. It isn't even really about me," she added. (Did she believe that?) "Mostly it's about himself."

"Okay," Simon said, knocking into her arm as he hopped off the curb.

"Your father and I have been married a long long time. People make mistakes."

"You said that already," said Kay.

There. So now it was a cliché.

Simon stopped short at the newsstand across the street. "It's okay if you guys want to get a divorce," he said, pulling open the glass refrigerator door. "Can I get a water?" He shook the wet off the bottle and looked down at the morning papers.

"Well, thank you for your permission."

"Donald's parents got divorced and it's not like his dad even did anything."

"That's enough, all right? Be a little sensitive." Deb draped an arm around her daughter. "Sweetheart, you want something? A Snickers or something?"

"Can I get gum?"

"And can I get this?" Simon held up a *Post*. "For the train."

"I'll buy you the *Times*."

"This is cheaper."

"I'd rather you read the *Times*."

"But this one has sudoku."

"Fine," Deb said, and bought everything. Thinking: We have raised two entirely city children. She and Jack had reared these urban creatures, so different from themselves, a southern boy and a suburban girl. Art and dance had carried them to the city, but what kept them—kept Deb, at least—was the sense that it all was happening there for the first time, would ripple out in lesser versions across the country, like touring companies of a Broadway show, like everything everywhere else was an echo of something that had happened there. She never took New York for granted, but it had never belonged to her like it did to her kids, and there was still that pane of glass between herself and where she lived, showing her her reflection, in the darker places, where she was afraid. How could she guess at what her children were afraid of, then? Were they afraid of anything?

Simon had started down the subway stairs when Deb called him back. "Listen." Pressing her palm against the strap of his bag. "I don't know about Donald's parents. I know that your dad is sorry, and I know that this takes time to figure out. And he knows that too."

"So, what, he's going to be sleeping on the couch?"

"Does that bother you guys?"

"It's just Donald is coming over tonight." He telescoped and untelescoped his *Post*.

It is so hard to know the right thing and so important to make it seem easy. "Your father will be in our bedroom, then."

That, as far as Simon was concerned, settled it, and Jack was permitted back into Deb's bed to steel the family from judgment by a fifteen-year-old boy named Donald.

(Though Simon would keep Donald out of it, he'd also managed a way of inviting the rest of the world in, with that stuff he'd said in the elevator, and now several of the building people, moms mostly, had begun to look at him funny. They looked at his parents that way too, and at Kay, though his family, surprise, hardly noticed.

The moms looked at him on afternoons in the elevator, where he felt himself cornered by their grocery bags and laundry baskets. He stared out the little round window with wire netting as the floors fell away behind it. Swallowing hard.

They looked at him and thought, Poor kid.

They looked at each other and thought, With a husband like that, might have guessed. Doesn't take a rocket scientist, no. Doesn't take a Freud.

They looked at their watches and thought, Two-thirty, what are you doing home from school?

16B was the only one to ask him questions. Like their medium, if he were a ghost.

She asked: "How are we doing?" *We.*

And then not just questions but mottoes, like, "One day at a time." This she said to no one, to the air.

Well wasn't it what he wanted, attention? Yes, in a way it was. But just as important now was to show how much he didn't need any. That he was handling it, without his too-young sister and too-dumb mother and his father who was the problem. And without 16B. Because he'd seen this story before, on night soaps and in his friends' parents' living rooms. He knew what came next, and he wanted to show the world and the building people, everyone, that he was ready. Divorce!)

Jerry and Elaine are married and living in Jerry's apartment with George next door instead of Kramer. George gets a letter by mistake from a woman who is having an affair with Jerry. He goes to Monk's to tell Elaine, and she is like, So? George says: "But she said she is sleeping with your husband! Jerry!" And Elaine's still like, Yeah, so? LAUGHS. George says: "She said she wanted him to lick her on the nipples!" Elaine puts her hand on the table like she's about to leave and says: "Listen, Peterman has me writing about urban riding crops. I don't have time for this." And George shouts: "She said she was going to suck him off until he came and that she would swallow it and that he tasted good and then that he should fuck her hard against the wall!" Everyone at Monk's is staring at them. Elaine says: "George, I don't know why you are shouting." LAUGHS.

. . .

"What are you writing?"

Kay snapped back into the mustardy yellow bus rumbling down the West Side Highway, delivering her class to the planetarium. Two braids hung above her head: Chloe Haber looking over the back of Kay's seat, squinting to read.

Kay shook her head, nothing, and tried to turn the page, but Brett Haber had popped up too, curious, and nodded at her sister, whose arm darted down and grabbed the notebook away.

"Stop," Kay shouted. She turned around on the seat and got up on her knees. "Stop, you guys. Just give it."

Up front Mr. O'Toole was standing with his back to the driver, counting heads. He had long hair for a man, and he was the one she pictured whenever anyone mentioned Shakespeare.

Kay slumped back in her seat, afraid to turn around again in case they were reading it. The year before, for her birthday, she had taken the twins on a trip to Six Flags. There had been room only for two more in the rental car, with her mother driving and her brother riding shotgun (her father, who'd hurt his shoulder and who didn't like roller coasters anyway, had stayed home to ready the cake and streamers). She'd invited Chloe and Brett because at the time it seemed possible that they together would become her best friend or that she could become their triplet. But it is not easy to come between twins, who grew up with their own language and sometimes still use it, on long car rides especially, a language punctuated with laughing fits

111

they swear are not about you but your brother, who has been very quiet in the front seat and is probably afraid of them.

Still, she could not look. What if they were looking at her? The bus was traveling south now down Riverside Drive, they were so near her house and she wished they would just let her off.

Maybe the twins could help. There were things in the box that she hadn't understood. Maybe Chloe and Brett would be able to explain what, for example, was cuming? Coming? Coming where? And going down—again, down to where?

Across Amsterdam and Columbus, toward the park. The bus eased into the curved drive reserved for visiting groups, and Mr. O'Toole raised his voice over all their heads, flapping open a garbage bag and saying to bring their trash to the front with them.

The twins stood over her. Kay looked up but couldn't quite tell. "Did you—"

"Don't talk to us."

"Perv."

Okay then. Right, okay. Chloe pushed up the aisle behind her sister, whose hand she was already taking, leaning in to whisper. Kay looked into the seat behind her and found no notebook there. And from the Haber twins, word would spread, to Chelsea and to Jess and to Racky, which meant to everyone, and they would call her weird and a perv and gross, and the thing is, maybe she was?

As Mr. O'Toole's students sat in the planetarium, watching supernovas become black holes under a great dark dome, Deb was passing the fountain at Lincoln Center, where water climbed and fell down a tower of itself, white in the broad day.

The guards smiled and nodded her in. They had been old then and were even older now. She walked around and down to the dressing rooms, through the maze of emptied halls. She didn't come around as much as she used to, though when Simon was born the girls had all fussed over him, the little prince. None of them had children—they still were children. There were so many new faces now, too many to keep straight, ones that looked at her without recognition. And what faces she did know were changing.

"Sit sit, five minutes," Izzy said, already turned half away as the door fell open. It looked like it would take more than five, with Izzy still in underwear and a bra bandaging

113

her chest. She'd grown so small. When they'd danced together, Deb had been the thinner one.

They were going to lunch because each had been waiting for the other to cancel. Making dates only to call them
off, it was how they kept in touch. *You're the only one I
don't feel bad about bailing on,* Izzy had told her once, *because you're like me and I know you don't mind.* The comparison flattered Deb, and it was true, that for her there was
a sense of relief in finding her time unexpectedly free, in
being allowed off duty.

But Deb, today, had not canceled. She thought it might
be good to talk to Izzy, who'd known her when. "I thought
you'd be in Saratoga?"

"Oh, I'm going, I'm going," Izzy said, as if Deb were the
one dragging her.

Sixteen years ago almost exactly, Deb had been in Saratoga too, rehearsing *Serenade.* She'd left the studio feeling
dizzy and walked alone down the hill to the family-owned
drugstore in town. There were pregnancy tests swaddled in
a Love Pharmacy bag under her bathroom sink back in
New York—she often missed periods—but none with her
there. She drank half a liter of water and peed in a public
restroom and sat in the stall, still dizzy, until there were
lines she could clearly see. Then the five-hour bus ride to
the Port Authority, which felt interminable and also like no
time, because next thing she was home and calling Jack,
and next next thing there he was, there for her to tell him
what, what is it? what? She knew by then what she wanted,
probably had known for some time what, and the question
was whether the universe would let her have her way,

114

whether Jack would act as she wanted him to. (It would; he did. Remember that: Deb got what she'd wanted.)

"We're doing 'Diamonds,'" Izzy said, perched on a chair tipsy with dirty clothes. "Poor Ash had to do it with Naomi all week because of this damn leg."

"I haven't seen Naomi. She's a little stiff, isn't she?"

"Stiff? She's a hulk. I have muscles too, but they don't *show*."

Deb leaned against the white block wall and watched them together in the lighted mirror. "They show a little."

"I know, I know. I can't keep it on. Anyway, Saturday's the gala. I just want to stay home with the dogs."

"Parties are nice, though."

"It's so boring and everyone's so old. I'll probably just start screaming." She sighed and began pinning back her hair. "*And* it's standing around all night that I really feel the tendonitis."

Sixteen years ago, Deb had gone back to Saratoga to finish out the summer season and found herself at last set apart from the others, as the one who would soon be two. She'd never been a leader, but for those few weeks she almost led, by natural happiness, by what people called *that glow*. Quitting the company gave it back to her, the love she'd felt and the fun of it. She stopped worrying about steps and became part of the whole. The music was new again. And Lincoln Center, when she got back, became new. Chagall and his angels floating in red skies. The cratered limestone of the buildings that seemed to her made of moon.

"Oh my God, and how are the babies?" Izzy asked, rubbing a wet wipe in small circles over her skin.

"Huge. Adults. I wish they were babies."

"Horrifying." She leaned close to the mirror, peered into invisible pores. "That you gave birth to something that's going through *puberty*."

Izzy was a personality, and Isabel Davey an altogether different one. The ditz and the diva—together they owned rooms. Deb had always been told that onstage she didn't have any presence, flash. Not an actress. Pretty face but shy, and serious. She couldn't help it—she was *thinking*. There was a brazenness she was missing, whatever mysterious quality allowed Izzy to play make-believe in front of thousands night after night. Every year that Deb was passed over, people told her not to feel bad, that these things were so often political. But she knew she'd never get the politics to work in her favor. She wasn't one of those girls, didn't really have wiles.

"Jack's opening was last night." On edge just broaching the subject, knowing where it might go, feeling she'd confess everything.

"Oh poo! I'm sorry I missed it. If I'd known I was going to be here . . ."

"Really, it's not—honestly things are a little up in the air right now, with Jack."

"Well, I'm sure it isn't dull. *God*, I miss that big, bohemian husband of yours. So smart you were, marrying someone just completely not from this world. You know, this is it for me. I'm not doing my legacy or whatsit any favors dragging it on. That's what Ash says, and he's right. Of course he's staying, if you think I *like* the idea of him here all hours with Marina Slutsanova."

"What will you do?"

"Get fat! Pump out a few kids maybe." That was just how she said it, and Deb felt doors close inside herself. "And this book that already I regret."

"What book?"

"Oh come on, I told you about it." She was picking at a spot on her cheek where there was no spot, only cheek. "It's my, not a biography, like a nonfiction—like memoirs. I'm writing it myself, and this woman from the publisher is helping me. Ash wants to do *Firebird* in the spring, to time it to the release."

"Iz, that's amazing. A book."

"Mmm." A hairpin in the corner of her mouth.

Deb looked away from her, looked at herself. "Do you want kids?"

"Oh, who knows? If I even can," she said, her hands in her hair. "I'm just talking, don't listen."

That afternoon Deb dialed Jack's cellphone, which rang unheard in the empty studio where he'd left it. Jack had spent the day working distractedly and didn't realize he'd forgotten his phone until he was off the subway. Climbing the steps he had a few minutes to spare but couldn't know it, and he set off in broad strides toward the planetarium, that giant, off-white aluminum sphere that seemed to levitate within a larger glass cube. The whole building had been redone about ten years earlier, paid for and named after a family that owned half of New York, his mother-in-law's apartment complex included, and had done similar work for the public library and Lincoln Center. The building it replaced had been brown brick and had looked a bit like a high school; Jack had wanted not to like the new one, but he did. The right thing for a planetarium. Like the Death Star embalmed.

In the lobby area where school groups were meant to collect, Jack waited amid the rainbow minefield of backpacks. The bags were cartoon huge, packed to capacity even on a day when the kids didn't need their books. They came in highlighter colors with reflectors on their outer pouches for crossing the street at night. Some were embroidered with initials: JSR, ASB, even SAD.

A clot of girls stood a few yards away, playing some type of game where it was his daughter's turn. She was spinning around and around as a blonde with thin arms trailed behind her, hands clamped over Kay's eyes. His daughter's legs tripped right over left, and Jack realized the blonde was actually leading, dragging Kay, whose pleated skirt twirled too high and whose body looked reluctant to follow her head. Some sort of dizzying game, though he thought she was laughing. Laughing and crying can look about the same.

Jack started to dig around for his daughter's backpack, which he did not think bore her initials but which he knew was pink. Pink or else red. When he found it, he hooked his fingers through the loop up top and looked to where the girls were still playing.

"Babe, let's go," he heard from one of the mothers, a woman in a long, black coat—though it was practically summer—whose approach to parenting seemed more assured than his own. She called again, "Babe," and the tiny blonde who'd been fastened to Kay let go and galloped over.

"Move. We've got karate and your brother."

The girl swung her head so her hair fanned out around her. She pointed at Jack. "He has my bag."

The black coat descended on him, and then Kay was

119

there too, but blondie hung back, like a shy person, though Jack didn't believe she was shy.

"I'm sorry. I thought it was hers," he said, pointing at his daughter. It came out strange, *hers*, like he didn't know her name.

The blonde's mother took the bag by one strap and slung it over her shoulder, where it hung incongruous with the coat. "How's Deborah?" she asked, to show him that they knew each other.

"Great. Very good. And you?"

The mother nodded. "Well, we've loved having Kay over. We've loved having all the girls." By which she meant, I have fed your daughter pizza and frozen waffles and rented her movies and put her in a warm bed or sleeping bag at night, and you do not know my daughter's name. By which she also meant, *We* equals myself and my husband together, *we* who are happy, and *all the girls* equals we have a house with many rooms and are popular at PTA meetings.

"Thank you, yeah," Jack said. "They're good kids," though they could have been monsters, how could he really know?

"Which friend was that again?" he asked when the black coat and blondie had left.

"Racky."

"And the mother?"

"Arlene. Mom doesn't like her." Kay found her own bag. It was purple. A purple monkey dangled from the zipper.

Out she walked with her head down, not calling goodbye to anybody. Jack wanted to ruffle her hair but was afraid she'd pull away.

"So what'd you guys see at the planetarium?"

She shrugged.

"Isn't it Robert Redford who does the space show there?"

"I don't know."

The afternoon was golden, sun filtered through the trees. They were on the edge of the park. "Hey, kid, it's summer vacation. Want to go to the playground? I mean, to the pond there? Feed the ducks?"

She was watching her feet, fitting each step into the octagons that tiled the pavement.

"Where's the fire?" He wanted them to have a nice time. "Ice cream stand over there."

"No," even though she did sort of want an ice cream. She was afraid that if she spoke more than a word at a time now, she'd cry. The day kept showing up in her mind in rushes, how on the tour her friends had kept as far as they could away from her and how at lunch they'd disappeared with her notebook into the bathroom. And how at the end of the day Racky had grabbed her with so much angry energy in her arms, like she was out for revenge, only Kay didn't know for what.

They were passing the pink brownstone wing of the natural history museum when Jack tried again. "Let's go in a minute. Let's see Brown Bear."

Kay was thinking she should have just said yes to ice cream, but she knew she couldn't eat it in front of him. She didn't want her father to have the satisfaction of meeting any one of her needs.

"Come on. We haven't gone to see him in so long, he might be Gray Bear by now."

She liked his bad jokes, but this minute she didn't want to.

"Might be Geriatric Bear." He felt her crumbling. "AARP Bear." He'd recently begun receiving their mail at home.

A smile was near to forming on Kay's lips, but really she didn't want to smile. Smiling wouldn't be true.

"Bet they've given him a cane."

"Fine. Whatever," she said, only to make him stop.

She waited for him on a hard stone bench under the *Barosaurus* while he bought tickets and found a map. They needed a map; it really had been a long time. They walked without speaking to the Hall of North American Mammals. Jack watched her out of the corner of his eye.

There was a deep-underwater feeling in the hall, lights barely strong enough to reach the green stone floors. The real brightness came from the dioramas, long-ago animals in faraway places. The bighorn sheep watched from rocky mountaintops. Two wolves were forever bounding through the snow. It was nighttime for the frozen wolves and their world glowed blue.

Brown Bear was really the Alaska Brown Bear, and really there were two, one up on his hind legs and the other on all fours, but it was the standing one they always meant, because of the way he faced them, looking interested and close to human, while the other chewed fish.

Something did seem changed about Brown Bear, though he was no older. Kay was the one who'd grown, and the bear was different to her for it. His claws, which had always been long and black, were longer and blacker and disturbingly thick. He was more real bear than she'd remembered, less toy bear and also less alive, as though her imagination could no longer animate him. Hadn't he used to look directly at her? He looked now somewhere in the middle distance, and she got the feeling if she pushed him, he would tip over.

"Same Brown Bear," Jack said. "You think he's had Botox?"

She hadn't wanted to show any interest, but she did ask what Brown Bear was like on the inside, and was he heavy?

"Not very, I'd imagine. You know, they take out all the organs—have they taught you taxidermy? Where they take all the blood and organs and everything out? They put formaldehyde inside to keep him looking good. Formaldehyde's like Botox. Then they use a mold to make the form, so it looks just like the real thing. See how shiny the eyes are?"

"They're real?"

"Glass."

She reached down to touch the raised letters: ALASKA. "So it's like what you do."

"A little." He wasn't sure if he should agree to this. "A little bit. And this way he'll last forever." Jack leaned over to look at the bitten fish, how they'd painted the scales iridescent.

Brown Bear, whose eyes of course were glass, though Kay hadn't realized it till now, it wasn't his eyes that had changed but hers. She looked at her father, who'd changed too. She wasn't sure why the things he'd done had hurt her, only that they had, but she could believe now, watching him, that he hadn't meant to, and maybe that mattered. She was eleven, and it was hard to be eleven, but also she knew that eleven was young, and if they could stay this way, these ages always, like the bear, she wouldn't mind, really.

There was an exhibit of live butterflies in another part of the museum, and they left Brown Bear to go to that. They stopped first in the Hall of Gems and the Hall of Minerals, where Kay wanted to look at sparkling things in their cases, pressing fingerprints over the amethyst and emeralds and yellow diamonds, pretending she was at Tiffany's.

"Choose one thing in the room to take home," Jack said, and she wondered if she'd played her game too clearly. "That one's mine." He nodded to the room's highest point, up three carpeted steps where a block of brown-and-blue rock had been mounted. The rock was something weather had done to copper, with a rough enough surface to scrape you up bad if you heaved yourself at it.

Kay made a face. "It's ugly."

"Well, good, you can't have it."

She chose the Star of India, a milky blue sapphire with a star blooming out from its center. "Five hundred and sixty-three carats," Jack read. He whistled. It looked like it would be warm to hold.

They went quickly past the meteors, more things Jack might take home with him; the early monkey people so shamefully naked; and the American Indian collection, totem poles and grim little masks carved from wood.

At last they reached the butterfly conservatory, with sunlamps that hung from the ceiling. Their eyes had to adjust at first to the colors—magenta and violet buds, so many greens on broad, waxy leaves—but then the butterflies emerged, or their eyes became able to see them. Shapeless white ones fluttered plant to plant like bits of tissue. A monarch perched very still on a plastic dish of something netted.

"It's eating," Kay said. "They eat with their feet."

"How do you know that?"

"We did them in school."

Beside a sign that read DO NOT DISTURB FEEDING, a brown-and-black butterfly was unrolling its tonguelike thing onto an orange slice. White stripes and orange dots festooned either wing.

Standing over a stained-glass-looking one, blue with black trim, Jack said, "You know people frame them, hang them up. No taxidermy required." He wasn't sure if she'd heard him.

She clapped both hands over her mouth, and Jack thought something was wrong, she was avoiding his eyes. Only then he looked to where she was looking, a little down. There was the monarch, moored but so gently on the uppermost button of his shirt, near to where a bowtie might be. It opened and closed its wings. Other visitors began to notice, to gather around him and pull out their phones for pictures. Jack stood still as he could, and proud, smiling like an idiot for other people's photographs, smiling because he could tell that his daughter was smiling too, behind her hands.

They'd reached a good moment, at the museum, though a lot of the warm feelings dissipated once they hit the streets. It was an observably later day than the one they'd stepped out of, and the hurt that for Kay had begun that Sunday, the distance Jack had felt from her ever since, these things were reintroducing themselves now—they both could feel it—as the streets grew more familiar and as they got closer to home.

Where, at home, Deb was packing and Simon was shouting.

"It's not *fair*. You can't *do* this to people."

"Simon, if you get a suitcase together now, Donald can still come over, he just can't sleep here." Deb was on her knees, half-engulfed in the hall closet, where they kept luggage and warm but ugly coats. She'd made her first very big decision. Classes, her own and her children's, had ended, and she would take the three of them to Rhode Island. To Jamestown, and the little house they owned with Gary, which they hadn't gotten around to renting out this summer.

She'd received a call not an hour before from Susan Haber, the mother of those awful twins. Her girls had brought something home with them, something Kay had written. Disturbing in nature, she'd said. Disturbing how?

"Well, sexual," Susan had said. "Obviously inappropriate."

"That doesn't sound like her."

The Haber woman had read some excerpts: "Jerry wants Elaine to show it to her. Elaine says, 'Oh God, I'm so—'" Susan coughed, and the words did sound like someone Deb knew.

She'd talked herself into Rhode Island in the (minor) frenzy she'd worked up waiting for Jack and Kay as the time under the TV changed from five to six, and in her head she'd talked everyone else into it too. Izzy had asked where they were summering. So? Here was summer. They'd meant to go every year. So? The last time they'd gone she'd been breastfeeding Kay. But what about the plumbing and pipes and gas or electric (she wasn't sure if it was gas or electric or if it could be both)? What about the breakers? Well, what about them? I'll hire someone, I'll hire someone!

She bought three tickets for the next morning train.

Unlucky for Simon to walk into that, Deb's electric atmosphere. His day was shitty already. He and Donald had stopped for burgers at the diner down the hill. With classes over, it was more crowded than usual, and they'd had to stand at the counter while Simon tried not to get caught watching Jared and Elena together in a booth that could

127

have seated four, and might have, had the Confucianism presentation not gone so badly. Mr. Dionisio had given them a B, low in the world of oral presentation. It wasn't the grade, he knew, that bothered Jared, who was already in at Emory, but that the script had come across stiff and embarrassing. Another group had handed in 108 blank pages on their topic, Zen Buddhism, and got an A.

On the train into Manhattan, Simon had for once been appreciative of his friend's talent at one-sided conversation, which today confined itself mostly to his position on a variety of superhero franchises. Thank fuck that Simon hadn't said anything yet about what had happened with Elena, who since that Monday had ceased to know him at all. A common thing in high school, selective social amnesia, especially among pretty girls. Donald got off the train two stations early to pick up his copy of *2K* with the plan of meeting back at Simon's house.

That plan was being challenged now, and he would not give it up. "What do you *mean*? There's nothing *in* Rhode Island!"

"There's country there. There's water and trees." She pulled a dusty duffel from behind two tubes of Christmas paper. "There are lighthouses. Will this work?"

"You're not *listening* to me!" He kicked the air behind his mother, which she could not see, and stomped his foot, which she could hear.

"Simon, come on!" She stood to face him, brushing the floor from her clothes.

"I never have *anything*. Don't you think I've been through enough?"

"This is what we're doing." She didn't shout, but she didn't have to. It was enough of a change just to sound this way, severe.

"Jesus, *fuck*."

"Stop."

"Fuck, it's not fair, *fuck*."

"*Stop*." There, she'd shouted. Also, she'd grabbed him by the arm, very hard, and held it until he pulled away.

"*Ouch*."

He went to his room, and when she came in a few minutes later, he was packing. Her voice was changed again, back to soft. "Sweetie? Sy? You can still have Donald over tonight, you know? Just not to stay."

"It's fine. I don't want him to come here."

"But you two could still—"

"I already told him no, okay?" He was grabbing clothing by the armful and dumping it into the rolly suitcase they'd bought him a few years back. There were still airport tags looped around the handle from the London trip.

"Okay. Well, if you change your mind."

"I still think this is the stupidest fucking thing."

She went back out to the living room, to knot toiletries inside produce bags from Fairway, and to watch the clock until Jack and Kay came home, ten minutes later. Deb studied her daughter, who didn't look at all changed from that morning—those words she'd written nowhere on her face—and she didn't want to embarrass Kay, didn't want to broach the subject the wrong way. When she announced her decision, Jack raised every objection she'd rehearsed already.

"What car will you use?"

"We won't need a car."

"If there's an emergency?"

"They have taxis there too."

"You know how much work that house is going to need?"

"I know, cobwebs! I'll deal with it."

"What about the pipes? Something bursts? I'll stay out of your way here."

"Sy's too old for camp and Kay doesn't really like it, right?"

Kay took her cue: "Not really."

"And I hate this city," Deb added, and went to pack her closet.

"You don't," he said, following her. In the bedroom he shut the door and asked, "Why?"

"Because, I can't—it's too confusing right now." She swung open the closet, disappearing behind the mirrored door, which reflected the made bed and bookcase behind.

"*Why* is it confusing?"

"Don't."

"I'm just saying the fact that you're confused, that means something. You don't think that's a good sign that means something?"

"I don't think we can have any kind of signs."

"But we should deal with this together."

"If we do that, then I won't make the right decision." Knocking the closet further open so that Jack was faced with his own reflection.

"How do you know what's the right decision?" Jack

moved closer in the mirror, saw himself say, "If *being with me* is going to influence you, how is that wrong?"

"You can't force me into this."

"Who's forcing? At all?" He'd gotten loud again without realizing. Wasn't he calmer than this? Wasn't he much, much calmer than he seemed? "Come on, I know. Don't go. Don't be out there alone."

Deb looked at him, her arms full of soft, woven things. "We won't really be alone. We'll have Gary." She hadn't meant to bring Gary into this. She'd gone off script.

"You don't know he's there now."

"He will be. We spoke," she said and went back out to the hall.

Jack's wife and his old college roommate spoke. Another of the small things that alienated him, in increments, from his own life, like coming home to find the furniture rearranged. Like the time the corner bagel shop had closed without warning. The bagel shop had become a hat store had become a place for pet accessories, tiny tubed sweaters and gold leashes.

He was being subtracted from everything, like a character made to look at the world, how life would go on, after he died.

The kitchen table does not disappear because the room is empty and the doors all closed, and other people's lives go on without you in them.

Fine. Fine except Kay, in the corner, was thinking of things she wanted to say. At the museum she'd faced down the idea that liking her father required treason against her mother. She'd faced it down and found she might not have to feel that anymore. For a moment she'd seen the way out through all that had happened, which was like looking down one end of a bendy straw: tricky. She couldn't see it anymore—she'd lost it somewhere on the walk home—but it had been there, flashing, when they were with Brown Bear.

It was something her mother couldn't see and her brother wouldn't try to, but she was not like Simon, she let things be taken away. Worry bullied her insides until she was back in her room, packing and putting on her PJs.

Worry brought out the quiet in her. She lay down on her bed and listened to the sounds her family made.

In the kitchen the stove clicked on. Rice slid in all its pieces from a cardboard box. The printer was running in the back bedroom, and she could hear the cheerful chimes of text messages arriving on the other side of the wall.

Her father, eating in the living room, fork to plate. Hard to get those stubborn bits. Her mother, carrying a sheet of paper to the fridge, snapping it on under a magnet. In Simon's room there were fewer friends to type to. People were going to bed.

Her mother on the phone with Ommy.

Her father turning pages of newspaper.

Her brother, talking without talking, late into the night.

Kay didn't think she'd slept at all, only then it was light out, and there was her mother dressed and ready and Simon sitting under a storm cloud in the kitchen.

They were out by the elevator, her father supplying the saddest send-off from the door, when Kay threw down her bag and demanded they stay.

No. She didn't. But she might have.

That would have been one way for life to go, of the thousands of ways it could splinter and fly off; it might have meant a new branch, or tree, if they hadn't gone away or if they'd taken Jack with them. If they'd gone the next day, the next week. Even if she'd said something and Deb had not listened to her. That would have meant something too. But Kay, like her mother, was slow to make decisions. She didn't trust her judgment and was afraid of being

133

wrong.

So Kay was still in the hall, throwing down her bag, even as she was in a taxi, her legs crowding the hump of the middle seat, her mother to one side, printed e-tickets folded carefully around the bar codes, her brother on the other, turned aggressively toward the window. Something pounding on the radio filled the silence and still she was in the hall, saying no, her eyelashes sticking together in points, her crying bringing out that vein in her forehead and her dress gathered up in small fists she pressed into her sides. In the cab they hurtled downtown fast—it felt fast—even as everything outside slowed. They leaned against a long, lurching turn onto Seventh. A man on a street corner stepped off the curb, his coffee cup held up and away like a torch. The cabdriver's name was Mamadou. And Kay was still in the hall, her brother holding the elevator, her mother bent down in front of her, clutching her mother's face and saying, *Listen*.

PART TWO

That Year
and Those
That Followed

They went. They were away two weeks.

Jack went too, a day or three later, though not to where they were. He brought the cat in a carrier to Ruth's, where it moaned, homesick, and scratched the back wall of the closet, behind the coats.

For eighteen days the apartment sat empty. Fine dusts and pollen collected on the windowpanes and the mirrors stood with no one in them. Nothing in or out of the closed-circuit space. Only the wireless went on, invisibly complicating the air.

Folds in the mostly made beds sank deeper into themselves. Stains stayed stains, in the hampers and dresser drawers. In the kitchen, a milk-clouded spoon fixed to its bowl and magnets drifted down the refrigerator.

. . .

Then they came home, to the Ruth-gathered mail rubber-banded on the dining table and to everything—the graduated spines of books, rosettes on the living room rug—that looked suspiciously still.

The third week in July, the AC blew only hot air and they sat in front of fans.

Jack moved into his studio and then to a larger place in Sunnyside, Queens, with enough space for his work to live at home with him and for the kids to visit, when they were willing.

Deb moved, too: the bed to the opposite wall. Pillows at the foot of it.

For eleven August hours, they had the hurricane and bodega bags of ice.

Simon and Kay saw all the summer disaster movies in one trip to the Empire 25.

Jack and Deb stopped being married to each other.

That fall, Kay joined the field hockey team at school and spent the season on the bench beside the cooler, pressing grooves into the foam of her shin guards.

Simon became more and more like (this). He carried his videogames into his room and hooked them up to Jack's old college television, which he got out of basement storage.

New Year's, and a new year.

In Sunnyside, Jack began to work with smoke. He hung strips of paper like canopies from the ceiling and set fire to whatever was handy and burned powerfully, learning to make the blued white wisps rise in ways he wanted. He made the Manhattan skyline as it looked from a park on Vernon Boulevard, and the 59th Street bridge, its steel crosshatchings, from underneath like a zipper to the sky. Also the Shea Stadium parking lot and new baseball field, named for a bank. He held the smoking things high to make the darker marks, low and away for the flittering, coffee-stain singes. The kids spent one of their million weekends there, and the sliced hot dog and pasta Jack made for dinner tasted like burning.

Spring came and no one filled the ice trays. The glowing green clock on the oven fell an hour behind.

Isabel Davey's book came out. The author photo, Izzy in high-contrast black and white, shoulders encased in something boat necked, made it impossible for Deb to find any-thing to wear the night of the party.

Deb? It's me. I tried your cell.

It's in the other room. In my bag.

What are you watching?

Jon Stewart.

Good?

Mmm. I haven't really been paying attention.

My Internet here is for shit. I can't stream anything.

You should call someone.

I've gotta get the guy in again. But it's these walls, though. They're concrete.

Listen. I can't really talk.

Okay, if it's a bad time—

That's not why… Jack, hello? That's not why.

Okay, yeah. Jeez.

Halloween. Reese's wrappers and the wicks of silver Kisses papered the streets like leaves. Ruth took Kay to Jack's opening at a gallery in Brooklyn, where there was only wine to drink and no one their ages.

In the kitchen, the oven clock synced back with time and Simon stood watching his Pop-Tarts revolve in the yellow hum. Deb said, "Maybe you should spend less time at sleepovers," and Simon said, "Sleepovers, Mom, really?" He laughed and shook his head and said okay. She asked how was Donald anyway, and Simon laughed harder and said, "That fag." She said, "Well, just please don't stand so close to the microwave."

Jack bought himself a Christmas tree and carried it home alone, hand-sized hole clipped into the plastic netting, fingers to blisters by the time he got home (no gloves).

New year. Snowflakes looked like skeletons of something else.

The oven clock became wrong again. Someone finally fixed it, so that the next November it fell an hour ahead. Kay auditioned for the school play, which was *Our Town*. She read for Emily and was cast as one of the mothers.

Ruth died. Jack went to the funeral, sat at the back and didn't talk much to anyone. Kay asked what did *levayah* mean and Deb shushed. "It means *to accompany*," Simon answered, showing her the bright white face of his phone.

Deb woke up earlier and earlier, at six or five-thirty. In the hall she turned the knob to Simon's room, and if the door was locked she knew he was home. When she washed his hoodies they smelled thickly of spearmint gum, skunk, and burnt leaves.

Nubs of paper towel began showing up in the carpet, wherever Travolta left a mess. Kay filled out an entry form online and eleven weeks later received a forty-eight by seventy-two-inch poster for a television show on the CW, which by that time had been canceled.

. . .

It took everyone too long to realize Simon was failing school. "Aren't your grades slipping?" Deb asked over his report card. "When were my grades ever good?"

Toward the end of his senior year, Jack and Deb agreed to send Simon to a wilderness retreat in Virginia for troubled teens. "We can't take him if he's an addict," the program director said in their overlit Manhattan outpost.

"We think it's just pot smoking," Deb answered.

"Still, anything more serious, we're not equipped for that kind of thing. If you want, there's a place in Utah—"

Jack said, "Who said addict? It's just the pot. It's fine."

For seven weeks Simon and eight other boys built campfires and ate dehydrated packs of Yankee Noodle Dandy and were called only by their Nature Names, which they were made to choose their first night there. Simon was Wind.

Night drained the bruisy skies. The world blinked and the streetlamps came on. Travolta died, in the bathroom, a few feet from her litter box.

New year new year new year. The ball thrown in the air comes down faster. The numbers grew too big, unhinged from anything that sounded like time or what kept it. Nineteen ninety-eight was a year. 2015, 2020, those were eyesights. Calendars and the *Times* became props from a space opera. Everyone was always putting the date wrong in the upper right-hand corners of things.

Jack had very few, basically zero, New York openings

after Stanley gave up the gallery. His art got smaller, actually smaller, with no more room in his Queens apartment, which did not now seem so big, and no room for it either in the world, which had grown enormously. A school in Arizona invited him to teach, and Jack left New York for good. Or forever, anyway.

Doors to new drugstores whooshed open for anybody just passing. No one knew anyone with an address book but still companies somewhere kept making them. Kay was voted Nicest Girl in the yearbook, but all she'd really ever been was Most Quiet. Simon went out of his way to walk on cobblestones because he'd heard they were good for feet, though he forgot it was Jack who'd told him. He crossed the street, hair growing, nails growing, wisdom teeth two months from cresting.

Deb kept teaching at the college, studio and then dance criticism, and started dating another ex-dancer, a physical therapist called Eli, also divorced. She went to the earliest classes at Steps, fastening her hair the way she used to. She leaned close to the locker room mirror to tweeze the short grays that antennaed around her head.

Kay went to a university in California, and when she came back her name was Katherine.

Simon stayed Simon, at a college in the city.

On his faculty ID card, Jack wasn't smiling. It was a webcam, and he hadn't even known they were taking it—no flash, no birdie. In the photograph, his face, half under hologram, came out swollen on one side like he'd just had oral surgery. Or squirrelly, which is what he said to the girl who took it, meaning that he looked to be storing nuts for winter.

On Craigslist, fewer people responded to rentals without photos. Simon got a deal on a brownstone apartment in Crown Heights, where each morning sparrows hopped their cotton-ball bodies along the fire escape and would not shut up.

Deb moved into Eli's Tribeca loft. Because of the market or for other reasons, she didn't sell the apartment uptown.

In Palo Alto, Katherine got a job at a start-up in a technology research park, which in everyone's head looked like Six Flags.

They used pens made from recycled water bottles, or they didn't use pens.

Every screen responded to human touch.

A mole on Deb's face turned out to be cancer, but only stage one. A little plastic surgery and the scar hardly showed. At the gym, she sat in the sauna, with the warped wooden door that snapped shut behind her, feeling surrounded by dock on all sides.

How does anyone get over anything in places where the weather doesn't change? If you live someplace where the seasons are all the same, how do you get over any one or thing.

When her kids came to visit she wanted to make them so

144

many dinners. I never washed a vegetable until I fed the two of you.

After a few years, people expressed surprise to learn Jack had ever lived in the city. The lope in his speech revived, a timbre he got not so much from Houston as from growing up around his mother. He looked like a carpenter or a woodsman, in flannel and quilted vests. He'd always dressed that way, but only here did it take the form of function over style. The irony being that in New York he had done the hard labor of a carpenter, a metalworker, even a glass-blower from time to time, and here his art grew ever finer and more precise, though now he had more studio space than he could fill.

He whittled figures out of chalk, colors mint and laven-der and Pepto pink, sidewalk chalk sold by the bucket at a dollar store in town.

The nice thing about the university health clinic was you could make appointments online without talking to any-one.

Katherine sent Deb an invitation to one of her company's sites, where users set up virtual houses and decorated vir-tual rooms with JPEGs of furniture they could never afford in real life. Deb made an account, then did nothing with it. She got their newsletters, though, from Your Virtual Decorator, announcing the week's most popular chaise longue. They bugled into her inbox at five in the morning, when she was usually already awake. She'd clicked the unsubscribe link at the bottom of the page. She didn't know how to make them stop.

You could also cancel appointments online, at the university health clinic. Under "Reason for Cancellation," there was an option for "Illness," but not "Fear."

A few days after his sixty-sixth birthday, the associate dean who was also his girlfriend brought Jack a bouquet of silver balloons he could see his face in. They sank from the ceiling and stayed at eye level, hovering in the hall. In the morning, he held them out the window, set them free.

Balloons in bare branches look like foil lungs.

All the weight lost made him look better before it made him look worse.

He seemed to spend a lot of time in the rec room, looking at his hands.

The school updated all its access passes, so you didn't have to swipe but just hold the card to the thing, and everyone had to take new pictures. On his second ID card, he was smiling but rained on, a little deranged.

Jack found, before he died, among his stack of accordion folders, a portfolio of sketches he didn't recognize. Two of

Katherine, around age ten, and a few innocuous still lifes—a cracked egg with the yolk pooling out of it—from the drawing and painting class Simon had failed in high school.

A deep ache in his bones began to wake him in the night. Blood began showing up in his stool.

You ok?
Aces
You get my message?
Saw you left one
You don't have to play it. Just happy birthday.
I sent you something in the snailmail
Where?
To your Moms
K cuz I don't have a doorman
It's an envelope
My very own envelope
Nothing six figures. Happy belated
Simon I love you
Love you lots

The cane tapping and the wheelie suitcase together sound like a horse-drawn carriage.

Sometimes a memory turned out to be only an old picture from an album, a still his brain had fooled him into believing.

And in movies, why are there dial tones anytime anybody hangs up the phone? Is this magical realism?

In the end, what killed him was a mass in his pelvis, the size of a grape.

The end is never a surprise. People say, Don't tell me, Don't spoil it, and then later they say, If only I'd known. Nights in old living rooms, on pullout couches left pushed in, light reflects against the glass where the surprises were. We thought we were living in between-time, after this and before that, but it's the between-time that lasted.

PART THREE

Jamestown
and Out West,
the Start of June

There are cobwebs in the bushes. See them, there, in the late afternoon, when the disappearing sun spins the fine sticky threads into gold.

In Jamestown, it was taking some time learning how to look at nature. On walks, Kay kept a few paces behind her mother and watched where the sidewalks ruptured enormously to allow the roots of trees. They walked the waist of the island, from their house on the east to the quieter docks on the west. "Crosstown," her mother joked.

Her mother joked a lot. And said, "We're in luck." They were in luck the very first day, finding the single red cab and lady cabdriver outside the wood-paneled Kingston station, even though Simon lost a dollar to the one vending machine. They were lucky again in the car, thinking they'd gone the wrong way, when the right sign sprang up out of nowhere, and all the signs that followed began making sense. It was hard to pull onto their street without starting to pass it; the block was so small: four or five houses altogether, leaned uneasily against a hill.

Deb had made up her mind to be lucky, so they would be.

On the three-and-a-half-hour train ride, reading time had given way to thinking time. They were barely out of Stamford when her attention drifted, book to window. Her eyes ticked telephone pole to telephone pole, the slack of cable between, and she wished she had music to listen to, Joni Mitchell, a strong voice behind sad lyrics, to better indulge her sense of story, as if she were a character and this a beginning.

So many times she'd thought she was living her story. From five to twenty-five, every wish she made—on white horses, on eyelashes, on thin candles dipped in frosting— they were one wish. Getting into the right school, the right company, the right casting year after year. Just give me this next thing. Ballet and Jack were the great arcs of her life. Motherhood was a different kind of chapter, without auditions. Possibly there should have been. Kids were the only Big Thing she didn't have to work to get, and she hadn't expected to find herself wanting in that old way again. Now she saw how there might be yet another arc, even two. Who could say this wasn't the first day of something— God, not the rest of her life, let's not say that, but something, maybe good?

She let her eyelids droop, and outside the day blurred to green.

. . .

The house at first seemed more plant than house, but behind the wisteria and morning glories stood two floors, a roof shingled different grays, peeling white trim. There was a porch with an overhang that sagged in the middle and a screen door with the screen curled half away. Bird droppings, too, to match the siding. They weren't even sure they'd found it, because the brush had grown up over the mailbox. "Oh." Deb worried the glass heart around her neck, tipping her head out the cab's window. "Here? This is it."

"How do you not *know*?" said Simon. Surprising just that he deigned to speak. He'd had to clear his throat.

Deb overpaid the woman driver, who'd talked on the ride about her own kids, all boys. "I swear, tell them one thing and they do the opposite. And me my whole life just wanting a girl to dress up."

"They're pretty great," Deb said, winking at Kay, whom she never dressed up.

To Kay, the house looked broken. Inside the furniture suffocated under heavy plastic. The lights were out, but Gary had left a note on the kitchen table. *Property to see up in Boston. Back soon, make yourselves at HOME!!* Kay had no memory of Gary, your practically-uncle Gary, he used to get you toys on your birthday, remember?—Which toys?—and either Deb could not name them, or—"I don't know, that nanoo nanoo creature, that Furby doll"—and Kay might remember the Furby but not the person attached.

"This house is *one hundred years old,*" Deb said, coming up behind her with a duffel bag. She stressed the age as if it were a good thing.

"Is it even safe?" Simon shot past them, suitcase high over his head. He let it drop onto the second-floor landing and gripped both banisters, swinging his legs out from under him.

"Of course it's safe."

"There could be an earthquake."

"Simon, just—cool it, okay?" Deb said. Kay watched her mother gallop down for the last of the bags. The stairs were bare wood and rounded at the edges, without carpet or rubber grips like the kind they had at school. When she turned she was face to palm with Simon's open hand, black with dust.

In truth the house was worse than Deb had expected. Gary, who only ever used the place for fishing trips and painting, hadn't mentioned any water damage, but from the base of the stairs, she'd already seen brown stains ringing the second-floor ceiling, shadows like something died up there.

From the porch the water was gray and glittering as the sun slumped low behind it. Dinner hour had settled onto the street: the clatter of silver and dishes, conversations drifting from open windows and mixing with the hum of crickets. Deb found something embarrassing in bearing witness to the ritual, the smells and sounds of families gathered together and eating.

There was nothing for them to do but eat, themselves.

. . .

She took the kids to a seafood restaurant a few blocks down the main strip, with outdoor seating and Christmas lights strung around. They stood staring at the menu: mussels and thirty-dollar lobster. The nicest place in town but nearly empty with high season still a few weeks away.

"Let's do Chinese." Simon pointed toward an orangey brick building.

Deb squinted. "I think that's a bank." Then she saw the sandwich board:

PEKING EMPIRE

The Empire took up only a corner of the building, which was otherwise ambiguously corporate. At the door they passed a locked freezer and a poster board advertising ice cream cones. Inside, pictures of food hung backlit above the register—the Seafood Delight, the Happy Family Special—the same photographs as at cheaper places they'd been to in the city. "Want to take it out by the water?"

"I could eat here," Simon said.

Kay nodded yes, here.

So they stayed in, though it was clearly more of a take-out spot, with just the one table, a yellow fiberboard that pallored everything. Red tassels dangled limply from a television mounted to the ceiling. The reception was poor and they tried to guess at the movie. The food was like anything they could have ordered at home, which was what Simon and Kay seemed to like about it.

They walked back in the darkening with Popsicles the

155

shapes of comic book characters, gumballs for eyes. To Simon they were leaving the mother ship, lo mein and Coca-Cola, comforts of home. He carried with him two spare cans of soda, fearing there'd be nothing at the house but tap. One fell as they came around a bend near their street, detonating and spraying the sidewalk, the hedges, his shirt.

"Whoopsy-daisy," his mother said, in a funny mood. "And then there was one."

The house had only three bedrooms, so the kids would share the one with twin beds. The overhead light had gone out, but luck struck yet again when Deb dug a pair of flashlights out from the supply closet under the stairs, one with batteries that worked.

Simon and Kay had never shared a room before, and when they got back it seemed they were sharing it with yet another hulking someone, the mass of Simon's clothes heaped on one of the beds. Before dinner he'd unzipped his bag and dumped everything out in one piece, sandcastle tight.

He heaved himself onto the other mattress, thinking how stupid it was that, before leaving, he'd sent Elena a message and that now, in this stupid house, his phone was out of network, and he could not get online. *Let's try to go without for a little while,* his mother had said, *like pioneers.*

Kay shone the flashlight on the back of his head. "Where are you sleeping?"

"I don't care."

"You have to pick one."

156

"I pick two."

"*Simonnnn.*"

"Obviously I can't sleep on both beds, Kay." He bounced off the thin mattress and grabbed the flashlight from his sister, shining it onto his block of clothes, geological evidence of his packing order. An oak dresser in the corner waited to steep his clothes in its weird, rained-on smell. He wanted only to leave things as they were, to each morning excavate socks and underwear without ever upsetting the cube, sliding the empty case over it like a lid when this trip was finally over.

Instead he knocked the pile onto the floor. He flapped the sheets his mother had laid out over the mattress, not bothering with the corner parts, while his sister went out to change in the hall. By the time she came back, he was under covers, in the same clothes he'd put on in New York that morning, remembering what he'd written to Elena. He'd seen her the day before, sitting on the sandy dirt by the gym with Jared, when he was coming out of his geometry final.

His message had started:

heyhey. whats good?

"Simon?"

"What?"

"What are you thinking?"

"It's not your business. Nothing." *heyhey. whats good? survive finals ok? what are u doing this summer? i'm gonna do some traveling, u?* It was too many questions.

"Simon?"

"What, Kay? I'm trying to sleep." He heard her turn away from him. Loudly he said, "I don't know what you

157

want," though sort of he did. His sister wanted to talk about their parents, but Simon didn't think there was anything to say. He couldn't explain why he didn't care, that there was something make-believe about all this that felt to her so real. He couldn't explain how it was like they weren't even there. Real life was his friends, school. He switched the flashlight off. A few minutes later, he switched it on again. He put it down on the floor between their two beds, pointed up at the ceiling, where it stayed on until morning.

The day they left, when he could no longer hear the elevator noises of his family falling away from him, Jack made himself a bowl of cereal and watched the morning shows, like a man who'd have the apartment to himself for a couple hours. There had been a moment in the hall when he'd thought of turning to his daughter. Just hugging her. But he'd been afraid of what Deb would say. He'd be accused of, what—physical influence? Something like that. Pressure by proximity.

Of course there was time yet, to fix everything. They'd stay up there, what, a week? A week tops. Or maybe they'd call and he'd come and join them. Definitely tonight Deb would call.

He picked up the paper from yesterday and read again the piece about his show. "Don't Take the Bayt." Very clever. Bravo. And they say journalism has gone to shit. "*We deeply regret what's happened. We were assured by the artist that the explosives had all been detonated and accounted for well in advance of the show, and we're looking now into what could have possibly happened."* Stanley, you ninny. Well, throw me under the bus. *The artist.* Fine.

He sucked milk from his spoon and returned the Cheerio fossils to the bowl. There was one of those talk shows on, with its women, all white and one black, all liberal and one conservative, all postmenopausal and one who still got her period. They were talking about postpartum depression, which Jack knew had nothing to do with having babies and which he got every time he finished a project.

He walked to the kitchen and added more milk, came back to the living room and lay down. Maybe it was the milk that made him sleepy, or it could have been all those women's voices. Maybe he was only sad.

Anyway, he slept.

Stanley was usually at the gallery Sunday mornings, and that was where Jack caught him, early, just opening up.

"Please, Jack, not before my coffee."

"One more go. A few weeks. *A week.*"

"Jesus, not before my vodka soda."

"People will come." Jack hit his palm against the hot brick. The sun made neither of them more agreeable. "Stanny."

"People *would* come, just not for the reasons you want." Stanley shook out his keys. "Rubberneckers. You want rubberneckers?"

"I'll take rubbernecking."

"My lawyers won't," he said, sliding open the heavy door. "Not until we know for certain this woman isn't building a case."

Inside it was not even cool. "Christ, you cancel the air in here too?"

Stanley pulled a triangle of handkerchief from his jacket pocket. "Everything's backed up for me right now. Emily's on vacation."

"Emily who?" Jack asked. Stanley pressed the cloth to his forehead, blotting away the shine. "You know no one alive uses those. You iron those?"

"I'm going to Venice," Stanley said, running up around the white spiral stairs, "for the *biennale*."

"Hey, who's Emily?" Jack called, hovering his hand over the receptionist's desk, her silver cup of cheapie pens.

"You *know* Emily." The AC clicked to life from the second floor. "You've met her a hundred times. My assistant, Emily?" Cold air began to fall.

"Oh, sure," Jack mumbled. This was *Emily's* desk. There was his note slid under the mouse. NO ONE MUST TOUCH THE DEBRIS.

"I fly out late Thursday." Stanley was spry coming down the stairs, knees high. "You know, Jack, maybe you should take a vacation."

"The bee-ehn-ah-lay? No thanks."

"Or whatever. You guys have a house. Take the kids and go. The city's a terrible cunt in the summer. Already it's murder." Poor Stanley. He was shining up again, surveying the room for what else to say. Jack looked down at the desk.

"Yeah, thanks, Stanny." He shook the mouse until the computer came awake, the desktop a beach scene, palm trees. "Thanks. I think that's just what we'll do."

Their first morning in Jamestown no one set an alarm, and still everyone woke up early. Hard to sleep through new places.

In the bathroom where Jack had done the tiling—tiny, white hexagons and black grouting, both dizzying and spartan—Deb relearned the eccentricities of the shower, fogging the mirror and making the faucet sweat over the sink. Out of it, dripping, she stood and examined her approximate shape in the mirror. Still the right shape, still in and out the right places. She rubbed clear her reflection and arched her spine, turned to look at the long back over her shoulder. And maybe she'd finally done the right thing, in bringing them here. Hopefully she had. With her hands gathering up her hair, she wondered how long they'd stay.

. . .

She took the kids (neither showered) to a cheery breakfast place where the juice came in rich colors, deep cranberry and orange bright as to have a light bulb inside.

"I thought we could go out on the water this afternoon," Deb said, "explore around."

"Beautiful out there, my gosh," said the waitress, weighted on either side with orange- and black-handled pots of coffee. Her skin had that downy look of age plus makeup, cheeks pinked with powdery moons. "You all been out to Newport?"

"Oh, years ago, I have," Deb said. "But not these two."

"You'll want to see the mansions there. And Trinity Church, that's something. Lotta history."

"We haven't had a chance to see much of anything yet," Deb said.

Simon and Kay stayed pointedly quiet. The waitress looked at them around the table. "Well then. Anyway, I'm sorry, what'll you have?"

Then everyone asked for omelets. Kay asked her mother for a pen.

"I don't want to go see churches," Simon said when the waitress was well enough away.

"What I *really* want you both to see is Rose Island." The islands were what Deb liked best about the bay, so many uninhabited patches of land with romantic, Brontë names: Patience, Hope, Prudence. Despair. Her first summer in Jamestown, she and Jack and baby Simon had gone over in the brown-and-gold rental boat that sputtered, and the man who did the weeding there had let them walk all around. *Careful of the gulls. They'll attack when they're nesting.* Deb remembered walking the perimeter, how the island really was shaped like a rose. Then a seagull ran at them and Simon cried, five months old and in her arms.

She leaned across the table, toward where her son was watching her daughter ink outlines around the drawings of cocktails on her paper place mat. "Simon, you've been to Rose Island before." She disclosed this like a good secret, gossip about someone else, someone famous.

"That's not how you do shadow," Simon said at his sister's drawing. He dragged a finger over the heavy line she'd scratched around a Tom Collins, smudging it. "You have it so the sun is coming from both directions." He made a move for the pen.

"Stoppit," Kay said, angling her body away from him. "They're not trying to be shadows."

Then the eggs came and covered the place mats, and they could not fight about shadows anymore.

Instead they fought about watering cans at the hardware store, souvenir magnets and ugly fleece pullovers at the gift shop. Take it, you'll be cold at night. You think you'll ever use that? I'm sure we have things like it at home. Where are those energy efficient ones, the ones that look coiled like telephone cords? But I want it. Gross. Put it back. It isn't a fashion contest; you'll be cold. No. I said no. I said enough.

At a bookshop that sold miniature electric fountains and miniature Zen gardens and even a few books, mostly titles from small presses about local lighthouses and walking tours, but also some fiction in back, Deb told the kids to pick out some summer reading.

Simon reappeared with a thick paperback. "Are you sure?" she asked.

"Why not?" He thrust it at her.

Deb was about to make a case for why not, but her eyes had already shifted focus to Kay, who was by the register turning the chirpy wire stand of bookmarks, a deck of them already fanned out in her hand. "All right, give it to me," she said, and added his book to the pile.

The sky began to look like rain, but if they were quick they could beat it to the supermarket, which was at the end of a long parking lot, spotted with a few sedans and a red pickup under blue tarp. A kind of junior-league strip mall, with a video rental store and a custom sign shop that advertised gold-leaf lettering for yachts.

"Stay by me," Deb told them. Inside it was cold and bright and hard to find their way. With her kids filed behind her, Deb felt more alone, remembering they weren't her company but her charges. Every time she led them down the wrong aisle, she tried to find something there they could use. She trundled the cart around corners and perused the flyer that had been left in it. She didn't know what to get, so she bagged a lot of fruit and took what was on sale that week, a brand of seltzer she'd never heard of. Supermarkets outside the city left so much squandered space between the aisles. Once, in a time before cellphones, she'd lost Jack's mother at a Sam's Club in Houston and was twenty minutes paging her at the register.

At checkout, she found the food was definitely cheaper

than in New York. A teenager with feathery brown hair and a divot in one eyebrow double bagged everything.

"Oh, wait," Deb said, stopping a can of Sprite midair. "You want that now, squirt?"

Simon shook his head no and turned away from the cashier, who asked, "Need this taken out to your car?"

"We're fine," Deb answered. They had four bags of groceries, another from the hardware store, and a paper sack filled with books. That there was no car, she was glad the kids didn't say.

In the parking lot again, the air had turned a live yellow. Deb would have stopped to call attention to it, how pretty, but they weren't walking anymore: They were carrying. No rain yet but the wind had picked up, catching the tarp on the red truck so that it billowed. Strange, the way it sounded like thunder.

Jack could see his mother-in-law from inside the revolving doors—could see, at least, the helmet shine of her white-blond hair poking up over the back of a leather chair at the far end of her marble lobby. After Stanley, he hadn't been able to go back home without having what to do there, because he knew what he'd do, which was laze on the couch and eat and watch TV while Deb continued to not call. Instead, at the studio, amid the beginnings of *Sculptural Improvisation*, he improvised too a reason for going away.

The lobby was where Ruth had agreed to meet him ten minutes from now. Jack was early because he knew Ruth would be. He carried Travolta in the cat box, thinking of the girl somewhere with her guinea pig in a box, and how this was what happened to animals when their owners found new ways of being selfish.

He'd meant to walk to Ruth's, but on the second or third block this had struck him as unkind, hearing the cat's claws drag against the plastic floor as she slid around. He'd put a dish towel in to homey the place, but it didn't sound like it was getting much use. He tried hailing a cab, but so close to rush hour there weren't any, and when the bus pulled up a few feet ahead, he got on.

On the bus, Travolta *mrowwww*ed and the other passengers looked in on her, making sympathetic faces. Jack stuck his fingers into the gated front and tried plucking the towel forward, so people could see it was there. She's eight, he wanted to tell them. We must be doing something right. As to the masking tape on the side, TRAVOLTA in black marker from the last trip to the vet, to that he wanted to say: My son, he used to love the movie *Grease*.

Jack caught the eye of the yawning doorman/concierge behind the desk and nodded toward the blond head across the room. No doubt Ruth had announced that she was expecting company, Jack S-h-a-n-l-e-y, and that they shouldn't turn him away when he came. She liked to make a production, his mother-in-law. She liked to think of all the things that might go wrong and plan against them. For fifteen years he and Ruth had enjoyed defying all that was conventionally known about husbands and their mothers-in-law. While Deb had preserved an adolescent sensitivity to Ruth's small digs and asides, Jack was able to laugh everything away. *Your mother's a riot,* he'd say, which Deb hated. *Debby, don't be mad; it's only that she and I, we're the same generation.* His wife hated that even more, not least because it was almost true.

What would he and Ruth be to each other now?

Jack came around the side of her chair, cat box aloft like a peace offering. Ruth pushed her headphones off her ears and stopped her Discman. "My tapes," she said, though she meant CDs. Ruth listened to books. There was one she especially liked about Aristotle on ethics, and another called *Don't Sweat the Small Stuff* that she lent once to her daughter and that Deb had returned unplayed.

Jack held the handle high so that Ruth could see in. "Look who's here," she cooed. He felt Travolta's weight recede toward the back of the box and set the whole caboodle down on the glass-topped table.

"Made it in one piece." He sat beside her, trying to seem easy, though the depth of the chair into which he sank surprised him. He was feeling very low. From his jacket pocket he pulled two golden cans of Ocean Whitefish Feast. "I can go and pick up some more now with the litter—"

"I've got litter." Ruth had had cats once too, though hers were dead some years.

"Don't you want some new? You're not going to carry that all from the store—"

"Jack, honey, I'll tell you a secret. They deliver my groceries. Don't worry." She laughed. "I don't carry a *thing*." The laugh was tired and a little angry, as if it bothered her, this truth about herself. She'd never signed off on getting old.

"Good." He nodded. "You shouldn't carry. I mean, you absolutely could, if you wanted, but it's good you don't."

"My friend Lorraine, you know Lorraine? She's the one that started me on it. She said, 'Ruthie, why are you killing yourself carrying?' But Lorraine, she has her own problems. She's not a well woman. Her feet—nothing serious. Anyway you know me, I'm such a dope, I said what did I need to be paying extra for? So I should hurry home and miss them? So they should forget a bag? Never did it. Never. Always carrying these big bundles home. *Years.*"

"That can be difficult."

"And news flash, Jack, I'm not rich. Lorraine travels, no kids, two husbands divorced—and wealthy men we're talking, not like my Norman." It was the kind of conversation Ruth could never have with her daughter, who considered such micromanaging of finances depressing, who would have found her mother's story tedious and self-exonerating. Fine, do it, Deb would say, but why do we have to *talk* about it? Jack had never minded Ruth's soliloquies. He had an idea of what it might mean to be lonely, of how bad it could feel. Ruth, widowed, had not remarried, as his own mother had. He understood that there were people who liked talk, who needed it more than others. And he did think she was funny.

"You're right, though. It makes more sense that you get them delivered." He felt relief that she could still be normal with him, and when the ethics of delivered groceries had been exhausted as a topic of conversation, when again they had fallen silent, he wondered if she was surprised at having slipped into their old ways so quickly, if she was even now regretting it.

"Look at him," Ruth said, turning her attentions on the cat. "Her, I mean. Isn't that bad? Well, mine were boys."

"I don't think she took offense."

"So," she said, picking an invisible thread from her blouse. "Deborah knows about your going?"

170

Jack held hands with himself in his lap.

"Honey, look," she said, leaning closer. "I don't get involved. Okay?"

"Thank you."

"I think you're an *ass,* and a *moron,*" she said plainly, her voice higher but no louder than before, "but I know my place, and this is not my place."

"I appreciate it."

"My girl's grown up, better or worse." She laughed that tired-angry laugh. "She has her reasons. What'll happen, who knows?"

The Shadow knows. Something Jack's dad used to say. Jack had never heard the radio show firsthand, but his father always made the line sound noirish and pulpy, with a backdrop of heavy rain. *Who knows what evil lurks in the hearts of men?*

Back at the studio, he called Deb.

"Hey," she said on the fourth ring. She still sounded like herself, and not so far away. Like she could have been just at home, and not in Rhode Island. Not on some other planet he couldn't reach. "What's up?"

"How are you? How's everybody?"

"Good. The kids are good. It's raining."

"And our buddy Gar? How's pretty boy?"

"Don't, don't do that."

"What shouldn't I do?"

"Gary's not here until tomorrow."

171

"Well, and you? How are you?"

"What do you want, Jack?" There it was. The other planet, orbiting.

When he told her he was flying out to the university that had given him the new commission, to meet the deans and see the space, she didn't sound all that surprised, even though she knew how seriously he didn't take them, these commissions.

"My mom can feed Travolta."

"I took her over there already. So she doesn't have to go back and forth."

"Whatever you guys work out."

"We worked it out, I told you." He wandered into the little half kitchen. Opened and closed a cabinet for no reason. "It's good to hear your voice."

"What do you expect me to say to that?"

Jack said: "You sound really far away."

Deb said: "I am."

When they were off the phone he dialed easy, laughing Jolie, to make her guess who was coming to town.

Howard Roark laughed.

His mom, as usual, had been wrong—wrong in this case about the ferry, which did not run every day, not until high season, and so they could not go to Newport, where supposedly there were shops and movie theaters and actual things to do. They couldn't go to the islands either, not that he wanted to. His mom talked about these stupid islands like the whole world was poetry. Simon thought that if nobody lived on them, it was probably for good reason. What a moron.

Howard Roark laughed.

And she also didn't think he'd like this book, which was why he was going to.

Deb had taken Kay on one of her walks, which, by now, hour forty-eight in Rhode Island, he'd already learned to decline. Simon wanted to be found reading in full view when they came back, but his mother would never catch him on the bird-shitty porch swing, so he'd gone down by

173

the docks, where the ferry wasn't, and where there were a few small shops in a row, two of which sold real estate. He sat at the round green table outside the sandwich shop that was closed. The table had a hole in the middle for umbrellas, the size of his fist.

He turned the book over in his hands. *"A writer of great power. This is the only novel of ideas written by an American woman that I can recall."* This was what Simon needed, to be dispensed a philosophy, a way of thinking and living and winning. He did not yet know precisely what objectivism was, but he knew it had something to do with ruthlessness as a way of getting what one wanted. Something to do with not being a tool. The cover art, besides, reminded him of Rockefeller Center, a man of gold gripping the sun, or fire. It made him think of ice-skating and of Radio City Music Hall, where he'd gone once to see the Christmas Spectacular.

Okay.

Howard Roark laughed.

Inside the sandwich shop, someone also laughed. He turned but saw only metal shutters.

Back to Howard, naked and on a cliff high up above a lake. So already that was pretty impressive. Definitely a cool opening. Simon looked out over the bay where the water was splashing, not like Howard's, which was so still as to look stony. Or no—it was that there *was* stone, around the lake, and that the water was more still than the stone. He was confused by *a pause more dynamic than motion,* but imagined it was like in *The Matrix* where the bullets are flying and everything slows.

Laughter again from somewhere inside the shop and

again he turned. Two voices, both girls'. He stood and moved a little ways down on the dock, nearer the water.

Howard was thinking how all the nature around him would be destroyed and put to use—the trees and rocks, for building—but not in the way Simon usually heard people talk about it, like it was something wrong or sad, like the animals would go extinct and the ozone would tear open and we would fry.

Just then a set of feet came slapping down the hill. He lowered his head and stared into his book.

It was only Kay, hurtling toward and then past him, to the pebbled edge where dock ceded to water.

"Jesus Christ, what's the matter with you?"

"We found a cat," she said, pointing. "Up the road. Mom's watching it, come see." She doubled over to breathe, like the low air would come easier.

"I don't want to come see. I don't care. The cats are everywhere here." That morning he'd already seen one skulking around the yard across the way.

The voices in the sandwich place were louder now, the door suddenly open.

"You're late" was the first thing she said to him, this girl the sun made hard to see, so that she was only a shape at first, hovering over him like a wave. "Lunch service ends at three." She stepped back into shadow, and Simon pressed his palms against the dock, turning himself around.

"Oh, we weren't—" he started. "I mean, I was just out here reading."

"Anything good?" Her lips were chapped and pale, and her hair blew a blond banner behind her, thick like it carried a lot of salt in it. She looked like someone who spent a lot of time outside, this girl, in shorts and a big T-shirt, sleeves rolled to freckled shoulders. She would know how to tie knots for sailing.

Simon held the book up, felt dumb about it.

"She can't read," called the other voice—the other girl, darker and smaller, now coming out from the shop.

"Shut the ef up, Laura. I read."

"Not books," the other one—Laura—shouted, and began locking up.

Simon looked back at the first girl to find her staring at him seriously. "What?" she said. "You don't think I read either?"

"Yeah, no . . . I mean, I just don't know you." He slipped a finger out from where he'd been holding his early place. "I don't know what you like."

"Well, now you do," she said, holding out her arm. "I'm Teagan." She must have been eighteen or nineteen. She had that friendliness, an ease that came with things like college, and time.

Simon stood and shook her hand. He was just barely her height.

"Here's where you tell me your name, if you want."

"Simon," Simon said, feeling his heartbeat visible.

"Teegs." Laura, by the door, windmilled her arms. "Can we *go,* please?"

"You asshole!" Teagan's smile buoyed everything she said. Simon wanted her to call him asshole. "Is this your sister?" To Kay she said, "I like your sandals. Where are they from?"

Kay looked down at her feet, and for a moment they all

176

did, contemplating the hot-pink jellies that passed for shoes. "They're from Harry's."

Simon explained that Harry's was in the city, then added, *New York* City, to be clear and just maybe to impress her. Kids he used to meet at summer camp, kids from places like Michigan, they'd always seemed impressed, assumed untrue things. "We're here on vacation."

"Yeah, no duh," Laura said, arms now crossed like for leaving. "That's what everyone here is on."

Teagan took a step away. "Well, New York. Don't be late next time." Where the shirt pulled tight, he could see the curved cup of her bra—like the sun, he could see it without looking. "The wraps here are *pret-ty* good."

Simon didn't say he'd come back, hoping to preserve any air of mystery the city might have lent him, but he was anxious already, knowing he would. He watched them go, and repeated her name to himself, Teagan Teagan Teagan, so as not to forget.

"She's cool."

Simon started, remembering his sister. "Isn't Mom, like, waiting for you somewhere?"

Kay grinned, reaching to pull her foot up behind her. "She's cool, and you're not."

Simon looked at her, teetering on one leg. He could see the day's sun already on her face, pinking her nose and cheeks, and he was about to say she looked like a hot dog, but she rocketed off quick as she'd come, up the hill, jelly shoes almost flinging themselves off behind her. She had never heard of cats that didn't belong to anyone. She thought they might as well be hers.

177

But the cat had gotten away. Deb watched it go while Kay was off looking for Simon. She'd asked it to stay, pretty-pleased it to, she'd even tried standing in its way. Kay pouted when she came back and blamed her mother, as Deb knew she would, and the nice time they'd been having came to a close.

"You keep doing it," Kay said on the walk back. "There, like that."

"I swear, I'm not looking at you any *way*. I don't mean to." It was their first chance to really talk since Kay's trouble at school, and Deb was often quiet, finding words to form the sentences. "Susan Haber called me."

Kay said nothing, seemed to quicken her pace.

"Chloe and Brett's mom."

"I know who," and she was definitely moving faster.

"So do you want to tell me, about what happened?"

"That's okay." Kay was nearly running now. They were almost to the house.

"Well, would you talk about it anyway, please?" Deb hurried after. "I'd like it, to talk about it."

"No! Mom—" At the drive she stopped, looking wildly around. "The only reason you *know* about it is because they were being spies on me. That's the only reason!"

Deb was about to say that it didn't matter how she knew, just that she did, and that she wasn't mad, not at all, but Kay's attention seemed to have darted away.

From the house, two weedy legs, blondly fuzzed, were barreling down the small hump of lawn, alongside but without heed to the flat stone steps, made no use of by this man who'd built them—who'd paid for them, anyhow. And he was still handsome, still startlingly well made, with his light eyes and strong jaw. Gary, Deb thought, looks so much the same.

"Sight for sore eyes," he said, spreading his arms wide. He swooped his tall and narrow frame down to Kay. "And you! Where you been, huh? All my life." With both hands he cupped the whole of her head, so it became a clay pot he was making. "Amazing."

"Yeah, we like her okay." Deb laughed. "We plan on keeping her."

The three spent an awkward moment around the kitchen table.

"I remember your age," Gary told Kay, as though this could mean much to her. "I hated school—hated having to get up that early."

"Oh, please!" Deb said. "Mornings are the worst. But I

179

don't know"—trying to draw a smile from Kay—"you don't give me *nearly* as bad a time as your brother. For him I need a bugle."

"And what is it for you now? Junior high?"

"Middle school," Kay answered.

"They're hard years," Deb said. "Much harder this time around than they were for Simon. Girls can be so, I don't know, *unkind* at this age. Gossip and what have you. It's tough. But we're hanging in there, right, babe?" She reached across the table to stroke her daughter's arm.

Kay drew both hands into her lap. That the two adults exchanged glances she knew without looking.

"Well," Deb said after a pause, "how's Nancy?"

"*That* . . . isn't really happening anymore."

"You broke up?"

"We just sort of petered out." He shrugged. "Didn't see a future." To Kay he added, "Nancy's my girlfriend. Was my girlfriend."

Kay thought that, whatever his age, it was too old for a girlfriend: There should have been another word for it.

Then Gary suggested he and Deb scare up some wine from the cellar.

"Sorry it's a total dust bowl down here," he called from the unlit flight of stairs. Deb was surprised how immediately it made her nervous, being alone with him. He pulled a chain that hung from the ceiling. A single bulb threw light onto the honeycomb of dark bottles and, over it, one of Gary's landscapes, which he rarely showed and didn't sell except through hotels and restaurants in town. Mostly fine, precise oil paintings of local harbors, lighthouses on the sound. They suggested an appreciation for small and simple things, one she didn't have herself but that she admired, hoped to cultivate. Jack said Gary lacked imagination, and vigor. Energy! He doesn't have any energy.

"Okay," Deb said, crouching down to survey the lowest rack. "What'll it be?"

He squatted beside her. "Deb, listen. Your email, it didn't mention . . . I heard what happened, about Jack's show."

"I guess maybe a white?" There was so much she didn't know about wine.

"He must be in a pretty bad state."

"Or red! Red we won't have to chill."

"Hey. Talk to me." His hand on her wrist. He might have been asking the time.

"It's not about the fucking show." She kept her eyes fast on the shelf, the shadowed cubbyholes. "There's been— someone else, you know?" Gary would know, wouldn't even have to ask whose someone else, hers or Jack's.

There had been a time, as Jack's first marriage was ending, when everywhere they went it was tables for three. They went to the opera and to shows, the twenty-six-year-old and her fortyish escorts. Three was supposed to be a bad number for groups—whenever Simon or Kay fell into trios at school, there was always one kid left unhappy—but they'd never been a true triangle, more a line of three connecting dots, with Deb at the center, the leader dot in vee formation, if they were geese. She'd liked the feeling, looking over her shoulder, of these men following behind. She thought they'd liked it too, being both geese or both college boys again.

"Are you surprised?" She pulled an inky green-glass bottle from the wall of inky green-glass bottles and blew the dust off it.

"You're an amazing woman, Deb."

Everything, that was how much she didn't know about wine. "We should probably head upstairs." It felt like they were hiding, down there in the dark.

In the small garden, Gary lit two glass lanterns, casting shadows to dance on the white-stone table. Simon was back from wherever he'd been. He and Kay leaned over the low brick wall, pointing out fireflies and arguing over who saw them first. You are lucky. You are lucky, you are lucky, you are lucky.

The next morning at airport security, Jack drained his coffee, deposited his laptop into a bin, and smiled at the guard, militant but for a French braid running the length of her skull. Taking off your shoes was one thing. Now apparently they could ask for clothes.

In terminals people hemorrhage money, on magazines, eight-dollar trail mix, batteries, and packs of gum. The confines make them desperate for these things. Glowing amber bottles of duty-free perfume: They slow to look. Flight attendants herd past the shops, monitoring the sales. That personal gumball machine, $39.95. Not low enough yet.

Jack bought a slippery pack of Raisinets and ate slowly.

He found his gate and a row of chairs nearby. Across from him a young couple stood kissing, the woman with tangled hair and a flannel shirt buttoned halfway, the man in tight black jeans. Easy to tell Europeans from the Americans. His own family looked American but not garishly so, not in the way the rest of the world used the word, as a derogatory term. Though still they were, recognizably *American*. It had to do with what was square or self-serious about them. Optimistic in their ability to circumvent misfortune. Neither he nor Deb would ever take up smoking again, beyond the occasional puff, or ride a motorcycle without a helmet. Ride a motorcycle period.

It is ridiculous to watch the planes take off. Heartbreakingly clunky and hopeful seeming.

A lifetime later, his section called, Jack walked the connecting hallway of large accordion-like segments, feeling like lint pushed through a vacuum cleaner. A quick glimpse of ergonomic chairs and entertainment consoles and private islands and on to the narrower aisle in coach. Then they were lifted up, as though seized by the hand of some giant. Always a miracle when it worked, every time a breakthrough in physics.

"Light bird today," he said to the flight attendant as she passed. He'd heard one of them say that once.

"We'll be fine," she answered dully, and kept moving.

As an eight-year-old he'd fallen in total love with a Pan Am stewardess who'd pinned him with a pair of wings. This was when stewardesses were younger and wore those costumes and when people were still allowed pins on planes. It had been his second time flying, the return flight from New York, the only time his father had taken him on one of his trips. They'd lived in a suburb of Houston, and Jack

Senior was always flying to different cities to meet with clients, see factories, take the general manager's family out to eat. The New York trip had been scheduled over young Jack's birthday, which was why he got to go along.

Of the city he remembered next to nothing. He knew they'd stayed three days and two nights, but not where, and that they saw a musical, but not which one. Jack did remember, because of his birthday, that it was near to Christmas, and that they went sight-seeing on a tour bus and then an observation deck, so he could see the building tops all lit up. His father gave him a coin to put in the telescope and Jack had looked, as far left and right as the machine would let him, for the Empire State Building, but he could not find it. "And why do you think," Dad had asked, "why do you think you can't find it?" Jack kept looking until the time on the telescope ran out, not because he still believed he would find the Empire State Building, but because his face was upset and he didn't want his father to see.

When Jack couldn't travel with him, which was the rest of the time, his father always brought back some trinket from the hotel gift shop. Jack knew, even then, how it enraged his mother to watch her son run to the door when the car pulled into the garage. The trinket would clutter the boy's room, become something she'd have to pick up off the floor. I am a single mother in this house, she'd say. Single mothers have jobs, his father would answer.

His father's job had sent him away sometimes five days a week, but it had paid for *all this,* and it really had been *all this,* plenty of space (too much space, his mother said), a maid who came by once a week to do the hard jobs, a banana-yellow Cadillac for his mother to drive around in. They had a color television and dimmers in the living room and a beautiful bar cart that his mother got the most use out of during the week, always going to the liquor store on Fridays to restock before his father got home. There were times also when she forgot, or slept late and didn't have a chance to go, and those times Jack remembered watching her hold a bottle of something amber under the faucet to get the level up, returning it to the cart a shade too light. All of five and he knew the color of bourbon.

They soared, higher. Somewhere a tray that should not have been open during takeoff rattled. Jack looked out at the sky and had to stop himself from smiling whenever the wing broke through another school of clouds. Flying was the same, even if the airlines had changed. They were run less like hotels now, more like branches of government. Stewardesses had become flight attendants had become security guards. They tell us that a nail clipper is not a nail clipper, a nail clipper is a weapon, and we become people who have had to imagine how a nail clipper might be a weapon. Maybe by splitting it down the middle, pressing the sharp end into the jugular of somebody. Of some body.

He leaned his forehead against the window. At this angle he could see a sliver of a woman a few rows ahead, the pulse of her temple. Probably trying to keep her ears from popping. Jack's own ears popped a little.

Maybe they're right, and we will be safer when we finally think of everything, of all the things that can do us harm, and make rules against them.

. . .

One hour later and thirty thousand feet in the air:

The *SkyMall* catalog had lost its charm. He felt cold but did not like the blankets in their plastic bags. They reminded him of felt, of a school project. He did not like the pillows either, in their gauzy cases.

The screen overhead showed they were leaving Eastern Daylight Time. The red arc on the screen began in New York, New York, and ended in Phoenix, Arizona, the little white plane blinking somewhere in between.

A few more hours, a little closer to the ground:

Jack woke to something cold and wet in his lap. His tray was open, a plastic cup spinning on its side, the orange juice he'd ordered everywhere, seeping.

"Excuse me," he called toward the front of the plane. A man across the aisle was staring. Jack gestured, palms up, toward his lap: *Can you believe this?*

"Hey. Excuse me," he called again. He pressed the silver button on the armrest, which made the seat recline, gave up, and went to the bathroom, pushing the door to make it fold open at the middle and punching it shut behind him. Waited for the light to come on.

He was wrong to believe he would ever evolve beyond those moments of wondering how he'd come to a particular place in life. Specifically, here, in this sallow light, rushing handfuls of water onto his shorts.

He dropped lumps of soggy paper towel into the toilet below the sign that said to please not drop paper towels in it. When he flushed, the bowl filled with blue and the sound was frighteningly loud.

The plane landed and no one clapped for the pilot. Off it, they stood together, all twenty of them, on the tarmac, or whatever that area was around the tarmac, and waited for the shuttle to arrive. Some fanned themselves. To Jack the blazing heat was a welcome respite from the cold on board the plane. It was thawing his insides, bringing him back to normal.

He did not think his shorts would stain.

Simon, because he was older, retained a stronger impression of Gary than his sister had. It was a negative impression, which is not to say it was bad, only that Gary's presence had always signified a sort of absence—the absence of his mother's attention, of his father's, the absence of any conversation directed toward himself. He found that to be true again the next morning, over breakfast—Gary-scrambled eggs and Deb still in her robe, laughing too hard at Gary's jokes and trying too hard to bridge lulls in the conversation—and then it was true in the afternoon, when Simon had announced he would be bringing his book to lunch down by the docks, and his mother, who couldn't take a hint, suggested they all go along with him.

God did him the small favor of filling the green table with fat old people who left no room, so they couldn't sit in front of the shop directly. "They're getting up over there," Kay said, pointing to a bench in front of one of the real estate places (their father had taught them to point with a finger hidden behind the other hand, which his sister actually did around people). Simon prayed the bench was far enough away that Teagan would not hear his mom when she said the day looked like a painting.

"Order me a turkey provolone," he said, not wanting to get so near as to read the chalkboard menu. He'd angled himself absurdly on the bench, legs to one side, his back to the store.

"But they have all these cute specials." Deb squinted at the sign. "Sea something . . . Sea Treasures? That's probably tuna."

"I think it's crab," Gary said.

"Turkey provolone and Sprite," Simon said, wanting to be done with it. He was wondering what the back of his head looked like, how long his hair had gotten on his neck and whether his shirt was wrinkled. Whether he was very recognizable from behind.

"The Beauty and the *Roast Beef*," Gary read. "Kay, that sounds like a good one for you. What do you think's in a Beauty?"

Deb shook her head. "Roast beef's too tough for her."

"It's too much you have to chew." Kay's arms were crossed and she hopped foot to foot, holding her elbows.

"Kay," Deb said, "I *asked* if you had to go before we left."

"I *don't*."

Simon ignored them as they walked away, opened his book to the where it was dog-eared. He was finding he had a lot in common with this character Peter Keating. *He wondered whether he really liked his mother. But she was his mother and this fact was recognized by everybody as meaning automatically that he loved her, and so he took for granted that whatever he felt for her was love.* He'd brought the book thinking it would give Teagan something more to say to him. Also because he knew, though not why, that his reading it irritated his mom ("So, you're liking that?").

They came back with a Cool Hand Cuke and two B-L-Ta-Da!s, which did look better than his no-name sandwich. "Sy, we were just talking about our new houseguest," Deb said.

"Mm." All morning a great gray cat had been turning up in the closet where Kay kept her clothes (mostly on the floor, his sister too stupid for hangers). *He did not know whether there was any reason why he should respect her judgment. She was his mother; this was supposed to take the place of reasons.*

"Sweetie, that's fine if you feed him," Deb said. "We're just saying you can't do it in the house."

"I'm not, Mom, *God*." Kay slumped nearer her sandwich. "Gosh."

Simon filled his mouth with meat and cheese. If he chewed hard enough, he could almost tune out the conversation. *Mother means well, but she drives me crazy.* He wasn't very far yet, but he thought when he finished that the book would be his favorite.

"The real stumper to me," Gary was saying, "is how he gets in there by himself, Kay."

"The front door doesn't always close."

"*None* of the doors close," Simon pronounced through his food. "Because Dad painted over the locks, like an

191

idiot." He took another mouthful and did not look at them. Easy because of how they were lined up on the bench, like ducks. Dad was not someone they'd talked about yet.

Deb sighed. "So."

"What?" Simon exploded. "It's not like he's dead." He felt great saying it because he was so right.

A stroller at the next bench began to cry. Deb shrunk from the sound.

"That's exactly what Grandma does," Simon said, lips curling. "You look exactly like her."

"Sy."

"I'm just saying."

Now his chewing was the only thing to listen to. After a minute Deb said, "I don't know, do you all *want* to talk to Dad?"

"It's whatever," Simon answered.

Deb was about to say something else, only there wasn't time because here, of course, came the inevitable.

The inevitable Teagan.

And what was she saying?

She was saying: *Folks.*

"Folks, how we doing? Hi." She said the last word directly to Simon, and it must have been obvious to his mother, to anyone listening, that she spoke differently to him, like she meant it, *Hi.* Then: "How are you guys liking everything?"

"Everything's wonderful," Deb said, and Simon could see all her teeth. "We love the names! Who comes up with them? Do you?"

"No, no, I wish," Teagan answered kindly. Simon was sure she didn't wish. "That's Brian—my manager, Brian."

"Well, tell Brian they're *great*." (Enough, Mom. She doesn't care.) "So yum," Deb went on. Now Simon did want to die. Goodbye and die. To Kay, she said, "Aren't they yum?"

Simon could see the slight nod of Kay's head, but Teagan, who did not know Simon's sister, who perhaps did not know what it meant to be shy, leaned closer, awaiting the affirmation that had already passed.

"Kay?" His mother was on that kick that came around every so often in which she tried to toughen her children up. Such phases were always triggered by friendly young people like Teagan and never lasted more than a few hours, at which point she'd feel guilty and indulge them the other way. At fifteen Simon had her all figured out.

"She said yes, she thinks they're great." His next look, to Teagan, said, I'm sorry for them, for this; I'm not my family, believe me. It tried to say all that.

"Well, thank you," Teagan said, more waitress than person. She lifted her arm, slid a pen from her ponytail. "Actually, though, we're just closing up the kitchen."

"Oh, dessert?" Deb looked up and down the bench like this was some kind of actual problem.

"Teagan!" the other girl, Laura, shouted from just inside the shop, where she was tearing apart a cardboard box. "Can you come help me break these down?"

Teagan clicked the pen on and off, saying they could think it over. When they were alone again, Kay said, "I wouldn't mind."

"Dessert?"

"Talking to Dad." They were back to that. "I wouldn't mind it."

Deb looked down at her pita and parsley and cucumber, what bits were left on the paper plate that had turned translucent in places, where the oil had touched it.

"I think," Gary started, "if your mother and father need some time apart—"

"No, it's—okay. Sure." She turned a cucumber crescent around with her finger. It became the beginning of a parenthesis, the bottom half of a smiley face. "We can do that. And we can call Ommy." She nodded like some kind of progress was being made. "She'd like that."

They were all unbearably slow at emptying their trays into the trash, Deb shaking drops from a can for recycling, not that there was any kind of hurry. It was only a little after three and once again there was nothing to do.

They'd just started up the hill when Simon heard his name being called and turned back around.

Teagan stood outside the shop waving at him, hair waving too in the sea breeze. She saw that they'd stopped and jogged after them. Simon stepped forward like a chess piece to meet her.

"You should come over tomorrow night, if you aren't doing anything. My mom's house." There followed a discussion of certain landmarks, the white church, the library—that's that low brick building, right?—and when you see the swing set with the yellow seats, that's it, across from the yellow swings.

"Yeah, I mean, I just have to see if I can. I mean, if I'm not doing anything."

When she'd gone, Simon wouldn't look at his mother or sister or Gary, his cheeks tight with wanting to smile. Instead he walked through them, opening his book, keeping the good feelings between himself and the page. *He thought that the world was opening to him now, like the darkness fleeing before the bobbing headlights. He was free. He was ready.*

The Phoenix weather was up over one hundred and dry everywhere except the back of Jack's neck and the greenhouse taking seed in the crotch of his shorts. A shuttle had carried him from baggage claim to car rentals, and now he was on I-10, driving himself for the first time in how many years?

On the road.

In a way, too easy, that the Hertz people should send him off like this, all because of the card in his wallet that vouched that he had money, and another, softer card, confirmation that once, at sixteen, he'd been able to parallel park. If human cells regenerated, what, every seven years, then wasn't he a wholly new person? Several new people, it felt like, and not all of them knowing how to drive.

He didn't see why renting a car should be any easier than buying a gun; a car was every bit as much a weapon. Driving was faster and more freeing than he remembered, how directly the wheels responded, a little left or right, coasting along as though in a spaceship, a future in which friction was a thing of the past. The highway, so flat, came at him in rushes that hung in the air before they were over, reversed in retrospect, in the rearview of the ridiculous red convertible he'd let them give him for a joke.

Like virtual reality. The world shimmered and Jack thought: mirage. With his sleeves rolled up, one arm on the car door and the other on the wheel in front of him, he kept noticing the sweated skin inside his elbow, glistening to match the road where it glittered, concrete flecked with glass.

So driving was giving him a bit of a thrill, everything winking at him under the hot sun, and he sped up to get a good wind going on his face, ruffling his hair.

Probably it *was* just as easy to buy a gun out here, where if you didn't look too close at the edges of things you could feel yourself back on the frontier, a place you'd never been but in your mind. At the sign for Tempe, he turned off the interstate and followed the guideposts straight to the university. He'd figure out hotel, motel stuff later. There was a Super 8. Might be fun.

The campus was mostly pink brick and palm trees. He parked in one of the visitor spots and followed the campus map to the art museum, then called the department line that always put him through to Jolie, who said to stay right where he was and that she'd send someone out to meet him. He got the feeling that she would have come herself if not for the heat. He had yet to see a person.

Standing in his own sweat made him irritable. He stood

in the shade of the building, stucco with tiny square holes cut out for windows so that he felt himself on the wrong side of a bunker. He kept an eye out. They were probably up there rock-paper-scissoring to see who would have to go down, and he half expected to see someone in a hazmat suit plodding over.

His phone came alive in the pocket of his shorts.

"Deb! Can you hear me, Deb?"

"I hear," she said into his ear, and the fact of that changed everything. He was less alone, less unmoored than he'd thought. *She called*. "Is it a bad time?"

"No, no." There was a space between them, and he waited for her to fill it. "I'm in Arizona."

"I figured. That's good," she said quietly, like maybe the kids were around and she didn't want them to hear.

"I'm glad you called me." He propped his elbow up into one of the square holes, trying to seem jaunty. "How is it there? Everything running okay? Hey, how's the weather?"

"It's fine. It's beautiful."

Jack nodded into nothing and, to fill the space again, said, "It's hot here. Hot enough to bake potatoes."

"I'm sorry," she breathed heavily into the phone. "I can't talk like this, about the weather."

"Okay."

"Can you hang on a second? Just, hold on."

What was she doing? There was a sound like something dragging across the floor, and then the white noise around her changed, became more outside. She was in the yard, or out the window. "Hello? Deb, hello?" There was more jostling, and why the hell had she called, then, if she didn't care that it was hot in Arizona? If she didn't care that *he* was hot in Arizona.

"Mr. Shanley?"

Jack turned, his elbow catching in the hole in the wall so that he had to twist back and try again. A spindly Asian man with a thin smile was walking toward him, hand out, thumb at the sky. That he should be in a suit was strange, with a jacket even in this heat.

"Deb?" Jack gripped the phone. "Honey? Can you hear me?" No answer. The Asian man stopped in front of him. He had a sticker over his left lapel, HELLO MY NAME IS with "Kevin" spelled neatly in red marker. "I have to get off here, honey. I'll call you later. All right." He put the phone in his pocket and shook spindly Kevin's hand. "Sorry, the wife."

"Know how that is." Really? You look twelve.

The museum, on the way in, had been appropriately dim, but upstairs, where they kept the faculty and staff, it looked like any office, white lights and low, gray dividers. It took a few tries to get them to stop calling him Mr. Shanley. Kevin offered him a bowl of candy, little Bazooka gums and squares of Now & Later. Jack answered, "Maybe later," and Kevin laughed. So did HELLO MY NAME IS Lissa, standing over by the copier, and HELLO MY NAME IS Missy at the desk with the most phones. Both Melissas, wasn't it funny? "What are the odds?" Jack said.

When Jolie emerged from her corner office, there was no surprise about how she looked. Her voice fit her just right: dark blond hair that hung flat, skin deeply tanned but

199

yellowy, maybe the wrong makeup. Big girl, though not quite in the way he had imagined—big on bottom, like a pear, with not much chest and stubby little arms.

The little arms she spread out at him. "Jack!"

He went in for the hug. "Jolie!" They were old friends.

That the line was dead by the time Deb got back, this was another of the steps she took away from the man she was married to, from the hope that he would ever stop behaving like the sun. She said his name a few times into the phone and was aware, on the outskirts of her vision, of her daughter's hand, waiting to take it from her, his daughter who wanted to talk to him. Deb had gone to ask her, Do you still want to talk to Dad, because I've got him on the phone, and you don't have to, he doesn't even know I'm asking.

Kay was here, for him, and now Deb would have to tell her that actually he was gone, that actually never mind. She redialed, but the phone rang and went to voice mail. "Shit." She brought the phone down to her lap. "Sorry," she said, and for a moment it seemed she was sorry just for cursing. "He must've lost service."

Kay swallowed, nodded seriously.

"He's in Arizona for that project, you know? The reception, he must be roaming." She touched Kay's hair, smoothing the front piece down her cheek and curling it around her chin like a comma, after this face and before the next one, all the faces her daughter didn't know she would have. "Hey. Hey. Isn't it beautiful out here, the country? Let's go for a walk." But her hand stayed where it landed, on Kay's shoulder. "Whatever, however things— What's important to me is that you're happy. That's the number one thing in the world to me."

"I know."

"Okay. Okay, good," Deb said and let her go. "Head on down. I'll be there in a minute."

Kay's footsteps disappeared down the stairs. Deb would talk to her daughter now, finally. She would hear all she had to say. But first she tried Jack once more, this time getting nothing, not even the rings.

Jolie gave Jack a grand tour that afternoon, safe within the confines of her arctic SUV, cold air pouring from every vent and blowing motes into his mouth and up his nose. She drove him in circles around the empty square where his piece would be, not even stopping to get out and walk around. Then up to the school's prize building, an auditorium that had been one of the last designs of a Very Famous Architect. He felt like he was on the plane again, anytime his arm drifted toward the ledge of the rolled-up window, Jolie looking at him like she was afraid of getting sucked out.

"Okay!" She parked, and only from the gutted square on the other side of the curb, a dirt hole where there should have been a palm tree, could Jack tell they were in a different lot from before. Jolie was between the seats, twisted as far around as her seat belt would allow, grabbing a large patent leather purse with one hand and stirring everything around in it with the other.

"What's next?" Jack drummed his fingers on the computer in his lap (no babies, dogs, or electronics were to be left in the heat). Did he sound genial? Genial was what he was aiming for.

"Next . . ." Her voice trailed off and she forgot to answer. "Shoot. Ah! Herewego." She wriggled back the other way, holding forth one of the five or six worst things Jack could imagine, outside of, you know, a shiv. A digital camera, lime green. "Next we'll go up and talk to some of the grad students real quick." She licked her finger and scraped dirt off the screen with her nail.

"You know, this visit, it was just to see the space. I haven't prepared anything."

"You just be yourself." The camera bugled on. "You don't have to say a thing."

Fathers have a way with daughters that mothers never do. Deb had never known Kay to stay mad at Jack, or to deny him anything. And Deb couldn't hold it against her; things had been the same way with her own dad. If her mother dressed Deb's wounds, her father was the one who kissed them to make them better. It was Ruth who'd scratched the satin from Deb's first pair of pointe shoes, who'd singed the ribbons to keep them from fraying and knelt with her daughter on the driveway, pounding the toe boxes against the asphalt while Norman sat in the living room with his tray dinner and TV. "Who won?" he'd say when they came in after.

Women were the real workers of the family; men got to be allies to their children. It was Ruth who'd scheduled Deb's audition at the school in New York, who waited among the other nervous mothers in the room outside, hands folded with mysterious calm over her handbag that always had gum and Band-Aids and tissues in it. And when the call came, when Deb was accepted, it was Ruth who drove the hour each way into the city, four, five, then six days a week, for classes after school and all day Saturday. Deb still didn't really know what her mother had done those Saturdays. Maybe took herself to eat, took herself shopping, window-shopping.

Norman came to this and that performance. He said, You'll be great. You were great. You were the prettiest. You had the nicest what-do-you-call-it. Your shape was the nicest of any of them, all those bunheads. Best legs in the group. My girl. And she'd loved him for it.

On their walks Deb and Kay went no particular where. This time Deb asked the clerk at the souvenir shop down the road about a piney old pub where she and Jack used to drink red ale, marooned on a residential street that the town had since grown away from. Through the shop window he pointed and she traced a line from his finger with imaginary string, across the water, where the coast curved and ebbed out again.

They set out on the broken road, inching along at first, trying to keep pebbles out of their open shoes. When that grew tiresome they let the outside in to mingle with their feet. A grassy field, tall and thick with ticks, thrived beside a dead meadow, as though the two lived in different atmospheres.

Deb stopped every so often to point out a flower she couldn't name or the way light changed the color of the leaves. "Look at that. Isn't that beautiful?" She'd always wanted to be a person who felt close to nature. Such a practical bond to have; nature was free and it was everywhere.

Kay answered, "Uh-huh," or nodded vaguely. She didn't suspect that she'd ever wish to grow such interests.

"You remind me of what you used to say, about where you wanted to grow up. Do you remember what you'd say?"

"That was stupid."

"Why? I don't think so."

"Mom, *because*. Nobody lives in Times Square." But Kay had wanted to, to live where the lights were always on and there were always people and so you were never lonely.

"Well. I understood," Deb said, thinking the city had done that to her daughter: safety in other people, safety in strangers. "I thought it made a lot of sense."

Forest green siding, BAR & GRILL neon never turned on— Central Bay Pub had not changed a day, apart from having reversed itself completely. Deb was sure it had been on the other side of the road.

Inside, the different wood tones bounced off the shuttered windows and brass, turning the day into night. Deb led the way to the bar, where they had their pick of where to sit, and watched her daughter struggle onto a high stool. A faded Orangina poster hung on a wall through the kitchen. They ordered two of those.

"Honey," Deb started. "I'm sorry. I'm going to bring this up again, and I don't want you to get mad at me."

"I know what you're going to say already."

"Well, okay, but it's not about that. Sweetie? It's about what *you* have to say. And, I just want to listen. And, any questions you might have—about anything, all this stuff,

207

sex stuff— Don't roll your eyes at me. I mean it." She squeezed her daughter's knee. "Anything that you have questions about or, because, believe me, you aren't going to shock me, all right?"

Kay was quiet. Then to her glass she said, "I just don't get what's the big deal."

"About what?"

"Like, if this is just what happens. I don't get why we have to be so upset."

"You don't have to be upset—I'm glad if you're not."

"No, but I am. I just don't get why." Kay covered her face and breathed out her nose. "It's so stupid."

"I know. It's strange. You want to think that what someone does with someone else has nothing to do with you. And yet it does. That's why we have these rules, to protect us from getting hurt."

"Are you hurt?"

"Am I hurt? Um, hm . . . Would yes be too scary an answer?"

Kay swished her hair, no.

"Then yes. I was hurt. Yes, what your father did was very hurtful to me." Maybe it wasn't right to let Kay see her angry, letting her know that this was a thing to be angry about, but Deb, sorry, wasn't a saint, and did, maybe, in bursts, want her daughter to be a little bit angry too. It hurt to see Kay, after everything, reach for that telephone, want Jack anyway, want to love him. It was where her daughter looked most like herself. She thought of her own mother, how she'd overheard Ruth once telling a friend, *Well, you know Deborah. She was the child who learned to walk by never letting go of anything.*

Kay began scrunching the paper wrapper down her straw. "So why do they do it, if it's going to hurt us? Because it feels good? That's *it*?" She wet the wrapper with a few soda drops and watched it unfurl like a snake.

"There are a lot of reasons," Deb said, though her daughter's had bottom-lined them all.

On the walk back, the telephone poles began to look like stripped, alien trees, without the armor of bark. They could see the coves of Newport across the bay, the roads that wound around them, in perfect miniature, cars with their high beams curving in and out of sight and new ones replacing them, as if on a loop.

"We don't have to call him," Kay said. "Dad."

Deb stopped. "Why not? It's perfectly normal if— I mean, we still can. We totally, totally can."

"I just don't want to anymore."

Jack thought they were going to a studio, but Jolie was passing the studios, also a sign for metal shop and another for neon, and when they got to the third floor, he understood they were going to a reception. Always there was a reception—everywhere he was being *received,* couldn't anymore just *arrive.* And then never a very elaborate reception—nothing like what the Very Famous Architect would get if he came, if he were alive with nothing better to do outside Tempe. A reception was an evaluation he hadn't wanted, his career laid out in rows of weak, sweet supermarket wine, prepoured a third of the way, his worth measured in cheapie plastic cups on a tablecloth made of hospital gown.

Here the four or five faculty members also wore name tags, and the students, not that there were many of *them,* not more than twelve, they wore tags too. The only one aside from Jack without a label was Jolie, who had him wrapped up in her little arm now, taking him in turns around the room like a show pony. And it wasn't that the nearer she got to him the more he wanted to run. On the contrary—paradoxically! the inverse!—he found the more he wanted to run, the nearer he let himself be. He tuned out the room, drank wine when he was led to it, let Jolie answer his questions and brush his tail. He neighed every time, on cue.

A long hour later, they were at a dark bar across the road from the Super 8, brass-stemmed lampshades reaching down from the ceiling. Jolie had announced, in the elevator down from the reception, "I don't know about you, but I could use a stiff one." By which it turned out she meant a Sex on the Beach, ordered loudly. Jack drank Scotch and together they split a basket of fries.

"So I'm sorry to hear about your show," she said. Jack looked at her and swallowed loosely, letting some spirit linger on his tongue, sink into the space where his gums met the soft slippery insides of his cheeks. "The explosion and all that."

"Yes, I knew what you meant."

"We still want the piece, if that's what you were worried about." She sucked in her cheeks as she drank. A smidge of lipstick kissed off on the straw. "If that's why you came all this way."

"I told you, I wanted—"

"To see the space. I know." She broke a fry in two—they were the thick kind, wedge cut—and held the halves to her lips. "Just saying."

Jolie ate more fries and Jack drank more Scotch. She said no to another drink, and Jack pushed back his stool and walked over to the bar.

He ordered two, took one like a shot right there. Jolie had her head down, her phone to one ear, and a finger in the other.

"My son," she said, hanging up as he came back with his third.

"You could've stayed on."

"No, it's fine. It was a message. I was leaving a message." She looked around the room. "You think it's quiet enough that he heard?"

A jukebox in the corner looked like it was just for show, with at best a radio inside it, and there was no one at the pool table either. "I'd say there's very little noise."

She nodded. "He's—you know, he's wanting to join the army. Or, the navy, he's wanting to join. They say that's supposed to be safer. He says."

"You don't look old enough for an eighteen-year-old."

She laughed. "You don't look old enough for a line like that." Most of the fries were gone, and there was still some peach schnapps pooled at the candied-cherry bottom of her glass, but he thought Jolie was a little drunk too.

He was aware of her crossing the street with him while he booked the room, and he was aware of her following him up and down the hall, of her shouting *"Bingo"* when she found the room number before he did. Probably she said something about getting him settled in or wanting to freshen up; he didn't listen.

The room was wall-to-wall green carpet and two huge beds of depressing floral, quilted and sheeny like the insides of caskets. He sat at the foot of one while Jolie ran the bathroom faucet. He was tired all of a sudden. Everything in the world was conspiring to make him tired. Sleep made him tired. Coffee made him tired. Scotch. Receptions. Handshakes. Two Melissas. The price of things, that all things had a price.

Brown Bear. Brown Bear made him tired, plus old. Also? When the woman you've lived with fifteen years decides she won't understand you anymore. When you know she could, only she doesn't want to.

And Jolie, at the bar, that moment with her son. When she had seemed to him sad, and a bit pretty—even then she made him tired. That she was losing her son, that Jack was losing, well, everyone, that everyone loses everyone, eventually. How can anything make you more tired than that.

So Jolie came out of the bathroom with her hands still wet, and she put one of those hands on his hip, and she rocked a minute where she stood, or the vodka rocked her, and the rocking was like a blip in the system that told him this too was not real. They both were tired from so much lost, and nothing was real, to either of them.

Jack moved her thumb out from inside his belt loop and said good night.

. . .

213

He could lie down knowing he'd done the right thing, sending her home, making himself alone. He arranged his weight on one of the beds and from his pocket pulled a yellow-wrapped piece of taffy. He'd taken some the second time it was offered, with Jolie waving the bowl at him— "Now & Later?"—and without Kevin around he'd only varied the joke: "Maybe a Later."

He gnawed at the wrapper with his bottom teeth and was hit right away with that banana smell that no actual banana ever had. His cell was dead, so he used the room phone to dial out, dial Deb, but he got only her voice mail and everything sticky. "Hey. It's Jack. I mean, it's me." Even drunk he could hear how drunk he sounded. He told her where he was staying, and he could not find any extension on the base of the phone, not even the room number, "but if you give my name at the desk, I'm sure they'll patch you through. Seems like we keep missing each other." No good, this missing each other. Different pages.

He didn't have the car. It was still in the parking lot outside the art museum. He flopped back on the bed and dragged his laptop onto his stomach to rise and fall with his breathing. The hotel Wi-Fi, big surprise, wasn't working.

Different pages. Another taffy. Only yellow, these taffies? He realized he'd done the wrong thing with Jolie, letting her drive when she was that way.

You know you've hit bottom when you want for solitaire, for *Minesweeper*. What can you do without Internet, and not even any music on the machine, which had been for email almost exclusively. Email and also a few audio files, here. He'd never played them, but right away he knew what they were, and right away he knew that he would.

Double-clicking the earliest, he heard their first clear error, by no means the biggest of mistakes they would make. They'd used the recording software that came free with his machine (but no games?), and neither he nor the girl had known about the metronome that had to be toggled off. So it had stayed on, ticking like a clock or a sterile heart, keeping time with them, with how much time they had.

Okay. I think it's recording. Is this okay?
Doesn't bother me.

Um. So I'm just going to start. I have this list of questions, but we can deviate from them.
Sounds fine.

Do you think it's an artist's obligation to address current events?
Current events?

Like September eleventh.
So really we're just talking about one event.

For the purposes of this conversation. Yes.
Okay. Obligation? Do I think the artist is obligated? No.
I think, good luck to her if she thinks she can avoid

addressing what you call current events. What's so fucked up in the world.

So nine-eleven was something you couldn't avoid addressing?
I had to get it out of my system, I guess. I guess you could say that. At the time, you have to understand, I was working only a few blocks from the World Trade Center. I was there that morning.

I wanted to ask you about that. You've since moved uptown. This interview is taking place at your studio in Hell's Kitchen.
I'm sorry, is that a question?

What motivated your move?
To Hell's Kitchen? I liked the sound of it. We're above a methadone clinic, I don't know if you noticed. So there's the atmosphere. And it's cheaper. They say prices downtown fell after nine-eleven, but no one told my landlord.

So safety had nothing to do with it?
I don't believe lightning would strike twice. Grand Central Station, Madison Square Garden. Maybe there. Really they should watch the Empire State Building. The Chrysler. That would be harder, for people. No one loved the Twin Towers, the structures themselves, like they do those buildings. The terrorists would know that if they watched a couple of New York movies.

You say a lot of inflammatory things I think without realizing they're inflammatory.
I realize.

You don't care about upsetting people then.
I care. The bullshit is that after nine-eleven everyone felt like a real New Yorker? Fuck that. You can't wait for tragedy.

You're from Texas, aren't you? Texas originally?
Houston, that's right. My parents are there still.

I'm sorry, I thought your father—I thought he passed away?
Yes. I'm sorry, yes, that's correct.

Talk a little bit about what you saw that Tuesday. How did you find out? Were you on the street?
I went out. I listen to the radio while I work. Can't hear it half the time, when I'm cutting or welding, but that's how I learned something happened. I saw, you know, what everyone saw. The stuff on television. The stuff that ran once on television and got pulled. People running. People tired from running. I remember I'd been walking a while in a loop when someone offered me a bottle of water. They thought I'd been, somehow, a victim. Maybe one of the ones who got out. I get dirty when I work.

There's this theory I have about your September series.
By all means.

You reminded me when you touched on the buildings. Instead of the towers, you chose to depict the victims—the actual physical people, the man on the plane, the woman in the office, the falling man—

Yes.

No one was willing to show those images. It was a kind of censorship.

Censorship is a strong word.

Where were those images then? Where else?

I don't think I can address all that. Clearly, what I was trying to do, I failed.

You got people talking.

Not in the way I intended. That's something artists say a lot, don't they—good or bad, as long as it gets people talking? I don't understand that. People are always talking. They're desperate for talk. They'll talk about anything. Most of what they say is stupid.

And if they hadn't taken the series away when they did?

Who knows?

If they'd let the pieces stay on view, you might have had a different reaction.

It's certainly flattering to think so. But I think that probably they were right, in taking them away. People didn't like them, didn't want to like them.

For what it's worth, I thought they were exquisite.
You saw them?

Only in pictures. I was in Ohio for college at the time. They're in a private collection now?
That's right.

Well, I wish I had seen them. Actually I wish I'd been in New York then, to see all that.
You mean on nine-eleven?

Is that awful to say?
It's natural. It was one of those rare important times, fully realized. A day that announced itself as history. That's exciting. I wish I was there, and I was.

You say you were downtown by the time of the attacks, but you live uptown. How early do you usually begin work?
I stay at the studio overnight some nights.

And your family?
They're very patient.

Is that of your wife?
That, no. That's a picture for something I'm working on now.

Do you still work off live models?
Sometimes.

219

Strangers or people you know?

Doesn't really matter. To me. Though it might matter to them.

I used to model a little, when I first moved to New York.

From the Super 8, he could walk to the minimart, where he bought an off-brand Big Gulp, and back to the bar, where he bought two more whiskeys, neat, and a vodka cranberry for the girl who sat down next to him and who would tell him his ChapStick tasted like piña colada. But that was Later.

In Jamestown, with the overhead off and the front door propped open, it was a dark summer morning indoors. The kids were still in bed. Deb looked into the fridge and decided her iced tea had cooled enough. She'd used the mushroom pitcher Jack had found once at a flea market in town. The ceramic bowl of it was carved with cremini, painted seventies beige and orange and brown. Two clumsy green leaves made up the spout.

She packed two glasses with ice and clutched them stinging cold against her dress and bare arms. Gary was at the great wood table, aiming a screwdriver at parts of a fishing reel and probably straining his eyes. "Whatcha got there?" she asked.

"Oh, I was thinking we might like to go fishing, one of these days. Maybe a birthday trip."

She sat, peeled the glasses from her skin. "You were always good about that, birthdays."

"Yours is easy to remember," he said, though not why.

She thought of the first birthday she'd had with Jack, when he was married and she wasn't. Her twenty-sixth. How could she have been sad about anything then? Crazy, stupid, tortured girl: She wanted to shake herself. Nothing is so bad, twenty-six. It had seemed bad, when Jack was two weeks with his wife in Cape Cod at some beach she'd never been to, and she was drunk from endless Bloody Marys at the endless birthday brunch her friends had arranged for her. She had chosen brunch over a proper party because Jack's plane landed that night around eight and he'd promised to make it over.

And had she even thanked them for birthday brunch, her friends? She'd become indifferent to them; they'd become boring to her: Their opinions were not his. She'd liked him immediately, and so much. What do they call it? Enchanted. A victory just to be with him, moments when he wasn't with anyone else. Why had that meant so much then? The five of them had split the bill without her, even though everyone was a dancer and poor, and Izzy had arranged to be out that night. "But call if you need me," she'd said, clearly worried that Jack would not come. Deb couldn't remember thanking them. She wanted to call them all now.

"God, Gar, how'd we get to be so old?"

"Flattering, thank you."

"It's just being back around all this stuff. This incredible, ugly pitcher." Its ugliness had made them laugh the first few times they'd used it. At one point she'd tried making it into a vase, but Jack said it ruined the flowers. "How many summers ago were we all cooking dinner together here? *Cutting the ends off snap peas* or something."

"Long time."

"Being in this house—We're even in our same seats."

Gary shrugged. "It's where I sit."

"And this is where I sit, and *that's* him, where he would," nodding at the empty end chair between them.

Deb turned twenty-six in her rattling apartment over the subway with all the lights off thinking, Come. Please come. Where are you. *Where are you.* Whereareyou. Jack made it, just made it, the way he *just* did a lot of things. It was eleven-something when he rang up from the street. He hadn't showered since Chatham and brought the beach in with him. Later, after he left in the small early hours—their affair gave her so much new time, blue morning time she used to sleep through—Deb stayed very awake in bed and stared up at the ceiling, dragging the soles of her feet up and down the mattress, feeling the grit of him everywhere. Now she was forty-one, nearly forty-two, and a little thrilled to be away from New York, and from Jack.

She was pressing the nails of her left hand into the dark wood, engraving small arcs in its waxy surface. "Someone should have dropped this pitcher a decade ago."

"Ugly things don't break," Gary said over his gear.

She would always know Gary, regardless of how long they'd been apart. She knew how he took iced tea. With sugar, sunk mostly to the bottom. Gary was a little bit of a place to come back to.

Jack's head was like a blister of brown liquor simmering under the mile of sun between the Super 8 and his car. He made it, each step a superhuman achievement, past the cardboard box of a campus chapel and the forsaken tennis courts around which the grass would not even grow for heatstroke, to the parking lot, to his ridiculous red convertible, long abandoned by the shade of tree in whose custody he'd left it. And then the car, when he got there, it wouldn't start.

He sat with the door open, one leg swung out and the other growing slick against the leather interior—shorts were a mixed blessing—and pumped the gas and tried again. He could have taken it as a sign, right, if he were watching his life from somewhere far away, like a character in a book or movie. The sign would have been to go home. Go home, go home. None of this is for you. Only in movies do we heed the warnings of inanimate objects with due reverence. In life Jack ran the heater on high until it started blowing cool air, took the cap off the gas tank, and made his own shade, his back to the sun and his silhouette cast across what parts of the engine seemed important.

He'd woken up alone in his hotel room, on the scratchy-moss carpet, between the enormous, funereal beds. He was on his stomach, with a crick in his neck and some drool pooled around the corner of his mouth that made him want to move never. There had been, what, many drinks. He'd gotten sloppy with that girl. Kissed her in the bar and again outside after her friends had gone home. Made out, like a teenager.

He remembered no name, only that she was studying audiology. Whether it was a joke or not, she did seem to have a thing for ears, whispering into his like to drive him crazy, which it might have if his senses had not been so dull and if all of it were not so thin and so obvious. He was re-lieved when she didn't want to go into the Super 8, and it was easy to turn down the invitation to her on-campus double because, while he was lonely, or horny, he was not completely stupid (despite all outward appearances). Plus, also, he had certain practical misgivings (specifically that he was drunk to the point where it might not work).

It took cycling the ignition ten more minutes before the car would start, but finally it did. Jack drove to the airport without any idea about flights and without calling Deb, without calling Jolie. It was a pleasure not calling, building a dam between himself and the voices reminding him of all he'd done, and hadn't.

He was glad to be getting rid of the red convertible, which, like the Super 8, had become a failed irony. Funny

225

for the Queen of England to stay at the Super 8, or for the Very Famous Architect. Not for you. In the shower he'd found an old washcloth, dried stiff, that betrayed the history of the place, the sad naked men and women who'd preceded him. If the washcloth was from the last person, or the one before that, or how far back did it go.

Jack knew he was behaving irrationally—that he wasn't behaving, period—which was why everything he did now, all he was permitted, seemed suddenly too easy. The Super 8 people, Jolie, the ear girl—nobody knew. The woman elevated up behind the counter at the car rental did not know, or care. Her job was to say yes. We do have an economy model available for one-way travel, yes. To Houston, no problem. We have a branch located at Bush Intercontinental, very convenient if you plan on flying out. Yes, sir, it's a sedan. Four-door. Sorry? Black, I believe. Yes.

Jack was going home.

That afternoon it was back, the big gray one with the yellow eyes that Kay had started calling Wolf. The cat had a way of making its body thin on the sides and squeezing past their bedroom door even as Simon closed it, running always to the same place on Kay's closet floor, the pile of her clothes a kind of bed or nest.

"It's going to give you lice or fleas or whatever," Simon said in the warpy full-length mirror. He was trying out his fifth shirt of the day, fifth of the last four minutes.

"He doesn't have lice," Kay said from the floor, where Wolf was kneading a red sweatshirt with his eyes closed.

"Just keep it out of my stuff."

"He isn't interested in your stuff."

"Yeah, okay," stamping on his shoes.

At first it looked like a pile of trash, the pots, buckets, and vases heaped on the fringe of pale grass outside the house that had to be hers. Not without some reluctance, either, did Simon decide it was hers, only it had to be, because of the yellow swings she'd mentioned, and because the number on the house to the left was too low and the number on the right too high.

There was a yard sale in front of it.

Or not a sale, because the cardboard sign, flat on its back and weighted with rocks, when he stood over it, read FREE! TAKE ALL! Most of the clay pots still had soil in them, and the glass vases looked not very well washed.

Simon rang the white plastic doorbell, which was slapped crooked by the door, and if it worked, if it did anything, the sound was not one he could hear. He stood on the porch that creaked under several rugs, and it was strange to have rugs outside, though he guessed welcome mats were like the same thing, and these might have been welcome mats, all overlapping each other, welcome welcome welcome. He thought about this so he would not worry about what was taking so long, if she'd forgotten the invitation, if he wasn't really meant to come.

At last he heard a high shriek and a "Coming!" then a thumping down stairs.

The door opened to a green-beaded curtain and, behind it, Teagan, in a simple white T-shirt and the same shorts as before. Her eyes were rimmed purple, thick Cleopatra lines that curved out a little at the ends, like fish tails. She held out a bottle through the strings of twisted plastic. Beer, for him.

"My mom's asleep," she said, nodding in at the living room as they passed it, but he didn't know if she meant they should be quiet. He couldn't see anyone there, only the back of the couch, and for a moment the reflection, in the black, glassy face of an ancient Sony Trinitron TV, of what could have been a body or could have been only a mass of sheets and throw pillows. Of the house he was ready to say things like, No, it looks great, in case she said something like, Sorry for the mess, which she never said.

They came out onto the back porch, which turned out to be the same porch as the front, wrapped around. "He made it," said a pair of legs high in a hammock. Pale and freckled legs, the girl attached near to upside down. An *Us Weekly* splayed open on her stomach, she held a cigarette in the air so that the ash, if it fell, might hit her face.

That "he" made Simon uncomfortable, as though they'd been talking about him recently. And there was another *he* that bothered him, but this one an actual person, sitting on the floor with his back against the railing.

"You know Laura, and that's Manny. This is Simon."

Manny tipped his beer. The whispery brown hair, the divot in one eyebrow, and Simon knew this was the cashier who'd bagged their groceries that first day, when his mother had called him "squirt." *Please may he not remember.* Simon pressed the neck of his own beer against his chest and twisted the cap, hoping it was the twisting kind, and when it fell off a light mist rose up from the rim and the cold left a dark moon on his shirt.

Teagan kicked off her shoes, soft yellow Keds, and climbed up into the hammock with Laura and Laura's legs. "So! Simon." She blew invisible strands of hair from her face. "Tell us something."

229

"Something," Simon answered. No one laughed, or even smiled. "Like what? I mean, I'm from New York. My parents have a house here? Um."

"What do you do for *fun*?" Laura asked, idly turning the leaves of her magazine.

"Regular stuff, I guess. Hang out with friends, play videogames."

"Gamer, huh?" Manny said. "Right on."

"Quit being a dick," said Teagan, though Simon hadn't realized he was. "Simon likes to read, too, don't you? Unlike some people."

"Well, my school." Simon swallowed. "I'm still in high school, and our school is like—"

"Wait," Laura said, looking suddenly, troublingly interested. "Say again?"

"Just, we have like a lot of electives at our school, so—"

"You know *we're* in high school, right?" Laura pitched herself forward, anchoring her chin onto Teagan's shoulder. She'd lit another cigarette.

Simon could feel all parts of him tighten. "I know. Me too."

"But," Laura went on, "the way you said *you* were in high school, like we weren't."

Simon tried staring only at the piece of ash that had settled in a curl of her hair. "Yeah. Yeah, no."

"We'll be seniors in the fall," Teagan said, "but Manny graduated."

"Oh?" he asked, turning to the boy on the floor. "What are you doing now?" Like this was a person he wanted to know better. The nick in his eyebrow he'd probably had

230

from birth, but here, minus apron, plus cigarette, plus *girls,* it seemed more like something he'd won in a fight.

Manny was no more interested in Simon than Simon was in him, or in anything—the world, it seemed like— except whoever or whatever was on the other end of the old flip phone he never shut or let out of his hand, pressing buttons that clicked. "Uh." He looked up and then back to his phone. "I've got a band."

"You *used* to have a band," Teagan said. "He works at McQuades."

At that, Manny snapped his phone shut. "Okay, it's my time." He grabbed the last beer from the tub of ice on the floor, mostly melted, and stood letting it drip as he and Teagan seemed to say something to each other without speaking. He might have been waiting for her to walk him out.

She didn't. "Fine. Later."

They listened to him leave, and for a while there were still four of them, the girls and Simon and the sound of Manny walking out.

"It's cool you guys have jobs," Simon said. "I want a job, but, I don't know, you need experience it seems like. Like, how do you get the first job if they always want you to have experience? It's a total catch twenty-two." *Catch-22* was a thing he always realized too late that he might not be using correctly but never remembered to look up later.

Teagan picked a cuticle. Laura stayed with her chin on Teagan's shoulder and began to blow smoke out her nose. Simon finished his beer and it didn't make him feel anything. Maybe he should have been going. He'd only just gotten there, but he'd delivered himself, or some version of self, and they were not interested.

Then Laura said, "Actually, Teegs, I gotta go too." She hoisted herself out of the hammock and into the same sneakers Teagan had had on before. She dropped her cigarette into the tub and *Us* onto the floor, where the cover flapped off at the staple. "I gotta be at that thing really early."

"Boo," Teagan said, but the way she said it and the way she threw herself lengthwise along the hammock made Simon wonder if it was at all possible that she could want to be alone with him.

Laura walked out along the wraparound porch, the same way that Manny had gone before. Now Simon's only questions were (1) was this on purpose? and (2) or should he leave?

Teagan dug her bare feet deeper into the hammock's open netting, toes curled around its strings. "So." She looked at him. "Are you going to ditch me too?"

"I don't have any things in the morning."

"Ha." She spun herself around, tried scooting out from the middle of the hammock, which she could not do well. It was the lowest point and where gravity wanted to keep her.

Simon left his beer bottle to buoy with the cigarette butts and, trying hard not to seem brave, sat down beside her. So that he became the hammock's lowest point, so that Teagan rolled a little onto him and for a moment their legs pressed.

Smiling, she asked, "Want to see something?" and stuck her tongue quickly out at him.

"What?" he said, not daring to laugh. She did it again, slower this time, and Simon could see a hole where she'd had it pierced. "Whoa, that's. When'd you get that?"

"A while ago. Manny did it for me. He's an idiot. Anyway, my mom made me take it out."

"That sucks." He thought for what else to say. "Do you get, like, food stuck in it sometimes?"

"Gross," she said, but laughing. "Sometimes. My mom's a bitch. Well, we're Catholic."

"Yeah, if I did that, my mom would be all," but he didn't know what she'd be.

"But you live in New York." She said it like it was worlds and not an Amtrak ticket away.

"It's not that great."

"Have you been to the Chelsea Hotel?"

"No. I mean, I've seen it. But I think it's being renovated or something."

"I just used to watch this movie a lot about Sid and Nancy. It's stupid. Do you like them, the Sex Pistols?"

"Sure, yeah. I mean, I'm not, like, *super* into them."

She nodded. "Anyway. My mom wants to move, but it's like, to her sister's in Providence."

Even in the shade, with the sun mostly gone from the sky, her skin held the summer in it. He saw that her blond hair was lots of blonds, a banana when it is first peeled and then at intervals after, as the air rusts it brown. Warm came off her shoulders, smelling like smoked suntan lotion.

"Tell me something," she said, though for a minute it had seemed they might do without talk, without anything to remind them that they were strangers to each other.

He asked, "What should I tell?" and she said, "A story," and he said, "About what?" and she laughed and said, "Anything," so automatically he started to tell her Everything, why they were in Rhode Island really, his dad's affair and the box he'd found (in this version he had found it).

"I thought that guy at lunch was your dad."

"Who, Gary? No, he's my mom's—I don't know. I barely know him."

And No, he had no idea what was going to happen, only it was Good for Them to Get Away, good for his mother and his sister, to get *perspective* (and, he didn't think he'd meant to, but the way he was telling it made it sound like a decision he'd made for them, as man of the house, which actually he kind of was).

The sky and Teagan's face got dark listening to him. She looked worried, a little impressed by what he had gone through, and it was pretty much exactly the reaction he'd been looking for in people, *this,* except then, when she asked where his father was now and he said "Who knows?" he might have given her the wrong idea, based on what happened next, which was, she touched his back and said, "I don't know where my dad is either."

This, where they were sitting, was her grandparents' porch, her grandparents' house where her mother had grown up. She had an older brother, Brady, in the army. Only twenty but married, with a daughter who lived with his wife's parents, in another town. "We don't get on, though. My mom calls Vanessa 'the mother and the whore.'" Men passed through from time to time—"like

234

your Gary"—but never stayed. Her father, she said, had been gone forever already. Since she was seven.

"But you remember him and stuff?"

"Duh. You remember seven."

He wasn't sure. The years all fused together without major milestones. Seven might have been the age he went to the set of *Sesame Street,* where his father's friend designed Muppets. Simon remembered that Oscar's trashcan, from which he'd hoped to collect souvenirs, had been trash-free and carpeted, also that Mr. Snuffleupagus was kept hanging from the ceiling.

So, seven.

Teagan pressed a pointed foot against the porch floor and started them rocking. She had a small, white scar on her chin, and he asked her where it was from.

"A swimming pool one time." Another kid had pulled her under.

"Ouch." What little space there'd been between them subtracted itself. One or maybe both leaned in, he knew only that first the space was there and then it wasn't, as if God or someone had pressed the delete key, and when they kissed it was the only sound, the suck of air as their lips arranged themselves against each other.

He was observing more than he should, sitting outside himself and trying to drum up a laugh when there was an especially loud smacking, or when her top teeth tapped his lower ones, which happened. The laughing was to show he knew when things had not gone the way they were supposed to. But she seemed to want him, this perfect girl. *She* wanted *him*. She had her reasons. He did not know them.

He thought if he told someone about it, it would not have sounded like much, just kissing, but it wasn't just. Already hot, they became sweaty. He was learning what he had never known about girls' bodies, that there was so much more there than the parts that get talked about. A whole person around those three or four places you were supposed to focus on. A neck that pulses under his thumb when she angles her head to kiss him there. A hip, where it is sharp in front when she is on her side and where it gets softer, further back, making him think of a pitcher's mound, the way it fills his palm. There are places that flutter and flex and so much symmetry.

They pushed and pulled at each other in the hammock that drew them both together, and the world turned blue around them. When the yellow light ticked on in the living room, Teagan fell apart from him, saying something about having to start dinner. She walked him out along the porch that was like a moat around that house, and Simon had to be careful not to trip into pots and vases in the tall, black grass.

She'd whispered goodbye to him at the house's edge, stopping short of the front window. "Hey," she said, her bright attention snapped to him. "Come back tomorrow?"

"Tomorrow," he answered, and it was a real thing he could carry home with him, real as a pot, or a vase, lying out on the grass.

Kay, from the upstairs window, had watched him go. Her shoes were on already. Into the closet she said, "Stay," and pulled the door almost closed, dragging a chair in front of it. Her mother, out in the garden with Gary, had only waved as she passed. There were new rules in Jamestown—there were no rules: Kay could go where she pleased.

It's hard to follow a person who doesn't know where he's going. Simon would slow and look around every couple of streets, so that she was always ducking around corners and once behind a too-narrow tree, feeling herself in a movie. Outside a gently bowed house with a junky yard he appeared no less confused, actually scratching his head before realizing this must be it. Kay waited behind a fence wrapped in plastic netting and counted Mississippis in her head.

At ten-Mississippi Simon was *still* not inside but looming like a scarecrow on the porch, looking down at his feet. Kay squatted low and looked back between her legs. Behind her stood a rickety swing set with yellow seats and rusted chains, one post tilted an inch up off the ground.

By twenty-Mississippi the house had swallowed him up.

She stood now, feeling the quiet of the street. Suddenly so loudly quiet. She'd followed her brother—why?—just to see what would *happen,* but she couldn't, of course, see; she wasn't invited. In her front pocket, she felt the hard of Simon's phone. She'd borrowed it while he was dressing, saying she wanted to play *Falling Gems,* and he had forgotten to take it back. If Simon had caught her following, she would have said it was to give it to him.

She wandered, past the church and the library with its sign that read RESUME WRITING TONITE 7, then came to a row of outdoor tubs under a clay-tiled roof. Rubber tubes dipped lazy into the water, collecting little air bubbles like straws in soda, or drifting up and breaking through the surface. That was where the gurgling came from, so many soft brooks in a row.

It was a whole world to which she wasn't invited, sometimes.

Sitting Indian-style on the concrete, the knobby outside parts of her ankles hurting, she pulled the phone from her pocket and found his name.

On the third ring, she heard her father still clearing his throat. "My boy!"

"It's me," Kay said.

"Pumpkin! I'm so glad it's you. You know I'm thinking of you a lot, all the time. How are you?"

"Fine," she answered, scratching a twig along the ground. It was over orange sodas with her mother that she'd made up her mind to call, that she could talk to her dad and it wouldn't have to bother anyone. "Where are you?"

"I'm driving. I don't know if Mom told you, I was in Arizona. I'm going to visit your Grandma Phyllis."

"Is she sick?"

"No no, just ah, a few things to sort out at the old house. How about you? Where are you?"

She described the concrete and the tubs of water.

"The basins! Old-fashioned Laundromats. People used to wash their clothes in them, before washing machines."

"Really," she said doubtfully.

"I used to get a lot of premium thinking done down around those basins. It gets much darker out there, not like New York. Here, why don't you hold me up to the water? I want to hear it."

Kay got up on her knees, bearing the sharp pain, and swung an arm over the side of the nearest bath, angling the phone at the corner that bubbled. When she brought it back to her ear, her dad was saying, "That's a sound you don't forget."

"Dad?" Between her fingers the twig bent and broke. "When are we going home?"

"Where's your mom? Are you with her?"

"I'm alone." She was surprised how sad it sounded, the way she said it.

"Does she know you're calling? Honey, you there?"

"I think I have to go now."

"You know we can talk whenever you want. You don't need to ask your mom."

"I have to go before it gets dark I love you bye."

239

The drive, some thousand miles, would take him two days. He slept a few hours at A Day's End Lodge in Las Cruces, making the rest up with naps, some-hour intervals in empty lots. He spent magic hours smoking by the side of the road, the sun slinking up or down the sky. Sitting on a rock or the guardrail, a few yards from where he'd pulled over, and the car sitting waiting for him.

The cigarettes he smoked in chains. He'd never been a real smoker, just around drinks and other people. With no one to talk to he watched the paper brown and burn, smoke curling and uncurling, mingling with the painted lines on the road. At a tag sale near a gas station he bought a set of longhorns, seven feet across, bound together with cowhide. He drove with them levitated in the backseat, rested on the open windowsills, points peeking out.

Whenever he rode out of the country station's range,

the radio would start to autoscan, searching for stronger signals. Spanish talk scrambled with Chopin scrambled with Evangelical preacher people for miles. Sometimes the poor radio couldn't find anything. Some places, nothing was out there.

Deb couldn't sleep. The pillows lumped too hard under her head and each position felt like a pose she was holding. Instead she sat, switched on the light, and stacked her enemies the pillows up behind her. So unyielding before, they were fine now, perfect for leaning and for reading. Gary at some point had stocked all the nightstands in all the bedrooms with books; here were historical novels about Pompeii and the Chicago World's Fair.

Good Gary. If only she could like his boring fucking paintings of boats.

He'd been so great with the kids over dinner, planning the next day's trip. Great with Simon, mostly, who was suddenly almost chatty, and full of questions—about fishing, of all things. Boys and boats. Who knew?

Those stupid paintings.

Or maybe they weren't so bad. Maybe she'd been thinking Jack's thoughts.

. . .

In the next room, Simon and Kay were also up, though neither knew it of the other. Simon faced the wall, poring over the time he'd had with Teagan frame by frame, poring over the girl herself inch by incredible inch. He flexed his arm muscle, pressed into the mattress with his fist. Trying to rehearse their next meeting, he invented answers to questions that kept changing. There was this fishing trip tomorrow. Maybe some kind of story would come from that.

Kay had noticed the change in her brother at dinner, and how her mother had seemed so pleased by it. It shouldn't have made her feel left out—she didn't see why it should have—only it did, not least of all because she thought she knew the real reason he was happy, that it had nothing to do with fishing. There were just too many secrets.

And today she'd made one of her own, calling her dad.

Deb still wasn't tired at all. Sure, it was night, but that didn't mean she had to lie still in bed watching the dark inside her eyelids. Also, sure, hard and unhappy things were happening, but she didn't have to hold still for them either. Why not not sleep? Why not not be sad? No need to be all-the-time sad! Everyone thought she needed this time to mope and to cry, but wouldn't it be great if she didn't? The important thing was to stay on your own side. *Remember whose side you're on.*

So only Gary slept, or was presumed asleep, who could say.

"Mother." Jack could feel Phyllis idling behind the front door, unsure. He'd parked the car midway up the drive and stopped to pluck a yellowy green clover, three leafed, from a seam in the pavement. Now, among the guardian mallards of the porch, he looked up and down, past hedges, across striped fields of grass, where lawn mowers ghosted pale ribbons, for the first stirrings of neighborhood watch. "It's me. It's Jack. I'm outside."

"Jackie?" The locks came undone, and the front hall revealed itself in pieces, new ivory bookends bearing up the same old books, and his mother, thinner, hair more black, inky, like she'd taken a Magic Marker to it. Didn't anyone tell her how ridiculous it looked? Someone should tell her. Charles.

"Mother, you look well."

Phyllis said it was such a surprise to see him, and come in, Jackie, what are you doing here? Would you like a drink? Something? Charles, he's out—you know he goes to church to get everything ready. Will you come to service? Well, sit down.

"My, but it's a surprise."

She called questions to him from the kitchen, where she never let anyone. Only Charles now had been granted access, every few weeks, to make his storied and bland jambalaya, which he packed into Tupperware and kept too long in the freezer.

No, Jack was not coming from New York. Tempe, in Arizona. I know you know where Tempe is. Yes, just passing through. No, Tempe isn't so close to Houston. New York's fine. Deb's fine. The kids.

Phyllis came into the living room with heavy crystal glasses trembling, tonic water over ice. Charles had gotten her off drinking, and tonic was the only thing she'd touch. Said everything else tasted like kid stuff. She went back again and brought out a saucer of saltines.

"Now, when are you going back?"

"I just got here, Mother."

"Oh, don't be bad," she said, sitting on the opposite end of the new blue-and-white-striped sofa and crossing her birdy legs. "It's only I wish you'd called ahead. And things with Deborah?"

"Everything is excellent. You make it like I can't come here—"

"Don't be ridiculous—"

"*Like I can't come here* without something being wrong. You make it this great imposition. When I thought it would be a nice visit."

"I only wanted to know how much to buy at the market."

"I don't need anything. If I need something, I'll go out and get it myself."

"Should I make up the guest?" She held her drink out in front of her face like a boxing glove, like it was her chin that was made of glass.

"I'll stay in my room."

Jack ate a cracker and watched Phyllis watch for crumbs. He held the plate out to her, knowing she wouldn't take any. His mother had started out beautiful and had stayed that way, pin thin, all through Jack's childhood. The general consensus back then, which she'd encouraged, was that Phyllis Shanley was a woman of remarkable self-possession.

It didn't have anything to do with restraint, though. It was never about not doing exactly what she wanted. Food simply didn't hold any interest for her, and she'd subsisted, through age seventy-five, on a mostly liquid diet.

"Well of course we are so glad to have you, Jackie, just surprised."

In a house perpetually renovated, so much history sanded down and refinished, it almost passed as a show of tenderness that Jack's old room had gone untouched. Almost passed as proof that the child was missed. Almost, but didn't.

Jack could hear how it didn't in the breaking sound the door made, unsticking from its frame as though the two had grown together, fused into wall. In the room he could smell how *much* it didn't, could taste it in the mildewed air.

The difference between what's kept and what's left. Jack's room had been left. Not saved but cordoned off.

He stood staring at an old poster over the bed, an illustration of an airplane in a mass of white clouds, Mick Jagger's mouth tattooed on the tail, his tongue out at you, AMERICAN TOUR 1972. There was not much to look at besides. The bed itself seemed miniature. The quilt flattened and thinned and its paisley swirls, kidneys in utero, flat too, another pattern he knew by heart.

When the hour came for Phyllis to have her bath, Jack pussyfooted into the kitchen and ferreted out the twisted sleeve of saltines from a cabinet over the sink. He ate them in the new blue-and-white chair that matched the sofa and let his eyes glaze over a week-old *Chronicle* on the end table.

When the garage door hummed open in back of the house, the floor and every wall hummed with it. Jack recrossed his legs and continued to scan the articles, one hand sliding the remaining four crackers into his mouth and tucking the plastic sleeve, half-folded, into his pants pocket. When the back door opened, Jack was inspecting newspaper columns, the shapes of them, like bar charts.

"Hello, Jack."

The old man in the foyer, holding a canvas bag up high against his chest so that it seemed a schoolboy's lunch, or a hat he'd taken off to be polite, this man *lived* here.

"Hi," Jack answered, the hard *h* hurling observable crumbs through the air. He stood and shook Charles's hand. "Guess you're wondering what I'm doing here."

247

"I suppose those are your longhorns outside the house." Charles was a few years younger than Phyllis, seventy-two, seventy-three—Jack didn't know exactly—but he seemed older than everyone, than Father Time. His questions weren't questions but assessments he'd made, data to confirm, grimly. God could make a man that way. Put God behind a man and he thinks he knows everything.

"I guess you're surprised to see me," Jack tried again.

"Your mother phoned up at the church."

"Did she?" Jack imagined his mother upstairs, frenzied over her adult son, calling her new old husband, the Prophet. *No, Charles,* she'd have whispered, *I have no idea what for.* "I hope I'm not a bother to you two."

"It isn't that, that you would be a bother." If it were possible to have *taut* jowls, that was what Charles had. They were broad and smooth, like Droopy Dog's. His skin was pink and looked impossible to shave, it was so dry. Skin that cut easily, would bleed a lot, if Charles weren't drained already.

"Well, I'm sure you all have your routine that I'm upsetting."

"Suppose we sit down after dinner and have a talk."

Jack didn't suppose he could say no.

From the plain and spoon-shaped, Kay sifted out the kind that looked like fish, with wide-open eyes and painted scales. Also the feathered ones, hot pink and yellow, which felt soft skimming her cheek. ("Gross," said Simon.) She'd been sitting, hunched, beside the cooler at the front of the boat, cataloging Gary's lures as they rode further into the blurred blue. She arranged them by type, by color, by which would make the best dangly earring.

Simon pressed his finger against one of the silver barbs, umbrellaed into three points. "I thought we were using worms."

"Oh, yucko," Deb said, yawning from under Gary's hat. "Be glad we aren't."

"Clouds are high today." Gary, at the motor, had begun to broadcast mysterious things about the weather, casting his words across the water.

Kay looked up, hands shading her eyes. It still looked like sky, but she could see how high clouds might be preferable to lower, hanging ones. Because, if it rained, the drops would not reach them, or would not hit so hard when they did. Or because high clouds left more room for the air, for it to blow around.

When the lines were cast there was nothing to do, the rods even rigged to hold themselves up over the water. Gary produced a barrel of pretzels, his fingers wide spinning off the ridged red lid, and they ate gathered around it, backs to the sun, heads huddled against the wind. Crunching into each other's ears.

Gulls shrilled. Kay searched the sky for them but brought her face down again quickly, to the deck and their passing shadows, swelling and shrinking and sharpening at the edges.

"Baby, you okay?" Deb touched her shoulder. "She gets a little carsick."

"Yeah." Simon laughed. "A *little*."

Kay leaned her head against the side of the boat. The water below kept up in little bursts, frothy and fizzing. The boat's edge was hot in a good, painful way.

Kay had forgotten the last thing about fishing—that there would be fish. Mostly they caught bluefish and stripers, too small, that had to be pulled off the hook and thrown back. Then a splash as the fish rejoined the water and Gary cried, "Good as new!" which seemed unlikely.

Simon got the real first catch. Shouted, "Holy crap holy

crap!" At the other end of the line, the fish thrashed silver bodied through the air. In the excitement Ayn Rand fell overboard. She bobbed along for a few waves before disappearing under the boat. ("What a shame," said Deb, faintly smiling.)

Gary collected the fish with a long-handled net, the kind for butterflies or scooping leaves out of pools. "He really hit." Captive, the fish held very still. Only when he took it in his hand did it come to life again, wanting to wag itself away.

"Yeah!" Simon shouted. "I'm the *man*!" His face filled with the kind of thrilled alarm Kay had seen on him only during chase scenes and the bloodier parts of movies.

"If he'd of hit any deeper, we'd have been cut off this way," Gary was saying. Kay folded all the way forward and gripped her sneakers, wishing to close her ears. "Because those teeth are sharp."

"*Sick,*" Simon said. "Mom, isn't that sick?"

"Very impressed."

Suddenly Kay didn't like Gary, how he looked cut from stone and how his toothbrush could have touched hers in the bathroom. How her mother looked in his hat. He went on, "Now, this would be a darker meat, which I like, but some people don't because it's oilier. Okay, now see where I've got him here? I'm just going to reach in there, all right? One, two—"

"*Siiiick.*"

Kay was hooking and unhooking lures from her laces when Simon's bottom half stepped into view. He flipped the lid to the cooler, pulling out the last of the soda cans two by two and lining them up along the boat floor as Gary planted the fish, white plastic bagged, into the watery ice.

A few minutes later, she heard it. A crinkle. Might have been only the plastic bag settling. Then she heard it again, louder. Crinkle. Crinkle.

For Kay, the day fell mostly away after that. The waves rolled the boat, and the boat rolled the cans, and parts of her rolled too. She had to pee. Simon had had to go earlier, and Gary had shown him where he could do it off the side. "The burden of our sex," her mother said. Kay hadn't been around boys peeing before, except maybe when they were small and she didn't remember. Not like she saw anything, only the way Simon stood with his back to her and didn't talk while he was going. Then Gary went too, and the sound of his pee stream was louder than her brother's.

She had to go so bad. The boat lurched. All of her lurched. The plastic bag crinkled. She wondered, because she hadn't seen, which lure the fish had chosen, feeling it was more her fault if he'd liked her earring. She could hear him, twitching, through the quarter-inch space below the lifted lid.

Nothing of the day would stay with her as much as that cooler and its faint but awful rustling sound. It was the sound she'd hear, the small coffin she'd think of, whenever she saw another of these blue-and-white coolers, packed with ice and glinting soda cans, at picnics, at field hockey, the whole next year at school.

"For what we are about to receive, may the Lord make us truly thankful. God our Father, thank you for your love and favor. Thank you for bringing a member of our family to share with us today."

In the restaurant, Jack was peeking. Or, no, Jack was plainly watching, his chin not even lowered, his hands folded on the table but not in prayer, not pressed at the palms like his mother's or Charles's. Here is the church; here is the steeple. Charles said the words, and they both were holding their eyes closed, not that Jack believed it. Who closes their eyes, really, in the middle of a restaurant— praying, as with kissing, who keeps their eyes really closed? Jack smiled, watching. Go ahead, call me out. Both of you, either of you, pretending not to see.

"Bless our loved ones who are near us and keep safe those that are far away. May we always be mindful of the needs of others, for Jesus's sake, amen."

Open the doors, and here are the people. Phyllis and

Charles returned to the room, to the middle of the mostly empty Shining Star Tavern where his mother's chief worldly concern had been getting a table.

The restaurant was Charles's idea, to save Phyllis from having to unwrap or defrost an extra meal. They took the Lincoln there, his stepfather driving, his mother on her special ass pillow, Jack in back like a little boy.

"This is our son," Phyllis said on the way in, addressing herself to the hostess, the waitress, the busboy, to everyone but the signed photographs on the walls, George Foreman and Walter Cronkite. The best use of family was having it in front of other people. Jack won them fewer points than a grandchild, and Wade, the seventeen-year-old kid who poured their water, didn't bear much witness, but it was something.

"They've redone the menu," Phyllis told him when they were seated, flapping her heavy napkin out of its fleur-de-lis fold.

"I don't doubt it."

"Redone the prices too."

His mother got her tonic with a garden salad, lots of pepper and dressing on the side. "And one of your chops," she said, patting Charles on the hand. "I never eat enough to make it worth ordering my own. Just one of his chops, that'll do me."

Jack got the ahi tuna, which came with wasabi molded into the shape of a leaf, outer Houston's soft stab at the urbane. Charles's chops turned out to be lamb, with sprigs of rosemary and a porcelain vat of electric-green jelly center plate. Phyllis made a show of choosing the smallest and most well-done piece of meat.

"Falls off the bone. He likes 'em bloody. Don't you, Charles?"

"Still saying baa."

"Jackie, I don't know how you eat that. I just cannot stand the smell of fish."

"It's very good, Mother. Good for you too. You should try it."

"Jack, how's work?"

"Now, is that going to smell up everything?" his mother asked. "Because we don't eat fish."

"You eat shrimp."

"I do not."

"Charles's jambalaya."

"Tell us about the art world, Jack."

"That isn't—that's not fish. Is it, Charles? Shrimp's not fish."

Jack wished he could order a drink, just a beer. Phyllis went through three sodas because what's that they say, about old habits. She guzzled tonic like it was wine, and wasn't she fooling herself with everything, not just the drink but the man, with Charles? Who the hell is this guy? Jack wanted to say. Who invited *him*. Simon's first Christmas in Houston, the boy not yet two, Phyllis's special friend had been an extra place setting at the table. The first time they said grace before dinner, the first time the holiday had seemed to have anything to do with Jesus.

"Shrimp's a crustacean," Charles said now and nodded.

"That's right. It's a prawn." Phyllis tapped her glass with a long, ovaled nail.

The drink is no drink and Charles is no John—Jack's father, John. John Shanley wouldn't know her now, the woman he'd married, she who'd bronzed poolside for hours, who'd held her liquor and herself in mink stoles. She who'd said *shit* under her breath and *goddamn* and who'd believed in, what? Not God. You traded in your silver Cadillac for a maroon town car and you let your anger atrophy, but it is not gone.

"Jack, I believe you were about to tell us how work is going," Charles said.

"It's all right. Don't know how much you've followed."

"You tell us about it." Charles dabbed a chop in mint jelly. "Any new developments?"

"Here and there." His mother's husband didn't read the *Times*. His mother's husband read the *Chronicle*. Still, there were always old friends someplace clipping newsprint with scissors from the junk drawer, dating the back and sending it, paper clipped and envelope tucked, out into the world. *In case you missed it! Hope you and yours are well.* Hope you and yours are still kicking. "Can't please everyone, but, you try to please a few people."

Phyllis was scraping her plate with a butter knife.

"Now how about those Yankees?" Charles said. "How are your Yankees doing?"

"I don't know. I guess they're doing well."

Charles smiled. "Not what I've heard."

. . .

The ride back existed in only two moments, the first as they came slow around a long bend, Charles up front saying, "We get some deer crossing, this area." Jack knew that they did. Even in the dark this road was familiar to him. Then, the sudden light bouncing off the garage door, the blank page that had snuck up on him.

Inside, Charles got down on the living-room floor in front of the hearth.

"I don't see why you need to bother with that thing, honey." Phyllis sat on the sofa, stockinged feet slipped out of her soft brown loafers. "In high summer."

"I've put on the AC, you won't cook." Charles clicked on the gas fire. "Jack should see how this works. Heck of a lot better than the logs you all used to use."

"Much better," Jack said. His mother and Charles had redone the whole fireplace and flue the first fall after they married. This was back eight or nine years ago—no, Jesus, eleven years: Kay had just been born. A chimney sweep had come and taken a steel brush to the insides, scrubbing off years of soot from the kindling they'd burned when Jack's father was alive. Now they got the chimney sweep in annually. There was some reason for it, a fire that caught once when Charles was younger—Jack didn't know the details—something like that had made him careful. One of those perfect-fit stories that make you say people aren't all that hard to figure out. Maybe it's true.

Phyllis went up to bed after the fire show, citing and reciting instructions for the clock in Jack's bedroom, how it ran a little slow and how the alarm got set, and Jack went with his stepfather to the dim and woodsy study, Charles's brown-Bible world, a cave apart from the fringed rugs and white wire baskets. When Jack lived there, it had been a sewing room and always empty. Now a gold-plated cross hung nailed to the wall, mixed with Charles's diplomas, degrees in business. A years-old cactus sat inert on the windowsill.

From his shirt pocket Charles produced the key to a cabinet behind his desk, and from there he pulled a half-emptied bottle of port. The only fermented thing let into the house, residents aside. "So, take a seat." The cork came out with a hollow pop, like an echo of the real sound. "It's a wonderful thing, you know, having children."

Jack stayed staring at the shelves, the embossed spines, discards from the local library. "How's this?" he asked, holding up a Reagan biography, its edges woolly with dust.

"You may borrow it. I want to tell you, it is a very powerful thing for Phyllis, seeing you grown. A man, with a family of his own. Please."

Jack took the glass, the measly pour of port, and sat.

"I know how proud she is of you. You should see the way she talks—about her son out in New York, how you've got yourself all this acclaim, about how there's the prestige—"

"It isn't—"

"Well all right, all right but that's what she likes to say to people. She likes to tell them all that, and about the kids and how you're married and how it's two kids, a boy grandson and a girl grandchild, and she says if she died now, she'd be complete. That she has everything. Now, I know a lot of that has to do with how proud she is of you, this life she sees you leading." Charles paused for a sip of garnet wine, but he must also have considered this a good breaking point, thought that even if the whole mountain of his argument was not yet visible, at least the mist had begun to clear.

For Jack, fog. "Thank you. That's always, it's nice to hear those things."

"Here's where we have our problem. Here's where I'm a little worried. You say things are all right at home."

"I do."

"And work, your career."

"Still do." Jack followed Charles's gaze to where it dropped on the desk between them, to the sand timer with the heavy marble bottom and brass casing. Phyllis used to keep it in the sun-room with what curios she deemed nautical. Called an hourglass, though it measured only thirty minutes. The upper half was empty now and for a bad moment Charles looked about to flip it over.

"Where I'm worried is where a grown man comes, flies, by himself—a married father—to stay with his mother on no notice—"

"I would have called—"

"—and behaves as though he were asked to come. And I don't just mean that he'd been invited. I mean unhappy to be here. As though it were not a matter of his own free, human volition."

"I thought we had a nice time tonight." Of course it hadn't been a nice time, but it was unlike Charles to say so,

259

or to notice. Dinner had been grim because their lives were like that, grim. Jack had been, he thought, only a fly on the wall. "The restaurant was a good idea. Thank you for choosing that."

"All right." Charles took another sip of port, set the glass down and turned it. It was a nervous thing to do, again not what Jack would have expected of him. He was working toward something, the old man. "Jack, now, I'm not your father. Never was one. God didn't bless my first wife and myself with children. Instead he saw fit to take her away, I'll never know why. But he blessed you, and Deborah, and I don't suppose it isn't trying. In ways I can't imagine."

"Okeydokey, Charles."

"I can't tell you how to be a parent, except to tell you words from one wiser than I. 'Train up a child in the way he should go, and when he is old, he will not depart from it.'"

Jack stood and turned back toward the bookcase. Books on theology, golf, the theology of golf. "That's a lovely sentiment." Rubbing his neck, he realized it hurt.

"You should be with your family."

Jack spun around. "Why is it so hard to conceive that maybe I wanted to check up on her, see how she was doing? My own mother."

"We seem to be missing each other."

"It's not like she hasn't had her problems. It's not like there couldn't be any cause for concern."

Charles pressed his fingertips together and touched them to his mouth. When he moved them away again, he said, "The thing I'm asking, Jack, is what do you need from her? What do you need that she can give you. Money?"

Jack was furious all of sudden. He'd been mad and now he was furious. "Does she even eat? Does she even eat food? Who's to make sure she does that, Charlie, you?" He came right up against the desk, standing over his stepfather, towering. "No. You probably have her going into raptures. *Seeing God.*"

"Don't turn this onto God. We've been down that path already. Don't make about God what is about me."

No, this is about something older even than you, Charles. Jack saw his problem in Charles's question: What do you need that she can give you. To which the answer was: Nothing? There is nothing I need that she can give me. Which is not the same as, There is nothing I need.

The problem was older than Charles, but Jack was too old for the problem. Such things expire. Your mother never would take the full weight of you, even when you were small and tried to be easy. Now you are heavy and her bones are weak; now is not the time to try.

"I know what you think." Charles leaned back against his chair, belly buoyed up as though separate, a large egg nesting under his checkered shirt. "I know what you think of me, my life. And I sure know how you feel about God. What I don't know is what you feel about your mother, but I am going to hope and pray and give you *benefit of the doubt* that you wish her only well. As I said, I'm not your father. But so long as we'll be under this one roof, I suggest, and suggest strongly, that we all put on a nice face until you get on that plane."

Jack spent the next day up in his room or out by the pool when he remembered it. In the bathroom he'd had a small proud moment finding his old purple trunks still fit, though in profile under the good lighting he had to admit that they hung not quite like before. His legs were thinner—that was what caused the nylon to gape out around his thighs. Also his ass had bloomed full. Maybe it was no real achievement, for thirty-year-old trunks still to fit. Was anything outgrowable that had a drawstring. Surely it had not always been this hard to see his feet.

"Why didn't you just take the key?" his mother said when he told her where he'd been. This was in the dining room, where sunlight still papered the walls but where, at six-thirty, it was dinnertime. Phyllis said *the key* because technically it was a shared pool, though because only the houses around their cul-de-sac were granted access, there was no lifeguard, and, while the women were supposed to wear swim caps, no one ever did.

"Don't need a key." Jack unsheathed his paper napkin from its porcelain holder. He didn't need a key because the fence around the pool was low and, like most every partition in the neighborhood, trespassable. When he went for a swim he still tucked his wallet in his shoe, but right at the heel, not even fingering it up into the toes.

"People will think—well, they won't know who you are," his mother said, passing around a limp salad. Dinner at the house was Phyllis slicing a beefsteak tomato on Bibb lettuce and delivering to her son and husband a half can of tuna each.

"I'll tell them then," he said, reaching for the bread basket. A grid of rolls, nicely thawed and reheated, that was dinner too, and a saucer of mayo with a miniature spoon, recurrently seesawing onto the table. Jack, since that morning's grapefruit, had already felt himself going hungry. He tried surrendering to it, embracing it as an ascetic would. Little food, plus the sun and swim. Not that the pool was much exercise—he mostly floated—but for the elixir chlorine. After a dip he liked to air-dry on his stomach, mouth resting on his bleached-smelling arms, and breathe deep, sucking up the arm hairs, which danced with the nose hairs and tickled his nostril walls.

"From their *houses* you'll tell them?" His mother's eyes ticktocked an appeal to Charles, who sat sorting the church mail, slitting envelopes open with a butter knife. She'd made her voice loud so as to reach, not just Charles, people in other rooms.

"No, guess not. Guess I'll just wave."

Other things chlorine did: It cleared his back of teenagery blemishes, drying them into pickable white nothings. It sluiced orange fudge from his ears, exhumed the crunchies deep inside his belly-button pit. Pool water purged him by the swallow or noseful, doses that made sterile his lungs and empty stomach. He basked monastic on his holey towel.

Later, upstairs on his invertebrate bed, Jack sat and he sank. Suddenly very close to his knees. The lamp went on with a tick. In the middle drawer of the nightstand, an old spoon, forsaken. He used to smuggle up ice cream, cups of yogurt, in zippered jackets. Phyllis had complained to the maid about missing silver.

His mother, this house, Charles, always they had this effect, of reminding him why he'd built what life he had, away. No reason it should be any different this time, only a hopeless hope for something else. For the feeling of home, which he was nearly sure he used to feel, somewhere here.

He bent between his knees and drew up the quilt. He saw the curve of his own weight dipped low between the bed frames. Also, the thing he was looking for, the orange rotary phone he'd had since high school, wound in all its cords. He dropped onto his knees and crawled with it to the jack by the window, where he used to lie on the floor and look out at the sky and talk to girls, or friends from his terrible band.

The phone worked—a surprise, hearing that digital ohm. His finger was slow to find the numbers, pulling each one through and waiting for the dial to whir back around so that it felt like he was calling from another time, when he was another person. The rotary made him young and tender toward himself. The rotary and Deb, the careful way she answered, not recognizing the number, and him saying, "Hi, it's me."

"God," she said somewhere in Rhode Island. "I saw the area code and thought your mother—what's wrong?"

"Everything."

"What happened?"

"Nothing, no. I'm just, losing my mind." He walked his elbows out behind him, easing himself down until he was lying back that same way he used to. "Probably I'm dying."

"You're not dying."

"You're right." He fingered the spiral cord, uncoiling it and wrapping it around his finger the opposite way. "Probably I'm not dying."

She asked if he'd been drinking.

"I've been with my mother."

"Why on earth would you go there? I'm sorry. *I'm* a little drunk."

"What's the occasion?"

"Nothing, talking to Gary. It got late."

"Well, so." He let go the cord and watched the bendy orange twist stubbornly back to form. "How is Gary? The worm."

"Why do you say that?"

"Okay, fine, I'm not. He's a worm, but I'm not saying so. Ignore me."

Like Ruth, Deb laughed when nothing was funny. Her laugh now meant: Right, ignore you. You make it so easy for anyone to ignore you.

265

"Would you put the kids on please?"

"You could try in the morning. You could call around ten."

"I think," pressing his fingers to his lids, "I'll be at church then," and that she really did find funny.

"So," Deb said. "How's the Arizona project?"

"It doesn't matter."

"Okay. Anything from Stanley?"

"How can I care about all that while this is going on?"

"You mean multitask? I don't know, Jack. You always seemed to before."

"I know I've been . . . not all the way here. Or there, I guess. You know, for years—ever since that September stuff—"

"Don't do that. Don't *use* that."

"Well, but it's true. I'm not using it, but it scared me."

"Of course you'd say it's work. Of course you say that."

"Let me finish, please. Before you say. You know how I get, these things, they carry me. What next. It's all I was thinking about: What next. Every day, what next. And nothing was good enough, and everyone had their eyes on me."

"With bated breath."

"Don't—You were there. You know what I mean."

"I *was* there."

"But what you don't know—or what *I* didn't—and I am trying to tell you something here, all right? I really, really am."

266

"What?"

"Is that, sleeping with someone . . ."

"Sleeping with someone *what*, Jack?"

"Yes, okay? Yes, she flattered me. She admired me. Like it was important, what I was doing. I think I thought if I could just hang on to that feeling—"

"Vampires do that. Parasites. You can't fuck somebody and have that not hurt us."

"Why?"

"Because those are the *rules*."

"This was never supposed to touch us."

"This *is* us. Every time you chose to be with her, you chose not to be with us."

"People don't have a limited amount of—affection, of interest."

"People have a limited amount of *time*."

"But, Debby, we fuck up. You of all people should know."

"What's that supposed to mean?"

"Nothing. Nothing. You know what it means."

"Don't you use that either."

"But why? It's how we happened. I, *we* fucked up."

"Please do *not* go there with me now."

"I'm sorry. I was making a point. You there?"

"It was a shitty, bullshit point."

"I know.

"It's your birthday tomorrow. Deb? You didn't think I'd forget?"

"Wish I could."

"Happy almost birthday."

"You stopped talking to me about your work."

"I didn't know that bothered you."

"I was so, I don't know, honored, or flattered, when you wanted my opinion. That you thought I could help you. I didn't know a thing about art."

"You knew more than you thought you did. Instinct."

"But I was so young, you know, and a *dancer*. God. I'm not a lot of things I used to be."

"You are more than you used to be."

"You talked to her about your work."

"It's how we met."

"You stopped wanting that in me."

"I want that in you now."

"Oh. Fuck off."

"So what *did* you think of the show?"

"Fuck off."

"Come on, tell me. What does it matter now?"

"Well. I thought you made a mistake."

"Obviously."

"No, stupid. I mean the Tigger."

"The whatter?"

"The stuffed animal, the Tigger."

"The tiger?"

"He's from Winnie-the-Pooh."

"They sell those all over the world, though, right?"

"In Ramallah?"

"I didn't say in Ramallah."

"It's just funny to me, since you bought it for him."

"I bought it. For Simon."

"Yes, of course for Simon."

"Will you let me come see you?"

"Don't, not—no."

"What you were saying about time, how when I was away from you I was with her, how we only have so much time?"

"I remember."

"You assume that when I was away from you, I was closer to her, but I was far from her too. I was running from her the minute it started, my own mistake I was running from, and where I ran was into my work. You see? It's why people have these messes. We make our lives impossible places to be, and that's when we do our work."

"Not everyone is like you."

"Well, that's what this was for me, more than anything. This was about work. Deb?"

"You want to know if I believe you, or if I believe you believe it?"

"Both. I do believe it."

"Both is I don't care."

"Okay."

"Both, I don't think it matters. Not one shitty bit."

"I understand. I get it. You know, I went to her apartment. She wasn't home, but I wanted to tell her what—"

"You saw her?"

"She was gone, I said."

"When?"

"I don't know, after she sent the package."

"So the very next day you're there."

"To tell her off. I wanted her to know what she did."

"I don't get why that mattered, to tell her that."

"Because she should know what her actions—"

"Who cares what she knows? You do, obviously. You saw her?"

"No, are you not listening? I didn't see her."

"Too bad, maybe next time."

"Listen to me."

"*No*. I don't trust you. I don't trust you I don't trust you I don't trust you. Say what you want; I won't believe you. It's too much. Definitely, *definitely* do not come here. You will not be welcome here."

She'd been down in the kitchen when they started talking, though she was vaguely aware, in the interim, of being other places too. Vaguely up the stairs, vaguely down the hall. Touching her face, absently, in the bathroom, in the angled mirrors where Rockettes of her receded endlessly. Staring into the empty hall closet, not seeing. She was at some point sitting at the top of the stairs and at some point sitting at the bottom. The phone warmed and sweated her hand.

There, on the last step, she became aware of her breathing.

"Deb, don't—don't do that," the voice in her ear was saying. "You can't say that. Please, Debby, don't do that to me. Don't tell me you would have let me come if I hadn't told you that."

She did not think she could tell the voice anything. Her throat had cracked open, and in place of lungs she had two produce bags. They seized, fuller and emptier than her actual lungs had been ever.

"What's—Deb?"

These bags! They took so much air and couldn't get rid of it fast enough. She thought: I am a bicycle pump. I am some kind of wind-powered machine. Her breath was something being done to her, violent and involuntary, like sneezing.

"Breathe. Debby? Baby, breathe. What's wrong?"

Wrong was that they'd talked themselves to where it felt natural, and it was good to hear Jack's cello voice, the one every other man's was higher or lower than. But talking wasn't natural, the words weren't right, and she'd let him too far in. That was what all the moving around had been about, as though new rooms could keep the minutes from collecting and catching up with her. Of course, everywhere she went, there he was.

She let the phone down but could still hear the hum of him against the step. She stayed that way for she didn't know how long. "I'm okay." Seeing if it felt true. She picked up the phone and said it again. And yes, she'd thought of telling him, yes, that if he hadn't confessed to her that last part, about going to see the girl, she would have let him come. It would be easy to say, but cruel, and untrue. "I wouldn't have let you come anyway."

"How can you make up your mind without seeing me?"

How was the phone this hot. She switched hands and wiped her palm on the step. "Because you'll come and you'll be sweet, and it won't be real, is the point."

"You're afraid it will be good."

"Obviously. Obviously I am."

"Fear is never a good reason."

"We're afraid of the things that hurt us. That, repeatedly, hurt us."

There was a quiet, and when he spoke again she almost didn't believe it, that this was the same—well. "You can't do it, you know. Officially, you can't make it so I can't see my kids."

"What, you mean legally?"

"That's your word."

"Wow. That's impressive, thank you. That's nice."

"I'm just saying."

"I'm just hanging up."

That night off the phone Jack wouldn't remember but in snatches. What he'd remember best was wanting, that he'd wanted for so many things. He'd wanted it to be an hour ago, or two, before the call, or a year ago, or several, whenever he'd started drifting. For it to be home. For home to be ten years ago. For ten years ago to be when he was still young.

Also, he wanted a drink, and for that he needed a crowbar. How else would he get into Charles's damn cabinet.

After two or after three, he crept down the stairs and into the study. He knelt in front of the cabinet and pulled the knobs, stuck the fat of his pinkie in the keyhole, rattled the thing.

He found a letter opener in the pen cup on the desk. It fit narrowly into the void around the cabinet door, knocked down and up against the metal bolt of the lock. He tried to pry the door and the opener snapped.

The lamp fell as he was spinning the whole thing around,

and Jack flapped his arms like a conductor—*silenzio!*—palms open to catch the waves of sound as they passed.

The cabinet's back was not fuzzy fiberboard but dark mahogany, no panel he could lift. Jack reached under and ran his hand along the bottom, and it was like this, on his knees, arm hooked under the thing like feeling inside a lampshade or up a dress, it was with this particular blocking that he became aware of his audience.

Charles, of course, and the hour was indeed after two or after three but, worse, was after four and just past five, five-fifteen, and here was his stepfather come down to help Phyllis with the coffee.

Sound came from the kitchen. He could hear the click-click-click of the gas range and his mother's low hum-song to herself, la-da-da, and he heard Charles too, who didn't have to say anything. A while later the sun was up and so was Jack, barely, for morning service, on the disagreeable planks of the church's first pew.

Train up a child in the way he should go, and when he is old, he will not depart from it.

Jack had to leave, quite immediately, after that.

Deb spent her birthday just how she said she wanted: lazy in her boxy blue sleep shirt, blowing the dust off old records with Gary. There weren't any presents, though Kay devoted twenty minutes to a card made with orange highlighter and printer paper folded twice, and when Simon came back from the sandwich shop, he gave his mother the rest of his ice cream.

The ferry was back to its weekend schedule, and for her birthday dinner, they just made the six-fifteen. The boat was small and tipped easily, which made the ride more fun, salt spray prickling their arms and necks and faces. Like the whole sound playing with them.

And Newport! Newport was where everyone had been hiding. The main square where the ferry dropped them was alive with people, polos and white shorts spilling out of yachts with funny names painted on: *Diablo del Mar* and *College Tuition;* sitting at outdoor restaurants, again with the names: The Black Pearl, The Red Parrot, The Barking

Crab; saying cheers over sparkling wine and lobster and clam chowder. Deb could feel her children's buzzing thoughts, *Oh, couldn't we just stay here where there are stores,* and where, yes, there are strangers, but none who will try talking to us?

At an Italian restaurant on the water, they ate as the last red crown faded from the evening sky and everyone paid too much attention to the food, zucchini flowers and orecchiette that Kay pressed inside out, like turning one kind of belly button into the other, and the plates soon were empty, slick with olive oil and needles of rosemary. The kids fell to listening and then not, as the grown-ups talked, a little about art and a little about the past.

Gary took up the wine bottle from the table and tipped the neck of it toward Simon. "Little for you?"

"I'm okay." Simon returned to texting under the table. He was used to his parents' friends slipping him thimblefuls of champagne at parties, as if they could win his favor that way, like it was some great boon.

"Who you talking to?" Deb asked, her eyes winkingly on Simon.

"Uh." His thumb darted around the screen. "Nobody."

"You're texting *nobody*?"

"This is like Odysseus," Gary said, scraping forward his chair.

Kay laughed and Simon pointed the phone at her. "You shut up. You don't even know what that means."

A rectangle of tiramisu was brought out, and the staff sang "Happy Birthday" halfheartedly. Deb took a deep breath, but it was the sea breeze that blew the candle out.

That night, Teagan said, she'd leave the door open. She remembered about the door but not the hanging beads, which Simon collided into a hundred small clicks, scattering out and into his hands as he roped them together. Holding them still, he waited for the sound of any thing, of grown-up legs swinging out of bed.

Inside the house was darker than out, without the moon, and his vision beat blue until there was light enough for him to let the beads go gently free and climb to where she'd said she would be waiting for him. Quarter speed ahead he crept, past the living room where Teagan's mother slept, a large mound before the tube TV, on mute. He heard the whistling way she snored, shallow, teakettle breaths.

At the stairs his hand reached for the railing, but he drew it back, remembering the loose post she'd warned him about. This was his first time on her stairs. Coming up on the landing he had to think: Don't trip. At the far end of the hall, he could just make out Teagan's name woodcut in pink-painted bubble letters.

The entrance to her room unsealed even before he got to it. She must have heard him, to be already on the other side, stepping back now to let him in. She wore a thin, white nightgown with satin strips ribboning the neck. At the hem it was broad and starched and stood apart from her. He watched her ease the door shut and couldn't remember if he'd closed the one downstairs.

Making it through the house was like a game he'd won, but nothing was won yet.

She sat at the foot of the bed, and Simon sat too. It was a high bed, with posts, that left their feet to dangle. The room, what he could see of it in the low light, was gently frothed, like the nightgown. Rosebuds bloomed up the walls and on the triangle of quilt between his legs, and something about how pale the pinks, how chipped the white wood and wicker, aged the room—still girlish but preserved—and Simon remembered that it had been her grandmother's. Over the dresser, Van Gogh sunflowers curled in a glassless frame.

Teagan bounced a little on the mattress and laughed air out her nose. "So."

"So."

"Yeah."

When Simon snuck out of the house, Kay was ready and on the move. She couldn't believe he was sneaking out, and in following him (again like in a movie), it almost didn't occur to her that she was doing it too. She felt like a secret agent, light-stepping through the kitchen to pluck her mother's phone from its charger. In case she lost him.

Clearly, *clearly* Simon was breaking the rules, only it didn't look like anything wrong because of the way he walked, without hesitation. Watching her brother cross Teagan's lawn, she could see the growing up of him, a little, where it had started to take root. It had started in his step.

Then he was inside—she hadn't even seen anyone let him in—and Kay was a little disappointed he hadn't caught her, even when she'd hurried her feet close behind. I'm not following, she was ready to say, even though it was all she could be doing. That and, It's a free country. Another line she never got to use.

She walked to the porch and sat on its lowermost step. The house was like a pirate ship alive behind her, beached up from the ocean bottom. The planks, the little rugs and the railing, everything she touched left a trace of itself on her fingers.

Simon and Kay had each taken great care stealing past their mother's door, a black-ops precaution that was actually unnecessary, because Deb wasn't in there. She was on the edge of the bed in Gary's room, wearing her sleep shirt and listening to Debussy on a turntable.

"You know, I bet I still know the steps." She stood and hobbled on one leg, arms akimbo. At her birthday dinner she'd had a few glasses, and Gary a few more.

"You should see yourself right now."

"No, wait, I—" She switched legs, laughing. "Wait, here it is."

Simon's hand found Teagan's on the bedspread. He kissed her mouth, the skin around her mouth, her cheeks, her neck. He breathed into her ear by accident, and she made such a happy sound that he returned there again and again.

In the unmoving dark of the porch, Kay ran a thumb over the buttons of her mother's phone. She looked at her own serious face in the camera, brightening and dimming the screen. She watched the time change and listened to her breathing. She wasn't sure if it was earlier or later in Texas, if there was much or any difference.

"Jack Cell" in her mother's phone. It went straight to voice mail, but she left no message. There was a slug on the step beside her. There were no fireflies that she could see.

In Gary's room, Deb was dancing. They'd stopped laughing. She kept her gestures small to fit the space, concentrating hard on the floor to follow the music. Throwing her hair forward over her face. The girl in *Afternoon of a Faun,* a part she'd always coveted.

"Hey," he said and grabbed her arm to stop her moving. "Happy fucking birthday."

"Thank you." A nod affirmed it. "I'm officially old."

He stood and slipped his fingers through hers, their hands left to hover in some kind of pact.

Teagan's hand: warm on his thigh, reaching the zipper of his jeans.

Simon's hand: brave enough to slip inside her collar and cup the skin just below.

Kay had walked home from Teagan's house before, but her father was right: It got much darker here, not like New York. She closed her eyes, thinking how long it would be before Simon came out, if he'd stay all night. Wondering what he was doing in there.

The night air slid over her cheeks. A sound behind her— she hadn't realized the front door was open. Open wide, beads tapping together in the breeze.

"Feel much different?" Gary asked.

"Being old?"

"Being wanted."

"That, oh." She laughed and turned toward the mirror, still playing with her hair.

Over his fly Teagan was making circles and figure eights and not really any sense, but it felt good, without knowing where her hand would go next. Simon's own fingers found her nipple, and she pushed into him with a long heavy stroke that he liked better than anything. His hand under her shirt forgot what it was doing, but her hand didn't. He could not believe this was happening in front of another person. He saw that she was waiting for him to kiss her, and he did, deep and hard and fast. It was enough for everything, for the whole night. If he could love, he loved her.

Kay slipped past the hanging beads. Up on her toes, surprisingly quick. Forgetting to breathe. Simon was here somewhere, doing things that required the dark and minimum sound.

In the living room, television light. Blankets and pillows charaded as people. Then she was on the stairs without knowing exactly how.

"Turn around."

"Make me."

He put his hands on her, thumbs pressing hard into her top shoulder bones. "Deb, you are the kindest, most beautiful, most—kindest—"

"Oh, you're drunk." She raised her arms as if to fly away from him.

Teagan was hooking two fingers into the loops of his jeans and leaning back, pulling so he'd follow. He climbed over her, clumsy over her, trying to keep his elbows locked. She slid one thigh between his two, braiding herself around him with legs stronger than they looked.

He would have liked to see everything better but was afraid now to pull away, didn't want to do anything that would turn out to be the wrong thing. He was pushing up her nightgown and she was pulling down her underwear and the more time that passed the longer he would have to think about what he was doing, the danger of getting into his head and outside his body. He was so sick of thinking things. Faster than the speed of thought, that was how he moved into her.

She cried so loud he nearly stopped, but as she cried she nodded. She reached a hand around and pushed him toward her from behind. As he moved her jaw fell open, and he could just make out the place in her tongue where the stud had been. He concentrated on the shadow piercing in her mouth, the hole within a hole, and tried to think only exactly about how it felt. He was glad she closed her eyes.

Kay stood very quiet at the top of the stairs.

Down the hall, the hard of something rapped against a wall, once, twice, but didn't sound like anyone wanting to be let in.

Suddenly she felt herself wanting to cry, and what was wrong with everyone, and what was wrong with her, and why was she alone here?

What was wrong, she didn't recognize. Didn't know

enough to know what she didn't understand, which was that she'd been feeling—for some time, but more now than ever—she'd been feeling—

There was one sharp, quick sob, definitely a person.

She spun around and tripped over her own ankle, landed on her knees partway down the stairs. Tears in her eyes from the shock of the fall. Unable even to perceive in real time what she was doing, which was flinging herself to her feet, running down and back out through the wave of beads, racing herself home.

Afterward the thing he most wanted to do was to collapse on top of her. But her head was turned off to the side and she was quiet, and so he stood, unsticking his skin from her skin, which seemed to want to stay touching, the soft sound it made, like peeling a Post-it.

He picked his puddled jeans up off the floor. "Did you hear something, before? I thought I heard someone walking around."

"It's just the house," she said, rolling her nightgown down from around her waist. He held her underwear out to her and was surprised when she pulled it back on, slick where he'd touched it.

Teagan didn't look at him again until they were down in the kitchen. There she handed him a peach from a wire basket and waited for him to bite into it. The juice ran down his wrist and he hoped she didn't hate him already. No muscles in his thighs at all. Together they tiptoed to the front door, which had been open the whole time, and she let him kiss her carefully good night.

On the walk back toward his house he knew he was happy, because his legs, only noodles before, wanted so much to run.

The record had stopped.

Deb was looking at Gary, and then she was looking beyond him, over his shoulder, to the partly open door, where she saw the shine of eyes, then a face. It was a girl who gave the impression of a second daughter, because Deb believed hers to be in bed already, lights out. In the dark of the hall, she appeared to have no body.

"Baby?" The face retreated into dark. "Honey, come in. Why aren't you asleep?"

The door eased open and Kay looked to be crying, indeed was all kinds of wet. Moons of sweat had pooled under her arms, and she'd scraped a knee.

"What happened to you? Have you been outside?" Because she had on her shoes.

She got her into a chair and brushed soil from the scrape on her knee, inwardly ransacking the bathroom cabinet, if they had any bacitracin in the house.

"Where else does it hurt?"

"No place." Kay leaned over her red-glistening knee. "Don't touch." She'd fallen twice on the way home.

"Baby, you have to tell me what happened." She squeezed Kay's waist, her shoulders, as though she could feel a break if there was one. "Where were you?"

"Don't!" Kay's hands threw fists when she felt Deb trying to touch her.

"Honey," Gary knelt down and held her by the wrist.
"You've got to tell us."

"Both of you, please! Stop yelling at me."

"We're not!" Deb shouted. Then, calmer, "Honey, we're
not. Okay? This isn't yelling. Gary, go get Simon please."

"He's not there."

"What do you mean?"

Her mother carried her back. On foot was the only way
Kay could remember how to get to Teagan's house; Gary
took his car and kept at an even crawl behind them, wheels
crunching the graveled ground.

Kay hadn't been carried in forever. She faced the opposite direction, arms gripping her mother's neck, the road
bobbing and blurring, Gary's low beams catching her eyelashes and the ends of her mother's hair. At corners Deb
prompted, "Straight?" Kay sometimes nodding into her
mother's shoulder, sometimes turning her head to be sure,
saying, "That way."

They were coming up the block when Deb saw her son,
very small, walking their direction. He seemed actually to
be strolling. Dillydallying.

"Which is the house?" she shouted, thirty feet away.

He stopped, then jogged to them. "What the hell—what
are you doing?"

"You don't ask me anything right now. Where's the
house?"

286

Kay twisted her head. "He's here. We found him. We can go home."

"Simon, which house?"

Kay yelled, "You said we were just going to find him!"

"I want to talk to that girl's mother."

"But you said!"

"Katherine, quiet."

"Okay," Simon said, "what the *fuck* is going on?"

"Fine, don't help. Just like him." Deb charged ahead, surprisingly quick under her daughter's weight.

"Just like who?" Simon hurried like a small dog after them. "Just like Dad?"

"Put me down," Kay pleaded.

"Here, is this it?" Deb had stopped in front of the wrong house. Both Simon and Kay hesitated. It would be the only thing worse. Deb could tell from their faces it was wrong and moved on to the next one, which she could tell was right.

"Here, Simon, take her."

"Mom, this is insane."

"I can stand!"

"She hurt her leg. Take her."

Simon did, awkwardly, Kay passing like an orangutan between them. Deb pulled her sleep shirt down over the short shorts that had been the only thing handy when she was blind angry and they were leaving. Gary killed the engine. Dark and quiet as she climbed the porch.

"I don't know *what* you did," Simon said, like a threat, into his sister's ear. They let a little go of each other, his arms loosening and her legs drifting down toward the pave-

287

ment. Kay slipped quickly off her brother, and he didn't try to stop her. She ran with her head down and crumbled on the curb two houses away.

Teagan answered the door. "My mother's asleep," she said when Deb asked to speak with her.

"Please wake her then."

Simon saw Teagan see him before she disappeared into the house. "Mom," he said.

They waited.

The woman Teagan brought back did seem to have just been sleeping, except she was fully dressed, in cutoff jeans that showed where skin sagged in bridges over her knees.

"Hello, hi," Deb started, "Mrs.—"

"Dignam. Deirdre," she said, sounding tired. "What is it? What's the problem?" She was thin everywhere but her stomach, which pooched out under a flower-printed top with frills.

"The *problem* is I have an eleven-year-old girl out there who came home in the middle of the night—hysterical, bloody—and that she was here."

Teagan's mother stepped out into the floodlight, her blond hair flat and sheer against her small skull. "I don't understand, tell it to me again."

"Just look at her!" Deb waved an arm behind her but only Simon was there, feeling his weight stacked in heavy columns over his feet. "Look, I don't— The reason she was here is, she was following my son."

"What the hell was he doing here? I don't know your kids."

"What? No, I know. It's just," Deb looked back toward

the car, touched her face. "I'm sorry. You have me confused. My son and your daughter were seeing each other. I guess you didn't know that."

"Seeing each other?"

"Yes, you understand? And they were together tonight, and, I guess they agreed to meet, you know, secretly, in your house."

"Just a minute"—suddenly shouting—"to get this straight. You can't keep your kids at home and that's *my* problem?"

"I'm not looking to cast blame. You misunderstand—"

"Your shit stains are sneaking into my house and that's on *me*?"

"We didn't know she was here." Teagan held her arms, steeling herself against Deb, or the night.

"And you!" her mother yelled, turning. "You think you can do whatever you want?" She pushed her hand into Teagan's chest, backing her up in increments. "Is that what you think?"

"Hey, hang on," Deb said. "All I'm saying is we should both, you know, do a better job monitoring our children."

"You had this boy in your room?" Her shirt's elastic shrugged higher around her waist. "After everything you put me through the last time, you learn nothing?"

The car door snapped open. "Deb, you need help?" Gary called.

Teagan's mother put one hand against the wall of the house and leaned on it as though each were holding the other up. For a moment everyone was quiet, but the silence was filled with other things.

The light was on in the upstairs window of the house next door, and Simon could discern two figures in the picture it made. The neighbor across had come out to watch, too. Looking up and down the block, he saw people appear like new stars, dotting the block. All those eyes and no one had noticed yet, that the eleven-year-old on the curb had been for some time gone.

Whom would you have had her call? There was their grandmother, there was Ruth, who would have come on the next train, but Deb had to stop turning to her mother, who was older now—who bought senior tickets at the movies now—and who shouldn't have to worry. And Gary was here, but Gary was still too much a stranger, would have required too much catching up.

And don't say no one. Deb was going to have help.

On the phone he asked mercifully few questions. As much as their history together was the problem, it was also what made things easy, the way it meant he knew when to shut up.

Deb reached him late; she reached him early. She reached him at La Guardia baggage claim, almost two A.M., where Jack was waiting very upright between Delta-blue columns. The longhorns had just made their triumphal way down the ramp. In so much bubble wrap they could have been a whole person, or a canoe. They failed to clear the first turn, jamming the procession of swollen Jansport duffels and tufted black Samsonites. He was glad to see them. He'd taken an evening flight out of Houston and had to change planes in Atlanta. It had been raining, and they'd held them at the gate an extra eighty minutes. He'd bought a two-dollar apple. He was tired.

His phone, when it rang, said "Simon-Cell," and he answered, "Pumpkin?"

"What? It's me. Jack?"

"Is your phone okay?"

"I can't find it."

"You should call and have it disabled."

"That's not—listen, something happened. It's Kay. We can't find Kay."

"What? Did you call the police?"

"I called. They sent someone, but he's taking so long, and I can't, I don't know what—I've been out with a flashlight, but."

"Okay. Okay, I'm coming."

At the mercifully barren Rent-A-Car, Jack got a minivan that could fit the longhorns when he slid them the long way between the front seats, where they bothered the gears. It had started raining here too. The pavement shone wetly before him and the traffic signals bled halos of light. He called Deb at intervals from the road. He beat the pads of his palms against the wheel. He did not stop.

He was in a hurry to be back with his family, feeling in a way that he was already. His happiness clashed with the conditions of his summons. He'd been hoping for a call, though he hadn't wanted it like this. His bliss at being wanted welled in lumps he had to swallow. Tricky not to get choked up over it, but it was important not to choke. He'd not been asked there to get weepy.

But Kay. He had to believe she was all right, that she'd done this, in a way, for him. She was his greatest ally, though too young and too quiet to sway the family vote: Her small voice held little weight. But she'd done what she could, in disappearing, like a magic act.

Three in the morning at the house and everyone was in each other's way. Out front a cop car had been parked some hours, white with POLICE splashed across its doors in slanted block letters, looking just like those windup cars Simon used to have, the small metal kind Deb was always stepping on sock footed. The officer who'd stepped out roadside asked too few questions, spent a lot of time adjusting his belt. Big-baby-bodied, he had a hard time getting the equipment clipped to where it was comfortable.

"I don't understand," Deb was saying. "What are your people doing?"

"I'm sure they're doing all they can," Gary said between rackets with the coffee grinder. Infuriating, how he stayed polite.

"It's all hands on the deck." The officer showed her his palms for no reason she could invent.

"What does that *mean*?" Deb shouted over the grinder. His hand radio gurgled and bleeped amid static din, a voice spouted ten codes. Sometimes he'd say into it "10-4," though nothing was 10-4 really.

It was six when Jack reached Jamestown. The sky was just beginning to wake. Lines distinguished themselves in the trees, setting apart each leaf. He stopped to let pass the morning's first jogger, a woman with earbuds and teal nylon shorts. He drove by the old library. RESUME WRITING TONIGHT 7. Jack knew the streets the way they say one knows the back of one's hand, though his hands, as he got older, had begun to surprise him.

Later he'd say it was a hunch, no more than that. He felt close to his daughter, felt he understood her thoughts, though his son was the more like him. Maybe that was why it had always been harder with Simon, because Jack could no more predict his son's actions than he could his own.

So, on a hunch he'd stopped at the water basins. If he'd been wrong, he never would have remembered trying.

She was there, with her knees up and her head against a dirt-dripped tub, asleep like the nerds who camp out all night for movie tickets. Deb's phone was on the ground beside her. She'd taken out the battery.

"Angel?" he said, sounding like his wife. He called his daughter every nickname.

Her eyes opened as though she'd only been feigning sleep, but she blinked at him uncomprehendingly, and her face was salt streaked.

He took up the phone and the battery and slid them into his pocket. "Come," he said, but already lifting her.

He carried her to the car. He couldn't think of the last time he'd carried her. "We're going home now," she said, sounding drunk or just young, and he knew she wouldn't remember any of this which he would not ever forget.

"I assure you, Mrs. Shanley," the officer said, "I've got every one of my guys out there looking for her."

"It's light out," Deb said, reshouldering her purse. "I can't just *sit* here."

Gary, carrying the old coffee filter and catching its drips, pressed an elbow into her arm. "The police know what they're doing. You should be here if she comes back. Try to be calm."

"*You* be calm, Gary. I can't find my daughter."

Simon was at the table, the heels of his hands pressed into his cheeks. "She probably just wanted to be alone."

"She doesn't get to be alone. Eleven-year-olds don't get alone time."

A car door slammed. Out the window, a dark green minivan sat double-parked beside the police car, effectively blocking off what traffic there wasn't. Between the cars stood a man, his back to them, though his family would know him anywhere. Bending to get something out from the shotgun side. Jack turned and the something was Kay, wilted in his arms.

"She's fine," he said when Deb came running out the front door. He set their daughter gently on the grass, checking to see her knees didn't buckle. "She's just sleepy."

Deb got down to the ground, held Kay by wobbly legs. "Oh, where *were you*?"

The others had come out behind her, Simon with his arms crossed and Gary with his coffee. "We know this man?" the officer asked.

"I'm the father," Jack said. "Hi. Hello, Gary."

"Jack," Gary nodded.

"Well, I need to radio this in," the officer went on. "Then there'll just be some forms."

"I'll do it. I'm the father." Jack pushed sweated hair from his forehead. "Found your phone too, D." He smiled, groping his wrong back pocket. He was distracted by so many eyes after being alone so long. Inside, the old house greeted him, chairs untucked at angles from the table and glasses splashed with water in the sink. His family's fingerprints on everything.

They had to lie down. Simon and Kay in their room, Jack beside Deb, she didn't care. Sleep clobbered them, left no room for thought.

Deb woke to an empty rest-of-bed. It was almost ten. She padded half-tired to the hall. The voices of men on the stairs.

They were standing in the kitchen together, Jack and Gary. They'd been laughing.

"You're awake!" Jack had a glass in his hand, her iced tea.

"I was just hearing about Houston," Gary said. "We weren't too loud?"

"No, you should have woken me." She walked to a chair, held the back of it.

"You needed it," Jack said, too cavalier. He swirled his glass, chattering ice.

"I'm fine." She looked at Gary twice, at the strap like a seat belt across his chest.

"Ah, yeah." He turned to one side, exhibiting the large, black bag attached behind. "I'm taking off."

"You don't have to." She looked at Jack, who shrugged, smiling. "I mean there's no reason."

"I was going to come get you," Gary said, though with the bag already on his back that seemed unlikely. He went on, something obscure about work and duty calling, and said to give the kids his love.

He hugged her one handed.

Jack got the door.

Deb stood holding down the chair, the chair holding her up, as they walked out to the car together, her husband and his friend.

As well as she knew the voice, Kay wasn't prepared, rolling over, to see the body that belonged to it. Jack, strangely occupying the corner of her bed, depressing the mattress, taking up space and blocking the light where there had been only light, and air.

"Hey, kiddo."

"Hi," she croaked, throat dry from disuse. "What time is it?"

"You slept," said Deb, sitting with Simon on the other bed. "I'm glad you slept."

Jack asked small questions that she answered smally, with her mother's help: about the cat they'd found, the fishing trip. It all sounded so nice, like someone else's life.

"Don't act like you care about all this stupid stuff," Simon said. The first thing he'd said.

"I care." Jack leaned close to her, "Sweetie? I want to know what you've been up to."

"Why don't you ask her what she was doing following

me?" Simon stood. "Huh? What's the matter with you?" Kay blinked once, then several more times, shuttering as if to keep something out. Or rather to keep something in. "Here we go again," he said, as the tears started streaming.

"Sy, cut it out," Deb said, pulling at him. "None of this would have happened if you hadn't been sneaking off."

"None of this would have happened if you both had just minded your own business," he said. "Seriously, what is your deal?"

"Simon," Jack shouted, but Deb had shot to her feet.

"Seriously, my *deal* is that you're my kid and I say where you go."

Simon waved his arms. "You're, like, obsessed. You know I'm not him, right? That I'm not Dad? I'm not actually doing anything wrong."

"Simon!" Jack tried.

Deb looked at her son, her husband, her son. Then she sat, and it was like something in her folding. "Do what you want. We go home tomorrow." She crossed her legs. "Just, wear a fucking condom, would you please?"

Simon looked at her, hard. It was the most adult thing she'd ever said to him. She might have said more, softened it, if they'd had more time. He was already out the door.

There was still some pottery on the lawn, but the sign (TAKE ALL!) had been brought in or thrown away. Simon made his charging way across the straw grass, treaded the matted carpets on the front porch. He'd armed himself with what to say to Mrs. Dignam, but around back the hammock lay with no one in it. His foot knocked a beer bottle, which rolled and tapped another. There were several, stood in a row, dark amber empties.

Teagan's room felt changed from the last and only time he'd been there. It had filled with sick. Almost noon, but she was in bed, a mound of flowered sheets softly breathing.

"Hello?" he said, like answering the phone. She shifted in her half cocoon. Crumpled tissues scattered and bounced to the floor, landing like origami cranes. "It's me. It's Simon."

There emerged the tangled blonde, and anyone could

tell she had been crying. She wore the puffiest version of her face.

"She didn't see me," he said.

Teagan pulled him to the bed, on his back, and her body curled over him, eclipsing his.

"So, we're leaving tomorrow, my mom says."

"I can't be here alone. I can't be alone with her." She breathed into his neck.

"No, but it's okay though," he went on. "I mean you really only have, what, another year here?" She began to sound and feel, in his arms, more upset. "Then you can go live wherever you want. Wherever in the world."

It seemed anything he told her could only stir up what sadness had settled. He let her shoulders shake into him and watched the ceiling as it bounced. "Don't, cry," he added, very quietly. She could opt out of hearing it.

Deb and Jack were still on the bed, still around their daughter. The first moment of levity had come in the form of the cat, of Wolf, who'd filled a quiet moment when Kay was all cried out, trilling strange meows from the closet. Jack had gone over and hovered his hands over the small gray body. "Not gonna hurtcha." He'd swept forward—something balletic in the way it was all one motion—and scooped the cat up around the middle, where its arched back made a handle for holding. Kay had smiled a little then, and her father had pounced, saying, "He wants to know what all the hubbub's about out here. Thought maybe he heard a can opener."

Yes, fathers have a way with daughters.

"Hey, what do you want to do today?" he asked. "It's going to be beautiful out, beautiful day. We'll get pancakes. Sun'll be shining, we can go out on the water. That sound good?"

"Good," said Kay, who noticed her father kept using the word *we*.

Deb had noticed it too, and that Jack had put his hand over hers on the hill of their daughter's hip.

Simon and Teagan slept an hour or two, or he slept them. Everything was changed from before; of course it was. The mattress so sinking he could feel the bones of it. She rewrapped her fingers around him, held him so tightly he felt pressed past her. He tried looking down, but her head was tucked high under his chin.

"I'm hot." He felt his heart against her, how it wanted to beat her away. "You hot?" He rolled off the bed and went to the window. "Probably from all the covers." Flattening his hands against the glass.

"Just, please," she said, and nothing followed it.

"Hang on—here." He pushed but the frame stayed stuck to the sill. His palms slipped and skidded squeaking up the glass.

Teagan made a soft wilting sound behind him. "There's a thing."

There was a thing, a little white lever in the middle of

the frame, which revealed itself to him now. He flipped it and the window sailed open. "There. Duh." A portal to the feeble breeze and slightly louder trees.

He wiped his hands on his jeans and found Teagan rolled away, toward the wall. The sheets had rolled with her, baring the longbow of her spine, the white nightgown bunched up around her waist. Sweat sharpened each of the fine, light hairs dusting her back's lower notches.

"Hey, what?" He knelt down by the bed, pulling her to him. She sat up but wouldn't look him in the face. "It's okay. You'll come to New York, in the fall." He felt he had only so much love, and for a brief moment, the scales had tipped in her direction. "We'll go to the Chelsea Hotel," he invented. "We'll go to the Statue of Liberty," where he had never been. "We will. You'll come stay with me there."

Then she hugged him, and if she didn't believe him, at least she was trying to.

When he left, she walked him out, down the stairs in case her mother was around. She even smiled a little, gentling the door open and drawing the beaded curtain aside so he could step out. There, on the welcome welcome welcome, thinking about whether it would be all right to kiss her. He didn't.

He took the back way, veering onto the street again when he judged himself far enough away. At the point where the hill began, he stopped and looked, the last place he thought he'd be able to see her, ghostly on the porch in her starchy nightgown that filled a little with air. But he could see her, too, hours later, lying awake in the sleep-

307

soaked room he shared with his sister, waiting for morning, and much later, when they'd gone back to New York, and for a long time after that. The little white sheet of her swaying. From the breeze, he thought, or from her feet, unsteady beneath her. And he did not know how he'd been so brave, or so weak, to leave her there.

That afternoon there was beauty in all the upstairs windows. "What did I tell you?" Jack had been bluffing, but Jack had been right. "Weather for allergy commercials."

They went out. It was a while since Kay had been with both her parents. She walked between them, bookended by them, playing on her mother's phone.

"I don't know what you do with that thing," Deb said, of the phone.

"Falling Gems." Kay cupped the screen to see by the shadow of her hand. They passed the shipyard with its fleet of retired-seeming boats, creaking rocking-chair noises against their ropes.

"Maybe I'd like a *Fallen Gem*," Jack said and smiled, pocketing his hands.

. . .

The metal-and-glass jangle of the door brought sound into the room, disturbing the otherwise quiet. The two waitresses were leaning with their elbows up on the bar counter, behind the revolving pastries. Their aprons and order pads made a small heap beside them.

They had the place almost to themselves, just an elderly couple at the booth nearest the bathrooms, and they sat by the window, Kay next to Jack and Deb across. The same rouged-up waitress as last time came with her pots of coffee to claim them.

"How we doing?" she asked, gesturing with the dark globe in her right hand, the coffee level sea-tiding inside.

"Excellent"—Jack leaned in to read the name tag—"Brenda! You know, I had a cousin Brenda, lived in El Dorado, Arkansas. Sweet girl, looked a lot like you too. You ever been to Arkansas?"

"Can't say that I have."

"Well, if you're ever in need of a body double."

Brenda smiled and Deb rolled her eyes when she thought Jack could see her do it.

The food came out all at once, dishes pyramided on the hook of Brenda's arm. "All right, herewego." All of it, the waffles but also the eggs, the hash browns and the home fries (which apparently were different), everything smelled of maple.

"Fantastic," Jack said, rubbing together his hands. "This takes care of me, but what are the two of you having?" Brenda laughed. Her perm trembled in ribbony pieces. "Laugh's the same too," Jack went on. "It's uncanny. You *sure* you've never been to Arkansas?"

"You really don't stop, do you?" Deb said when Brenda had walked away, close to floating.

"I'm sorry?"

"I just didn't think she was your type. Peanut? That looks yum." Kay, still absorbed in her mother's phone, had poured half the syrup onto her dark and shining waffles, filling them like an ice cube tray.

"You're not serious," Jack said.

"What's to be serious about? Everything's great, you're great. I'm glad you're great. I'm glad you get to come and be the hero, to the kids, to Gary."

"Look, can we not do this in front of our daughter, please?"

"Oh, because you're so good at protecting her."

"Deborah, I'm begging you—"

A plate landed with a smack facedown on the floor, and it took them each a moment to realize it was Kay who'd thrown it, and another before syrup began oozing out from under its edges, creeping along the floor.

"Kay, we don't do that," Jack said.

"I hate you," Kay said. She said it to her mother.

"Katherine," Jack started.

"Don't." Deb rose. "Let her, it's fine." She edged out of the booth. "Please would you just excuse me a minute." She went outside, chiming the bells again, meandering un-straight lines. Jack and Kay and Brenda with the coffee pot watched her, but Deb, through the window, appeared to be looking for something dropped.

. . .

311

The younger waitress came and cleaned the mess up.

Light spilled through the spotted glass, showing up the fingerprints and days of rain.

And Deb, who knew so much about form, knelt clumsy in the sun and turned away her face.

PART FOUR

That Year
and Those
That Followed

They went. They were away two weeks.

For eighteen days the apartment sat empty. No light bulbs burned out. The four stone *putti* over the television did not correct themselves, Spring beside Fall, Summer with Winter.

Only the wireless went on, invisibly complicating the air.

Then they came home, to the Ruth-gathered mail and the air conditioner, slowly breaking down.

Jack moved to a larger place in Sunnyside, Queens. Deb moved the bed to the opposite wall.

They stopped being married to each other.

. . .

Spring came. The glowing green clock on the oven fell an hour behind.

The girl who wrote the letter, the girl who loved Jack, spent some time in Pasadena, in her childhood home. Then she moved back, became a temp at a LEED-certified sky-scraper overlooking Bryant Park, where strangers left sticky notes on her monitor.

New year. Kay spooned all the cookie-dough pieces from a pint of ice cream and tried to cook them. You could still see most traffic signs after you closed your eyes.

The girl who wrote the letter found two books in her temporary desk: a guide to city restaurants and *The Professional Secretary's Handbook*. *Your image is the portrait you present to the people with whom you interact. Avoid continual emphasis on "I."* There was a rose pressed into the chapter on telecommunications, dried to a chart of time zone changes country to country.

Some April mornings the clouds looked like cottage cheese. There was something very punishing about dry-swallowing pills. Travolta died, in the bathroom, a few feet from her litter box.

At the desk above Bryant Park, the girl who wrote the letter wrote other things, wrote stories about what she had done. She stayed late sending pages to the office printer.

. . .

After years in Eli's Tribeca loft, Deb finally sold the apartment uptown. It was raining the day Katherine flew home from California to clear out her things. Simon waited to meet her on Seventy-second Street, under the patchy shelter of dormant AC units. She came toward him from the west side of the street, skipping a little over real and imaginary puddles. A street vendor barked "*Um*brella *Um*brella *Um*brella" beside a table of phone accessories and pashminas under plastic sheeting.

They went to eat, studied the menus.

"When did you—" Simon made scissors of his fingers and snipped the air around his ears.

"Oh, a little while." Reflexively touching her head.

A minute later he said, "So I'm thinking, you get the blackened catfish." Katherine laughed. "And I will have the *broiled calf's liver,* because that's got to be good here."

An old joke between them, something they'd gotten from their father: the idea that all diner menus had to be, in some sense, bluffing. "Wait, what about this though, the scrod?"

"Where are you finding that?"

"The specials? It comes with mushrooms."

"Comes with—all right, never mind. We're both getting that. Do you think they'll have enough back there? Multiple scrods?"

"We'll ask."

Katherine paid the bill while Simon plucked dusty mints from the bowl by the register. When she pulled out her wallet, a strip of toilet paper flew out too. The mess of her bag was the first time Simon wondered if her life was not all the things she wanted it to seem.

Outside, the *Um*brella vendor had gone back to being a phone cover and pashmina vendor. He gave them a quick once-over, maybe thought they were together. Lots of couples look related.

On the quiet ride uptown, Simon touched the taxi's plastic partition. "Ever since we were kids I could never see one of these things without picturing it, like, embedded in my neck, you know?"

The diamond flecks in the sidewalks were never diamonds, and the black spots weren't dirty gum. Some were, but most weren't.

In the lobby of their old building, the doorman asked if he could help them. "We live here," they answered. "Well, we used to," one said. "We have keys."

Acknowledgments

An inevitably incomplete list of inevitably insufficient thanks to:

Noah Eaker, alarmingly insightful editor and jelly-bean benefactor, and everyone at Random House, especially Susan Kamil, Caitlin McKenna, Barbara Fillon, and Janet Wygal.

Elyse Cheney, who went so far above and so far beyond. Also the wonderful Alex Jacobs, Adam Eaglin, and Tania Strauss.

Jonathan Safran Foer, impossibly wise, impossibly generous, simply the best.

The remarkable writers I have been lucky enough to call my teachers.

The Lillian Vernon Creative Writers House at NYU, and Deborah Landau in particular. Also the Bobst Library, for its late hours and lax policy on outside food.

The Rona Jaffe Foundation, for making my time at NYU possible.

Some of my favorites, for their feedback and my sanity throughout: Austin Bone, Anna Breslaw, Julie Buntin, Rebecca Dinerstein, Jane Esberg, Grace Kallis, Tiffany Peón, Sarah Peterson, Jennifer Rice, Nina Rouhani, and Shiva Rouhani.

My family: Robert Pierpont (tireless reader), Bob and Mary Pierpont, Shirley "Baba" Roth, Allan Roth, Doris Garcia, and Diana Garcia. You have given me so much.

And to Claudia Roth Pierpont, the most good. Thank you for always coming to get me.

ABOUT THE AUTHOR

JULIA PIERPONT is a graduate of the NYU Creative Writing Program, where she received the Rona Jaffe Foundation Graduate Fellowship as well as the Stein Fellowship. She lives in New York City.

@JuliaPierpont